TIME WARRIORS

A Time Warriors Novel

D1826657

AMY JARECKI

ISBN: 9781087938158

There are times in a person's life where destiny leads them to people of influence; people with the charisma, strength, and perseverance to change lives. My sensei, Mr. Marc Wilson is such a man. He taught me to live the life of a warrior where peace, love, and respect is central to all.

Chapter One

"Success depends upon previous preparation, and without such preparation there is sure to be failure." – Confucius

The aggressor's eyes blaze right before she launches an axe kick aimed to crush my head. A rush of adrenaline ratchets higher as I lurch aside. Breeze from my opponent's foot skims my face. My nerves jolt. Labored breathing thunders in my ears. As I continue to cross-step in a circle, time morphs into slow motion while the fighter is thrown off balance by her miss.

She staggers and drops her guard—an invitation to attack.

Lightning fast, I spin, my gaze snapping to my target. As I whip around, my leg darts upward with a hook, my foot striking the side of her helmet.

"Break!" shouts the judge as the girl falls to her knees. "Kick to the head. One point red. Tied, four to four."

Backing to my spot with my fists at the ready, I jog in place trying not to wonder if she's hurt, refusing to allow guilt from my kick to creep past my hardened warrior's armor. Yeah, I know her name. They announced it before mine. But she's not a name right now. She's the enemy.

The judge offers the girl his hand. "Are you okay?" He's acting concerned—giving her time to catch her breath. Good for her—not so great for me.

My heart's hammering like a snare so I steal a second to close my eyes and draw a deep inhale. I'm in the best shape of my life and I'm sapped, my muscles burning like blue fire. We're too evenly matched and the next point wins. This chick is good. Fast, too. The best I've ever faced with a vicious roundhouse kick. God, if I hadn't ducked in the first round, I'd be sprawled on the mat watching Tweety birds fly around my head.

And I can't lose. I'm so close, so damned driven. I have to prove I'm good enough to all the normal kids out there—the ones with real families—the ones who kiss their moms every night.

"I'm fine," my opponent replies.

"You sure?" the judge presses. His job is to be cautious.

Maybe my spinning hook was harder than I thought. Lucky, too.

My exhale whistles through my lips as I open my eyes, stance tense, ready for the next round.

An old man is watching just beyond the mat. Asian. White hair. He's bent at the shoulders and leans on a gnarled cane. But his gaze bores through me like honed obsidian arrows. Something in the intensity of his stare grips me—throws me completely out of my zone.

The judge moves back to the front of the ring and holds up his hand. "Sparring stances!"

Before my next heartbeat, my mind blanks, taken over by one thought.

Chakra.

A spark of energy bursts at the base of my spine and shoots up through the crown of my head until my entire body radiates energy—but not the power of a warrior—within a millisecond, nothing matters but being. My concentration zooms in on harmony, oneness, and peace.

Crap!

Here I stand in the midst of the most important karate match of my life, the score is tied, and I'm focusing on inner tranquility? Have I lost my mind? I won my open-hand kata, my weapons kata and, if I clinch the gold medal in sparring, I'll have a clean sweep. That's what I'm here for. Right? To prove to everyone on the planet I'm not a loser. The culmination of my high school career is on the freaking line and my adrenaline shuts down. Instead, I'm at peace with the universe, staring at some old man's laser eyes?

"Spar!" shouts the judge.

I blink, my gaze shifting to the adversary across the mat. Aware my body is ready, I wait rather than attack with my trademark full-on blitz. My head doesn't quite believe it. Even a voice at the back of my mind shouts, "The aggressor always wins, you idiot!" Then why do I dance around the girl and wait for her to make the first move?

The insane part? I know what she's planning. I already see her attack in my mind.

A wicked glint flashes through her eyes as she explodes with an eagle kick vicious enough to sever my head from my body. My heart rate doesn't even spike. I take a single step off the line, spin to the right, and land a backfist to the side of her helmet— not flashy but effective.

The girl reels, her eyes stunned like she's never lost anything in her life.

"Winner!" The judge's voice sounds as if it's in a tunnel as he points to me. "Backfist to the head."

Still eerily calm, I bow. I've just achieved my life's goal and I'm feeling this Zen thing. Going with it, I offer a hand to my opponent. "You were awesome."

She scowls as she shakes it. "Not awesome enough. I thought I had you."

"So did I."

"Huh?"

My shoulder tics up. "Either of us could have won." I look for the old man. Strange. He's vanished.

"It's Genesis, right?" she asks.

"Yeah—and you're Ziana?"

The girl nods as she takes off her helmet revealing bleached blonde hair, pulled back in a ponytail. By the purse of her lips, she's pissed but trying to put on a poker face. A bad one.

"Come on," I beckon her with a wave of my sparring glove. "They're waiting for us at the medals podium."

Ziana slumps. "Wonderful."

"Hey, just making it here is a big deal," I say, as a matter of fact. After all, this tournament is for the elite, by invitation only. Every single contestant is a champion in their own right. Yeah, I'm the Nevada sixteen-year-old champ, even though I never feel like one.

"Sure," says Ziana, picking up her bag. "Tell that to my mom."

I look across the stands until I spot a middle-aged woman glaring at us. I'd like to ask Ziana to tell her mom to go a few rounds with me. I might joke about it if I knew her better, but I keep my opinion to myself. Besides, at least the girl's lucky enough to have a mom—or a parent who bothers to show up for that matter.

I see my best friend, Rex, heading this way with one of trademark shimmies and flashing me double hook `em horns. God if it weren't for him I'd be one hurting unit. I answer back with a grin and a power fist, then steal another glance across the stands—just to see if by some amazing change of mind, my dad decided to hop on his Harley and drive to Los Angeles.

Nope. Not one familiar face up there.

When will I ever get it through my head that Dad's not going to change?

Still, my heart goes numb.

Story of my life. I'm Genesis Mans the sixteen-year-old parent...to my dad. Yup. That's me. An ass-kicking caregiver. Mom died of breast cancer when I was twelve. I credit her for my solid foundation, but that's as far as my nurturing went. The only other person on the planet I want to see here is my mentor, Sensei Soto. He got me in, but he couldn't make the trip because I'm the one who teaches his classes when he's not at the dojo in Mesquite.

Why should I be disappointed? At least Rex's parents let him come with me. Isn't that miracle enough?

I open my arms as my bro swallows me in a bony embrace. He used to be shorter than me, but I swear he's grown a foot during sophomore year—now he looks like a stick figure with neon-green hair. It's sort of a role-reversal thing. I'm the badass truck-driving girl and Rex...well, he looks great in pink nail polish. At least it works for us. He wants to go to some elite cosmetology school back east—live the whole city slicker life with an apartment in New York, working in an upscale shop. I'm all for it. He bleached the tips of my curly black hair and it's totally a professional job. He says I look like Becky G, with Beyoncé hair and wicked eyes, but he's an ace at saying things to make me feel good.

He smells like popcorn and I squeeze him every bit as tightly as he hugs me. "You rock, Batgirl! I knew you'd show 'em. Blondie didn't have a chance."

"You kidding?" I ask, giving his long bangs a flick. God, I'm so glad he's here. "She nearly ate me for breakfast."

Rex practically retells an entire play-by-play of the match as we head for the podium. We met in kindergarten at the dojo. When it comes to martial arts, the dude isn't bad, he just can't bring himself to hit anybody.

After I take my place on the top tier, a suit drapes the gold medal around my neck. I wave at the crowd and they politely applaud for the winner from nowheresville. How the hell did I ever make it this far, and what's next? My heart lurches as it hits me— in a week, my sophomore year is over and juniors are supposed to be deciding about colleges and their futures. Yeah, Dad and I have talked about it some. I've batted around the idea of starting college online so I can teach at the dojo and help out at the Muddy Hollow—Dad's biker bar in Bunkerville, Nevada—a place outside of Mesquite so small it's practically a ghost town.

But is that what I want? Here I stand, a freaking national champion and the future is gripping my throat with the force of the jaws of a tiger. About now I'd like to have a crystal ball to ask a gazillion questions about my destiny.

Right.

That's never going to happen. I'll figure it out. I'm tough. I'm independent. I'm confident. Well, I'd like to think I'm confident. Don't tell a soul, but the whole confidence thing throws me. I doubt anyone has figured it out, though, because I have a better poker face than Ziana.

"Smile, you two," says the lady holding up my phone while Rex and I balance the trophy between us.

I grin—more out of surprise since she knows my name. Sure, I won the tournament, but I'm still an unknown. The gold medals around my neck clank as we raise the ginormous cup. It's heavy and that totally rocks.

"Where are your parents?" she asks, handing me back my phone.

"Nevada," I reply as if that explains everything. I thank her and tuck my awards inside my bag.

Rex gives me a nudge. "How do we look?"

I click on the image and show him. "I think we're a team, and hey my eyes aren't even red." They're amber and, for some reason, pictures usually make me look like a Sith out of *Star Wars*.

He waggles his brown eyebrows. "We're the two best-looking dudes here."

I glance up to the empty stands. "Yeah, now that everyone's gone."

"Shut up."

I just shake my head and laugh. Before we head out, I check to see if Dad or Sensei Soto have responded to the texts I sent a few minutes ago.

"Anything?" Rex asks. He's the only one who knows how much I wanted my father to be here. Dad ought to be in the bar about now, though it shouldn't be too busy yet. Sensei probably won't respond until later.

"Nope." I stoop to slide the phone into my bag and as soon as it drops from my fingers, it dings. Faster than a rattler pouncing on a mouse, I snatch it back, sliding my finger over the print scanner.

That's my girl! Send pictures!!

I fire off the trophy pic with Rex and Dad replies immediately.

I am in awe of you! Drive safe. See you when you get home, champ!

"Not bad," says Rex, reading over my shoulder.

"Yeah, and I'm guessing he's sober." I don't know how Dad does it, but he nurses a beer during his shift and then drinks himself into a stupor most nights. He thinks I don't know how much he drinks, but I've always known. After all, I've been looking after him for over four years.

I fish the keys out of my bag. "You ready?"

"Want to find a DQ?" he asks, following me to the door.

"Not in this town." Holy hell, the traffic is insane here. On the drive down my life flashed before my eyes no fewer than seven times. And Bunkerville is hectic if you see two cars on Main Street. "Maybe we'll find one when we stop for gas."

"Well, in that case, I gotta pee."

I sling my bag over my shoulder. "Okay. I'll meet you at the truck."

Outside, only a few cars remain in the lot. Right away, the hairs on the back of my neck stand on end. I don't know what it is, but something about this place is making me edgy. Speeding my pace, I glance over each shoulder. Nope, nothing. It must be the humidity or whatever.

Nearly to my Ford, I see him. Not with my eyes, but my mind launches into hyperdrive just like it did in the ring. He's coming at my five. With no time to think, I drop my bag and turn in a crouch, my guard protecting my face.

The hooded man throws a spinning hook. His leg hisses over my head as I bob and weave beneath, aiming a roundhouse to take out his knee. But he defends with a move I've never seen before, sweeping my leg higher, knocking me on my ass.

God!

The worst place for a fighter to be is on the ground. I roll to my shoulders and spring up, sidestepping away, out of his reach.

I'm panting, totally freaked as my mind screams, *"Stay alive!"*

His face looks like death as he comes for me. His eyes filled with fire, his teeth bared. Goddamn, this isn't a sparring match.

This is real.

I leap toward my truck. But I can't reach the handle. With no other choice, I whip around and prepare for another attack.

"Back off!" I shout, using my toughest badass voice. "Save it for the ring, asshole!"

The man practically stops in midair. Dropping his hands to his sides, he steps away and bows. "Congratulations, Genesis. You just passed your entrance exam," he says, speaking in an East Indian accent.

Positive I've never seen this maniac before, I stare at him like he's a complete loon. The guy shows no emotion, backs a few more steps, then turns and heads off—not for the gym and not for any car I can see.

Every fiber of my body is shaking as I spot my keys on the asphalt. Just as I stoop to pick them up, Rex comes running. "Hey, you know that guy?"

My eyes almost pop out of my head while the keys jangle in my trembling hands. "You saw him? That maniac freaking attacked me!"

"Seriously?" Rex pulled open the passenger door. "I only watched him bow and walk away."

"Yeah, after he tried to plant a foot between my eyeballs." I skirted around to the driver's side. "Then when I told him to back off, he bowed and said I passed my entrance exam."

"What kind of freak does that? Entrance exam? To what? The Death Star?"

I slam the door and jam the key into the ignition.

"He's a psycho—see why I didn't want to find a DQ until we hit the road?" I pull up the directions home and throw the truck in gear.

"Should we call the cops?"

"No!" I say, taking a right into traffic. "I just want to get the heck out of Los Angeles."

What a whacked-out day. I'm taking home the grand champion trophy but all I can think about is what happened to me in the ring with the old man—which I haven't even told Rex about yet. And even weirder, some guy who has clearly achieved a fifth degree or higher attacks me in the parking lot and then says congratulations? Who would believe me even if I did call the cops?

Chapter Two

"The strength of a nation derives from the integrity of the home." - Confucius

I don't know what I hate more, Mondays or my alarm. Right now they're pretty even because I've already pressed snooze twice and the stupid thing keeps going off.

Groaning, I roll to my back. Ow. Since the rush faded from Saturday's wins, I've found a gazillion bruises. The one on my right shoulder blade is the worst. I got it when I sprang from the asphalt in the parking lot.

Rufus, my cat, is licking my face and purring. With a sigh I run a hand over his fur.

"Meow."

If I ever wanted to sleep in it would never happen because of Rufus. "Give me a minute," I say, pushing the blankets aside and heading for the bathroom.

It's our routine. I get up at five, feed the cat, eat a bowl of high-protein cereal and then head downstairs to clean the bar. The only time I'm allowed inside the Muddy Hollow is when it's closed, and that's only from three in the morning until when Dad opens at noon. He says his hours are noon to nine, but he usually stays until closing, which means

I don't see him much, except when he takes a break to have dinner with me.

He won the bar in a poker game before I was born and we've lived in the apartment above ever since. It's like a 1970s retro thing complete with cheap faucets and an olive-green refrigerator, but it's comfortable. I keep it clean like Mom used to—well, I'm not as tidy as her, but ever since she passed away, I've tried to pick up after myself because she would have wanted it.

Rufus finishes his kibble while I'm still shoveling almond granola into my mouth. He jumps on the table and stares at me like a stalking lion.

"You've already had yours," I say.

But the cat inches closer, lulling my resolve with those soulful feline eyes as if he hasn't been fed in weeks. I grab the milk and pour a little in a dish. I'm such a pushover. "What would you do without me?"

Rufus swishes his tail as he drinks. The sly feline. Then he struts away and decides to ignore me because I've given him what he wants.

After breakfast, I brush my fingers over Mom's bronze dragon statue before I head downstairs. The top of its head shines where I've petted him every day. We don't have many reminders of Mom in the house, but she always said the statue was handed down through about a gazillion generations. Mom was born in San Francisco but other than that her family is a mystery. Dad, too. He's an orphan and never talks about his childhood.

I guess I look most like her, high cheekbones and all. And though I have Dad's eye color, my eyes are cat-shaped like Mom's. My hair is curly like my father's. I'm not sure I like having curly hair. Of course, Rex would emphatically disagree.

I'm slender like Mom, but muscular like my father, olive-skinned, too. Sometimes I go on and on making comparisons. The bottom line is I'm Genesis and I guess I look like me.

Downstairs, the bar smells like beer and biker-dude sweat. I start with the men's room because no matter what, it's always gross. And after a whole night, the lady's room is rarely much better. But with the industrial cleaner Dad buys for the bar, by the time I've finished cleaning toilets, wiping counters, and mopping the floors, it smells clean. Too bad it won't last.

A knock comes from the front and I peer beyond the neon "beer" sign.

"Excuse me." A man in a FedEx uniform taps on the window.

Broom in hand, I open the door, ready to use the handle as a bow staff just in case I need to fend off an attack. FedEx doesn't usually show up this early.

The guy holds up a cardboard envelope. "I have a special delivery for Genesis Mans. Needs a signature."

"I'm Genesis."

"Do you have ID?"

I fish out my license, trying to figure out who would be sending me something so important it required my signature. I haven't ordered anything. I hold up the ID. "Here."

He has me sign a handheld device and, after bolting the door, I put the mop away and head up to the kitchen, turning the envelope over in my hands. It just has my address and is stamped, "*Property of the United States of America. To be opened by addressee only. Signature required.*"

Talk about weird. I slide onto a chair at the table, tear away the tab, and pull out a letter.

Dear Genesis,

Congratulations on your win at the World Teen Martial Arts Championship. You have demonstrated a high level of achievement both physically and mentally and we are pleased to offer you a position at the Military Academy of Martial Arts in Utah...

My heart just about leaps out of my chest as I grab my phone to Google it. I'm totally psyched—shaking with excitement, which isn't like me.

But the bubble bursts fast enough. There is no Military Academy of Martial Arts. Unless I want to go to West Point...in New York, not Utah.

Right.

I'm sixteen. Even if I could get into West Point, I needed to finish high school first.

I groan. Why would anyone want to play this kind of trick on me? What did I do to deserve someone's wrath? Win a tournament? Worse, who would pay to send me a hoax via special delivery?

I shove back my chair but stop when the next paragraph in the letter catches my eye.

This is a highly secretive organization which has operated in the United States since 1798. Only the elite are recruited. To better acquaint yourself with your courses of study, details about our location, and our expectations of your commitment, the following link and password will be available to you for forty-eight hours only. Congratulations. We look forward to seeing you report for duty on June 1st.

Report for duty? Highly secretive? It still seems like a hoax.

As I drum my fingers on the counter, curiosity gets the better of me. I key in the URL and password into my phone.

At first my screen goes black like my cell's being taken over by some creep on the dark web.

I'm about to X out when there's a bit of static before the website loads with a red rock arch against a blue sky behind the title *"Military Academy of Martial Arts"*. Below it are pictures of an ultra-modern campus that looks practically sterile. I click on a video that shows students doing katas, weapons forms, everything I love, except they're all fantastic— I mean unbelievably talented with aerial moves that hardly seem possible. Whoa, one guy somersaults over a brick wall and breaks a board with his forehead *and* another with his heel on the way down.

I salivate as I read further. It is a military academy like West Point or Annapolis, except in addition to a university, it has college prep classes for high school juniors and seniors.

I've never heard of such a thing. Going to school with college kids? That rocks...though I'll bet they keep the preppies separate from the undergrads.

Reading on, it says the academy has been created by a coalition of allied governments in the interest of international peace. I search for more on the peace thing and get nowhere. The site lists the college prep courses and then provides some sketchy details about the degrees they offer—history, languages, information systems and more. Cool, there's even a specialist in Asian fighting techniques.

I'd totally major in that.

But I'm skeptical. It looks unreal. And it probably is. I mean, I've been doing martial arts all my life and I haven't heard of this place.

Glancing to the letter on the table, I tap my finger on the signature. *Grand Master Li.*

I've never heard of him.

Is this too good to be true? What about Dad. What about Rex? He'll be eaten alive without me.

A moan comes from the back bedroom—my father's room. Dad's usually sawing logs about now. A rock sinks to the pit my stomach. He must have pulled an all-nighter.

Not again. I check the clock. I need to move fast if I'm going to make it to school on time.

Duty forces me trudge down the hall and tap on the door. "Hey, Dad, you in there?"

He grunts and I go inside. The place smells like a booze distillery.

He's flat on his back and there's an empty vodka bottle on the bedside table. Giving me a half-cocked grin, he blinks lazily. "You done cleaning already?"

"It's time for me to leave." I grab the bottle, noticing he's cradling a picture frame. "You promised you wouldn't drink up here."

"Special 'casion."

I crane my neck and my heart twists into knots. He's holding his and Mom's wedding photo. How did I forget? Yesterday would have been their twentieth anniversary. I should have said something. I should have sat up and waited for him to close the bar.

"I'm sorry," I whisper.

He clutches the picture tighter. "So am I."

"It still hurts super bad, huh?" I know, because not a day goes by when I don't miss her.

Dad rolls to his side, putting his back to me. "Yeah."

"I'll call Nancy and put on a pot of coffee."

"You're the best, sweetheart," he slurs.

Giving him a sad smile, I choke back tears and kiss his temple before I head for the kitchen. It hasn't been this bad for a long time. Sure, Dad drinks every night, but usually stays sober until well after he opens. As a general rule, he stops at closing time and more-or-less passes out after he makes it to his bed. About six months ago we made a pact not to have alcohol in the apartment, and I think he's been pretty good about it. After all, he owns the bar downstairs, he can drink all he wants there. I pour the rest of the vodka down the drain while I speed dial Nancy. She answers after one ring.

I toss the bottle in the trash. "Can you come in?"

I feel like a jerk having to ask, but Nevada law says I can't work behind the bar until I'm twenty-one. If I covered for Dad and was caught, he'd have his liquor license revoked. For a second, I think that might not be a bad idea—it would mean no more bar and no more alcohol on the premises, but then it would also mean he'd lose his livelihood.

"Double time?" This is the deal. Nancy always works from six to close. If Dad can't function, she opens at ten and gets paid double.

"Yep."

"I'll be there—need a couple more hours of sleep though."

"Thanks."

When I hang up, the website for the martial arts academy is still my phone and my heart twists into a gazillion knots. I can't leave my father when he's still hurting so much. It just wouldn't be right.

Besides, the place just seems too good to be true. It's got to be some sort of hoax. I X out. No use wishing for things I can never have. Dad needs me and with Mom gone, I can't leave him hanging.

Tossing the letter and FedEx envelope into the recycle bin, I try not to think about it. I put on the coffee and fish out some ground beef to thaw for tonight's dinner. I don't mind being his sidekick. After all, he needs me. Things haven't been easy for him these past four years. And in a way, it's nice to know how much he loved my mother.

After he drinks a couple cups of coffee and takes a few aspirin, he'll be back on his feet by afternoon— or tonight at least.

Life could be worse. Right? And, hey, only a few more days and I'll be on summer break. No one's going to give a rip if I'm a half-hour late for my history class.

The best thing about the last day of school is we go home at noon. Even better, the awards assembly will take most of the morning. I probably would have stayed home if Rex weren't kicking it off with the historical fashion show he's been planning for months, but there's no way I'd miss it. My bro even recruited the cheer squad and got some musical theater company in Las Vegas to loan him the costumes, but he's mostly psyched about doing the hair.

It's before the bell, and I head for the cafeteria but the first thing I see is Rex with a pair of pink fairy wings taped to his back. Under most circumstances, he would be fine with the wings, but he's surrounded by a mob of dudes on the fast track to the College of Rednecks.

I barrel through the circle and stand beside my bro. "Knock it off!"

Tommy is a junior linebacker with more brawn that brains. His face is about an inch from Rex's and he's completely ignoring me. "Oh, yeah, pretty boy? You need your dyke girlfriend to stick up for you?"

Growling, I wedge myself between the ox-brained junior and Rex, raising my palms to show I don't want trouble. The last thing I need is a fight in the final week of school—and I'd be the one ending up in the principal's office. The thought makes me shudder. "I said stop, okay?"

Tommy grabs for me. But I'm faster. I duck under his hand, nab the back of it and torque downward—not too hard to snap his wrist, but hard enough to bring tears to his eyes. "You want me to tell coach what you're up to? 'Cause I'm sure you'll be suspended come fall—you'll miss the first game at least."

Weighing over two hundred pounds, the linebacker whines and drops to his knees. "You're going to break my arm!"

"I could, but I won't unless you don't back off." I give the others an evil eye, warning them to stay away. They all know I'm lethal. Thank God not a one lifts a finger to help their idiot leader.

"We were just having fun," says a sophomore. I'm guessing he has the IQ of a rat.

I shove Tommy away and straighten, folding my arms like a bodyguard with Rex at my six. "Anyone else want a go?"

"Freak," he says as he struts away, the others following, giving me a load of dirty looks.

I force myself to take a calming breath before I turn to my friend. "You okay?"

"Yeah." He flips his flashy bangs out of his face. "I'm just glad we're outta here for the summer."

"You can say that again."

I lead Rex to our table, tugging off the fairy wings. "Are you excited to leave for your vacation?" His family rents a place in Oceanside for two weeks every year.

"I'd be happier if it were tomorrow."

I slide onto the bench. "Sunday will be here soon enough, bro."

"Yep—and you're still coming to the awards ceremony?" he asks.

"If I don't get expelled in the next two hours," I say with a snort. "It could happen. Especially if I have to keep scaring off football players."

愛

The prelude music for the fashion show is already playing when I arrive at the auditorium. I take a seat at the back so Rex will easily find me when his part is over. He asked me to be in the show, but I'm allergic to cheerleaders.

As the music fades, Rex steps through the curtains and walks to a mic at the side of the stage. "Good morning ladies and gentlemen." He sounds totally professional. God, my heart is hammering faster for him than it did when I was sparring against Ziana. "To open the awards ceremony, the fabulous Virgin Valley cheer squad presents to you Fashion Through the Ages."

I can't believe he's put all this together as the girls glide across the stage in fabulous gowns and hair that's out of this world—especially the

Renaissance, baroque and Victorian eras. The medieval period is plain and the Regency is simpler with lots of curls. But since it's an awards ceremony, the show only lasts about ten minutes.

After the principal takes the podium, I slide down in my seat, ready for a cat nap.

"Hey," Rex whispers as he slips beside me.

I throw an arm around him and give him a peck on the cheek. "That was freaking awesome."

"Really?"

"Totally. You are a rock star," I whisper. "I mean, New Yorkers aren't going to know what hit!"

"Shh," says the lady beside me—she must be somebody's mom.

I purse my lips and sink lower in my seat.

Just when I close my eyes, Rex nudges me and points to the right. His sister is waving at us and I give a quick wave back.

"Not her," he says, shifting his finger.

"Oh. My. God."

My Dad's here.

I pull my phone out of my back pocket and check the time. It's quarter past ten. Heck, his alarm usually goes off at ten.

I glance again. "Why is he here?"

"Volleyball trophy?" Rex asks.

"Not unless he found out about it from someone else."

Later, I almost fall out of my chair when Sensei Soto takes the podium.

I look at Rex. "Did I miss something?"

He spreads his palms and shrugs while Sensei adjusts the mic.

"As many of you are aware, I either have or have had the pleasure of instructing several Virgin Valley students in martial arts. But there is one student among us who has excelled at a very high level. You may not have heard the news, but Genesis Mans clinched first place in her age division at the World Martial Arts Tournament in Los Angeles last week."

He stops while the audience applauds. The arid Sahara takes up residence in my mouth. I'm positive the section of the crowd over by Dad is clapping the loudest, except maybe for Rex right beside me. I give him a nudge and a little eye roll. No one at school understands me. Karate is what I do. It's what keeps me sane and drives me. I breathe the art. It pulses through my blood.

But nobody here gets that. To them I'm a freak.

"I'd like to say how difficult it is for a contestant to make a clean sweep at a world level match." Sensei pulls my trophy out from under the podium. He keeps talking while I glance back to Dad. He's the only person who could have brought it here. My throat closes while I blink against the sting in my eyes.

My father glances over and gives me a thumbs up while Sensei beckons me.

When I don't move, Rex jabs me with his elbow. "Go on."

I manage to swallow and zip up to the stage.

Sensei shakes my hand and pushes me toward the podium. I shake my head at him but he gives me one of those looks that says do it or die.

I peer out across the student body and start to shake. Public speaking isn't my thing. "Um...I, um, didn't expect this," I say, forcing a smile. "I guess I wouldn't be standing here if it weren't for Sensei Soto and all the years of training—or for my Dad who got me started."

I raise my trophy above my head. "Thank you!"

I bow to my sensei then head for my seat, feeling lame, but psyched, too. Dad came. Does he have any idea how much having him here means to me?

Grinning, he meets me in the aisle and wraps an arm around my shoulder. "I'm proud of you, Princess. I'll see you when you get home."

愛

School is dismissed right after the awards ceremony and when I walk into the apartment, Dad's in the kitchen, leaning against the kitchen counter with his arms crossed like he's been waiting for me.

"Hey." I sling my backpack onto a chair. "You haven't opened yet?"

He grabs a power water out of the fridge and hands it to me. "Thought we ought to have a little talk."

My father wants to talk? I twist off the lid and slowly lower myself into a seat. "Okaaaay. Am I in trouble?" I don't think I'm in hot water—I mean I just saw him at school, but then again, maybe he heard about my confrontation with Tommy.

He takes a chair, turns it around and straddles it, crossing his arms over the back. "Maybe."

"Huh?"

He slides a slip of paper in front of me and taps his finger on it, his black eyebrows slanting over those intense amber eyes.

One glance and I know what it is. My face burns hot. "Did you pull this out of the recycling?"

"Yeah."

It's not like him to even give the recycling a second glance. I mean I catch him all the time throwing aluminum cans in the trash. Call it a sixth sense or whatever, but I know "yeah" doesn't even come close to the whole story.

Dad smiles, before he wipes it off, drawing his fingers from the corners of his mouth to his chin. "It doesn't matter how I found that letter. Fact is, you're going."

"Seriously? I thought it was some sort of hoax." I study the letter again, thinking of the guy who attacked me in Los Angeles. "*Congratulations, Genesis, you just passed your entrance exam.*" He scared the crap out of me but, come to think of it, he didn't leave a scratch. "Have you heard of these guys?"

"Yeah, and it's not a hoax."

"Okay." My brain's buzzing on overdrive. Something's not clicking and I want to get to the bottom of it. "How do you know for sure?"

"I just do."

Typical Dad response, skirting the issue.

I wonder if he's ever had the Zen thing, like I did. After all, he's a seventh degree. "So, they've contacted you?"

His lips disappear into a thin line as he nods. "Look, I think this is a great opportunity for you. You love karate. And you can't be serious about staying in Bunkerville."

My jaw drops while a gazillion warring thoughts rocket through my head. Most of all, I sense he's not telling me everything—just like he never talks about his childhood. I swear I know Rex better than I know my own father.

I was so psyched after I opened the envelope. I'd do anything to go to a martial arts school. But I what will Dad do if I leave? Though he has his secrets, we've practically been joined at the hip these past four years. "What about the bar?" I ask, even sounding lame to myself. "You always said we're a team, right?"

Rolling his eyes, he gives my shoulder a gentle rap. "You think I can't live without you?"

"Excuse me, but only Monday you crashed. What's going to happen when I'm not here to call in help? Or make you coffee?" I want to say "or clean up your puke" but just can't make my lips form the words.

"Maybe it's time I stop using you as a crutch." He swipes a hand over his mouth. Lord knows that wasn't easy for him to admit. "You can't throw away the opportunity of a lifetime because you're worried about me."

I blink, Mom's dragon catching my eye. What would she do? Would she go?

Yeah. She'd go. She'd want it for me almost as much as I want it for myself.

It would be the most awesome thing on the planet to go to a school that develops my skills—turns me into a honed warrior like the students in the video.

Dad moves a big, callused palm over my hand and squeezes. "Do you *want* to stay in Bunkerville?"

My foot taps under the table. I can't look him in the eye. "No," I whisper, pulling my hand out from under his. "You really want me to go?"

"Angel," he says. "I've always known one day you'd grow wings and fly away. If all that's stopping you is my *problems* then you have only one choice."

I press the heels of my hands against my temples. This is a major decision we're talking about here, something that will affect both of us, massively changing everything. I'll be leaving my school, my dojo, Rex. God, Rex will spend junior year with fairy wings taped to his back.

"Wow," I blurt, surprising myself.

The corners of Dad's mouth turn up. "You'd better go pack."

Chapter Three

"The journey with a thousand miles begins with one step." - Confucius

On Saturday morning Dad takes me to the Casablanca Hotel to catch a Greyhound for Moab because students aren't allowed to have their vehicles on campus. After our talk, I realized he was totally right. Except I haven't thanked him yet. Maybe I'll save my breath until after I've seen the place.

"You need money?" he asks, pulling my truck into a parking space.

"I'm good."

He reaches across the cab and brushes my cheek. "I want you to know you can always come back if it doesn't work out up there."

"I know." I stretch over and wrap my arms around his neck. "You're my dad. I love you no matter what."

"Me, too, Angel."

My eyes prickle as I kiss his cheek. I can't believe this is really happening. "Stay off the sauce, okay?"

"Seven days sober, baby."

"Awesome. Now make it fourteen."

He kisses my forehead. "Call me, okay?"

"Promise. And thanks."

"You got it," he says, squeezing my shoulder. "Love you."

"Love you back."

If I don't leave now, I'll get all weepy-eyed and I don't want Dad to see me choke up. I hop out, grab my duffle, and climb onto the bus. As I take my seat, the old man's already driving out of the parking lot.

I'm gonna miss that truck. Him, too.

I listen to an audio book which passes the time and, once we arrive in Moab, I'm met by a girl wearing jeans and a pink camo t-shirt. The only thing giving her away is her desert boots—definitely military issue. And she's super fit. Otherwise, her dark blonde hair is pulled back in a ponytail and she isn't wearing any make-up. Not that she needs it.

She steps forward and thrusts out her hand, her biceps bulging out from under the sleeve of her t-shirt. "Genesis?"

I wipe my sweaty palm on my shirt before I shake her hand. "That's me." Usually I'm not the nervous type, but I only found out I was going to be here less than a week ago and I'm still grappling with reality. Rex is already on vacation with his parents in California and here I am in the middle of nowheresville heading into the unknown to attend a school with so many secrets no one can Google it.

Okay, I cut myself some slack. Anyone in my shoes ought to be nervous.

"Welcome," says the girl. "I'm Grace, and I'll be your mentor—at least until you discover your calling. You need help with your bags?"

"No thanks," I reply, swinging my enormous navy-blue duffel over my shoulder. "I packed light." Honestly, I packed according to the list we were given which said uniforms were required on campus and they would be issued upon arrival. Most of my gear is underwear, socks, Under Armour for cold weather, my favorite blanket. It's an afghan, really. Mom made it, and if anyone gives me crap about "my blankie" I'll deck them. "Are you picking up anyone else?"

"Nope. You're the last of the new recruits."

"How many are there?"

"Not many—a dozen or so, I think." She examines my face, making me worry if I have mascara smudges. "You have the most amazing eyes. They're like polished amber. Do you wear contacts?"

"Nope—inherited the color from my dad and the shape from my mom—cat eyes they say."

"Cats or no, it's a Gucci combination."

I'm walking a little lighter as Grace leads me to an off-road Jeep—sand-colored, definitely military. I toss my bag in the back. I'm a little surprised my class is so small, but who am I to question anything? I'm still not even sure this is for real. If it weren't for Dad's insistence, I might even be worried about climbing into an army jeep with a girl who looks like Barbie on steroids.

I sit in the passenger seat and fasten my seatbelt while Grace revs the engine. "Are you a student?"

She checks both ways and heads north—back the way the bus came. "I'm a blue belt."

I nod wondering why she's at an elite school for martial artists if she's only a blue. "Do you like it?"

"The academy is awesome, but I'm the first to admit it's not for everyone."

Before we cross the Colorado River, Grace turns onto Route 128 away from the flow of traffic.

"The school must be pretty remote," I say.

"It is. As the crow flies, it's only about thirty-five miles from Moab, but it'll take us over an hour to get there."

Though the altitude here is a fair bit higher than home, the landscape is similar. It's dry and dotted with sagebrush on a background of red cliffs.

Grace glances over the top of her sunglasses. "I suppose you're nervous about what it will be like. I know I was."

"A little." Hell, yeah. I'm as nervous as a Chihuahua who's high on caffeine. I take a deep breath and transport myself to a meditative state. Though I got there super-fast at the tournament, I've been working on chakra meditation since the day I walked into Sensei Soto's dojo. Once the sense of calm pulses through my veins, I say, "A dozen juniors doesn't sound like much. What am I getting myself into?"

Grace laughs. "Everyone's asks that at first. It's on account of all the secrecy."

"Exactly. And why the hush hush?"

"You'll find out." She smiles like Mom used to whenever I asked what she got me for my birthday. "First of all, you won't be a junior."

Alarm bells blast in my head. "Huh? I know it's a college, but it's also a prep school for high school juniors and seniors, right?"

"It is, but we're all martial artists—we just have varying skills. First years are white belts—those are the incoming high school juniors."

"White?" I ask, my voice shooting up. Jeez, I haven't worn a white belt since kindergarten.

"Don't let it bother you. Most of us have black belts and above in various disciplines when we enter. White just means you're in your first year. Then if you make it six months you'll earn a yellow. Second years wear orange, third years blue, and fourth purple, fifth brown. Only sixth years—seniors at the college level—wear black."

My mind cogitates the news. First and second years are high schoolers and wear white through orange. College freshmen wear blue, sophomores purple, brown for juniors, and finally black. "It sounds like we're all lumped in together—college and prep."

"Not for academic classes but there's crossover in technique classes." Grace signals and passes a tractor. "Instructors wear red belts and Grand Master Li wears red with a black border."

"We get to train with the Grand Master?"

"He's the head of school—generally he trains our trainers."

"That's cool."

"You'll meet him. He always talks to the new recruits at orientation."

"Awesome." I rub my fingers over the armrest. "What was it you said about finding a calling?"

Grace drums her fingers on the steering wheel. "It's basically your major. White belts don't have to worry about it. Students select specialties because they excel in various courses of study like computers, history..."

"Martial arts?" I ask.

"Sure—at least the ones who are natural born fighters. *They* usually lean toward degrees in Asian history and fighting techniques."

"That's why I'm here. Absolutely."

"Sweet."

My anxiety eases a bit. After all, I'm not easy to impress and I was blown away by the martial arts exhibition on the academy's video. But then, it could have been all for show.

"Isn't it kind of weird to start now?" I ask. "What about summer break?"

"We don't really have a summer break. Don't get me wrong, our breaks are just different—a couple weeks here and there rather than a huge lump of time off. Unless you're on a mission..." she said, her voice trailing off.

"Mission?"

"Oops. I probably shouldn't have mentioned that." Grace glances at me and cringes. "Um...they'll tell you what you need to know at orientation. Anyway, white belts never go on missions."

"Okaaaay." I bite my lip for a second, waiting for her to say more. When she doesn't, I try another tack. "So, I'm guessing these missions aren't for some church. What sorts of things do the students do? Where do they go?"

"Seriously, I can't say." Grace flicks on some tunes and raises her voice, "It's top secret, you know what I mean?"

Secrets? Just like Dad. I'm used to secrets, but now I'm jumping from living with one person with secrets to an entire school of them. What the heck am I getting myself into?

My head bumps the headrest as she plows through a pothole.

Now the road crosses the Colorado River. A skeleton of an old suspension bridge dangles on the far side. For some reason, the ruin reminds me of my dad and how losing Mom broke him. Like he said, maybe not having me around as his crutch will actually help. I hope it does.

I watch the scenery for a while I bob my head to *Yummy*. "So, you said you're a blue belt?"

"Yep."

That means she's a college freshman. But I need to associate the blue belts with year three. The belt system makes sense to me. After all, I've grown up with it. Achieved my second degree black belt last year—not that it matters now.

White belt. I snort. I guess they have to put the first years in their place just like every other school.

Grace flips on her blinker. "We're going cross country from here. It's a bit rough in places."

The dirt road starts out smooth enough but that doesn't last. After a few miles, the potholes are like land mines and Grace turns up the volume loud enough to make my seat vibrate. We drive over rocks and up steep slopes, and finally, the road entirely peters out. We hit a section of sheer rock and I don't see any tire tracks at all.

The jeep fishtails—not a quick jiggle, but it skids down an incline, jerking from side to side like the Incredicoaster at Disney.

"Are you sure you know where we're going?" I yell over the rev of the engine and the blast of music, gripping the handle at the top of my door and the armrest on the other side. My body goes airborne, and I'm caught by the seatbelt as we sail over a ridge.

We hit nose first and Grace's head whiplashes against the headrest. "We have about another twenty minutes of this."

If we live.

I've been four-wheeling before, but this is extreme on another level.

By the time the red adobe, flat-topped buildings come into view, my teeth hurt from clenching them. "They really don't want visitors around here do they?" I shout.

Grace turns off the tunes as the Jeep rolls onto a smooth road, giving me a chance to check out the place without my eyeballs rattling. The campus isn't big—about the size of a small college. I already love the architecture. It blends in with the surrounding red cliffs. I turn and look behind us. We've driven through a narrow chasm. Now we're surrounded as if the academy is sitting in the middle of Mother Nature's fortress.

At the far end, the crag slopes upward to a striking rock arch, the top twisted like the back of a Chinese dragon—kinda like Mom's dragon. My heart flutters as if some sort of energy radiates from the gap and I bend forward for a better look. Crystal blue sky shimmers through the chasm. Oh yeah, I'm hiking up there as soon as I can.

"Are we in Arches National Park?" I ask.

"Nope. This property is government owned and protected by a state-of-the-art electric barrier."

"So, how'd we get in?"

She points to the Jeep's console. "Didn't you see me push the red button?"

I hadn't. But then I'd clenched my eyes shut more times than I could count. "But don't hikers come this way? Are they zapped? I'll bet that makes the news."

"Not so much," Grace says, not volunteering anything further. It's probably another one of those need to know things.

Another secret.

She stops the Jeep outside a building with a lot of windows. There's a silver sign over the doorway that reads, *Women's Dorm.*

"Oh, and cell phones aren't allowed. I'm supposed to take yours and check it in to the office." She holds out her hand. "Don't worry, you can get it back any time you leave."

I hand it over. "My friend Rex is going to think I don't care about him anymore."

"You'd better send everyone on your contacts an e-mail and let them know you've gone silent." She slips my phone into a zip lock bag that already has my name on it. "Come on. I'll show you to your room. Your uniforms are already there—maybe your roommate, too."

"I have a roommate?"

"Sure do. I even think you might know her."

The common room of the dorm is so clean it looks as if it's never used. There's a kitchen area, a big-screen TV and short-backed couches in red and green. Grace is walking too fast for me to take in much detail, aside from the lattice sliding bamboo doors as we pass them. She stops at the end of the hall and knocks on room one-twenty-two.

"Just a minute," says a voice while footsteps approach.

After the door slides open, I cough out a gasp. I thought Grace was joking when she said I might know my new roomie. The face staring back at me shifts from a friendly, smiling expression to disbelief. For a second, I'm thrown back to the tournament and the final match. My adrenaline shoots through my veins as I tighten my fist around my duffel.

"Hey," I say, finding my voice.

Ziana Davis purses her cobalt-blue painted lips. "Genesis? What are you doing here?"

All smiles, Grace gestures inside. "I heard about the tournament. Isn't it cool? First and second place are rooming together."

Ziana doesn't budge. She stares at me with those sapphire eyes as if her fingers are about to grow daggers. The girl has incredibly white skin like she was born in Iceland and has never seen the sun. And though her hair is bleached platinum, she has super dark roots to match her eyebrows. I'm guessing her natural color might be chestnut brown. It curls around her jaw in an asymmetrical bob—the cut suits her.

After another awkward pause, I push inside. "It's good to see you again."

The room is narrow—desks with cupboards and lots of shelves on each side. Laptops, too. I see Ziana has already claimed one.

"Orientation is at five. You don't have much time. Make sure you're in full gi uniforms," says Grace sounding way too chirpy. "So...*um*...I'll let you two settle in. But hurry."

The door slides closed and Ziana moves in behind me. "Tight quarters, huh?" she asks, sounding like she's recovered from her initial shock.

"Yeah," I agree. "But something tells me we won't be spending a ton of time here."

"You're probably right." She walks on and gestures with an upturned palm as if she's giving a tour. "I took the bottom bunk and the closet on the left."

"Okay." Beyond the desks, there are two cupboards side by side. I open the one on the right—there's hanging space on one half with seven shelves on the other. I finger one of the white gis along with pants and a belt. "Is this mine?"

"Yep. We all have two sets—and you'll find four t-shirts on the top shelf."

Opposite the closets are futon bunkbeds. They're recessed into tidy boxes with cupboard-like doors for privacy. The bottom bunk is unmade, so it appears I'll be climbing a slatted ladder every night to get to my rack. Ziana definitely took the better option, but I suppose it doesn't matter.

I set my duffel on the floor and open the zipper. "How long have you been here?"

"Two days."

"Wow, and I thought things happened awfully fast for me."

"They happened faster at my house," Ziana says, as if the recruitment process was a competition which she won because she arrived first. "As soon as the letter came, my mom chartered a flight."

"Chartered?" I ask, searching her earlobes for gargantuan diamond studs or something. But she's not wearing any jewelry—only her white gi, without her belt. "That sounds expensive."

She tosses her hair. "We never fly commercial."

I take out my afghan and sling it up to my bed. "Must be nice."

"My dad's rich. We live on the beach in Carlsbad. Do you know where that is?"

"No idea." I'm not about to tell her I live in an apartment above a bar in nowheresville Nevada.

"North of San Diego."

"Awesome." It takes me about sixty seconds to unpack the rest of my gear and fill two whole shelves. I wouldn't be surprised if Ziana has Gucci luggage and her closet is chock full. I can't help but shake my head. I'm rooming with Lady Gaga with a combative streak. Given I'm the most competitive person I know, it's probably not a good combination.

I close my closet and climb part way up the ladder to check out my rack. "Do you know what our schedule will be like?"

"We'll get it at orientation, but the workout facilities are to die for. I'm totally going to rock weapons class."

Why do I already want to strangle her? We'll be wearing white belts for a reason. That's because there's a boatload of upperclassmen who are leagues ahead of us in everything. Didn't she watch the video?

"Cool," I mumble. My bed cubby is more spacious than I initially thought. The mattress is really soft and the sheets and blankets are all white. At the back there's a lamp for reading and room for books.

I hop down and check the clock. "I'd better change."

"So, did you drive to Moab?"

I shed my jeans and t-shirt, folding and putting them on an empty shelf. "Greyhound bus—from Bunkerville, Nevada. Have you heard of it?" I ask, deciding I might as well lay my cards on the table. After all, we're all wearing white gis and white belts and I'm guessing we're all on scholarship, so it doesn't matter how much Daddy makes.

She shakes her head. "What's in Nevada besides Vegas?"

"Just drive to the end of the earth and just before you fall off, you'll reach my hometown—all thirteen hundred and three inhabitants," I say pulling on one of the academy t-shirts.

"That's amazing," she says, and she doesn't sound sarcastic.

I step into my white pants. "Why's that?"

"Because you beat me and I have access to some of the best martial arts schools in Southern Cal."

"You don't know Sensei Soto. Or my dad." Shrugging into my gi, I tie the side laces then grab my belt and flap it under Ziana's nose. "Where's yours?"

She huffs and opens her closet. Yep—it's totally crammed full of clothes and shoes. I almost laugh. Where does she expect to wear heels in the middle of the desert?

She gives me a snort over her shoulder, looking way friendlier than when I walked in. "I can't believe they're making us wear white."

Chapter Four

"Real knowledge is to know the extent of one's ignorance." - Confucius

The assembly hall is stark white with chrome chairs. There's an Asian mural on one wall—cherry blossoms, Chinese writing, pagodas—peaceful things. There are big windows letting in plenty of light which makes me feel warm. Maybe I'm a child of the sun because I love to be bathed in light. From the window is a clear view of the red-rock arch. I don't know why, but I want to stare at it. Is the dragon shape natural or altered by man? My guess is it's a wonder of nature.

Ziana and I move toward a group of white belts standing at the back. On the stage there are five senseis. I recognize them by the red belts they're wearing over black gis.

Oh. My. God.

The man who attacked me in the parking lot is one of them. Shading my eyes with my hand, I look at my toes.

Holy effing crap!

"Who are they?" asks Ziana.

"They're the first-year instructors," says a dude wearing glasses. He's of average build and looks like he belongs on *The Big Bang Theory*. Grinning, he thrusts out his hand. "I'm Elias. My brother is a blue belt. Ask me anything."

Ziana clutches her hands over her chest as if she's horrorstruck. "Your brother tells you what goes on here?"

"Well, not everything exactly. But he totally thought I'd like it here."

Flipping her hair, Ziana tips up her chin. "What belt level are you?"

"Ah..." Elias looks to his midriff. "White."

"You know what I mean, we're all champions."

"Champions at different things." Elias takes a step back. "Sure, I've been taking karate since I was a little kid, but my specialty is computers. Won a national science award. I want to work in command one day—as long as I can pass the physical."

"Command?" I ask, keeping my back to the stage. "What's that?"

"It's where they do research and support. You know, IT stuff."

The pieces of the puzzle aren't all fitting together for me. "But I thought everyone here was to be trained as an elite fighter—sort of like Navy Seals, but martial artists. And what about the..." I lower my voice. "Missions?"

"Shh." Elias holds a finger to his lips. "They're watching us."

"Missions?" Ziana whispers in my ear.

Turning his head, Elias cups his hand beside his mouth like he has a secret. "One thing I do know is there's more to the Military Academy of Martial Arts than just cranking out elite fighters like the Marines."

I examine him, narrowing my eyes. The Marines may have been an option for me if I hadn't been planning to stay in Bunkerville.

"Everyone find a seat," says a female instructor standing behind the podium. It doesn't take long because there are only twelve of us. Once we're settled, she continues, "I'm Sensei Nakamura. Welcome white belts."

We all applaud while I check around the room for Grand Master Li who ought to be wearing a red belt with black trim, but he's not here.

Nakamura is so short she can barely see over the podium. "I'm sure it goes without saying you all were handpicked for this top-secret institution. And I can speak for every sensei in the school when I say we are all looking forward to working with you. You will call us sir or ma'am just like in the military. Each of your instructors will train you on various disciplines of martial arts and, in addition, each of us teach classes as well. I will train you in judo. I also teach Japanese and Asian history as well as other languages of the Orient."

She asks the teachers to stand and tell us about themselves. Sensei Santos teaches Filipino weapons and warfare as well as English and math. Sensei Bashir specializes in weapons, medieval history and science. As a weapons enthusiast, I'm liking him better already. Besides, I know he's an ace. After all, he scared the crapola out of me in a parking lot.

Sensei Schneider teaches European history with an emphasis on the Dark Ages. Sensei Okoye is from Nigeria and teaches Egyptian, Greek, and Roman history as well as the ancient dialects.

By the time Sensei Okoye sits, my head spins. Do they really expect us to learn a gazillion languages at once? I am pretty good at Spanish. I glance over my shoulders and by the gape-mouthed stares of the others, I'm not the only one thinking there's no way I'm going to learn Japanese, Latin, and Egyptian Coptic on top of everything else.

"Ahem," says Sensei Nakamura. "Our goal is to stretch your limits. We're looking for the most dedicated and the most talented individuals. But I'll tell you now, not all of you will earn your yellow belts."

"I'm earning mine," blurts Ziana like she's asserting herself as class leader.

I clench my fists until my nails dig into my palms. Sure, I'll fight to get my yellow if it kills me but bragging about it isn't going to endear me to my teachers.

"You will do well to remember confidence is a virtue, but arrogance is a vice." Nakamura takes a moment to stare down my roomie, then she smiles. "Every cadet will receive his or her schedules first thing in the morning."

Ziana raises her hand this time. "Excuse me, but don't we choose our own schedules?"

The sensei makes a face like she's just eaten something way too sour and she's about to spit it out. "*White* belts do not. The faculty must first assess individuals and identify their aptitudes. Those who make it through the first term are then allowed more say into their courses of study."

"But—"

Before Ziana can utter another question, Sensei Nakamura holds up her palm, demanding silence. "This is not a time to ask questions but to listen. Now, please join me in welcoming Grand Master Li."

Everyone applauds while a side door opens.

"Oh my God," I whisper into Ziana's ear.

"What?"

"He was watching us spar at the tournament."

"No way."

"Yes way. I looked straight at him. He almost threw me out of my zone." He did throw me out. And something passed between us that took me to a higher level but I'm not about to admit it to Ziana or anyone else at the moment. I've thought about it a lot since the tournament. It was as if he took me into a zone where I'd never been before. But how? I'd never seen him before. We hadn't even talked, but ever since the tournament my reflexes have been a little sharper.

And I don't know why.

Li's gnarled cane taps the floor as he climbs up the stairs. His head is bowed, his movements slow and majestic almost as if he's performing a tai chi kata. I move to the edge of my seat, dying to ask him if he had anything to do with the outcome of the tournament. But I know the answer is no. I won, fair and square.

When he looks out from behind the podium, his face is every bit as weathered as I remembered, but his eyes are even more incredibly hawkish. He takes his time panning his gaze across the class. I want to smile, wave, and thank him for his calming influence during the match, but as soon as the idea enters my head, those obsidian eyes are piercing through my skull.

Again, an overwhelming sense of calm fills me and I know I've made the right decision to come here. I almost feel like I belong, like I've always belonged. Maybe destiny was waiting for the right time. Just being in the same room with the Grand

Master makes me want to work hard, to strive for excellence.

"Thank you for your introduction, Sensei Nakamura," he says. Li speaks with a Chinese accent. "It is always a pleasure to meet a new group of enterprising recruits. During your six-month initiation period, I ask you to focus on your studies and apply yourselves to the task of earning your yellow belts. Always remember that nothing matters aside from this single goal. Though I would like everyone to progress, the level of dedication and perseverance required does not suit all students."

"It suits me," Ziana mumbles.

He stops and takes a sip of water. "As for our history, in one way or another, this institution has been in existence since the time of ancient civilizations that are no longer—the Phoenicians, the Egyptians, the Mayans, the Macedonians, the Qiang." He pauses after the last—a civilization I don't recognize, but the mention of it makes an icy chill spread across my shoulders. It's eerie, like the feeling I got in the parking lot when Sensei Bashir was behind me in the parking lot.

I involuntarily shudder while Ziana squirms. I sense she's about to raise her hand and mention something about the inception in 1798 like it says in the letter. I give her a stern look and she folds her hands in her lap, but her foot is tapping as if she's about to jump out of her skin. I inhale to the count of six and focus.

Li spreads his arms wide and I'm surprised at how long his reach is compared to his height. "As you are aware from your introduction letters, The Military Academy of Martial Arts was started by President Adams in 1798, brought to Philadelphia from war-torn France. Our graduates are employed in all areas of the military and hold many positions in law enforcement as well as the intelligence community. If you remain, over the next six years, all of you will have the opportunity to develop yourselves into elite warriors. And by warriors I do not necessarily mean fighters. I am referring to the attainment of the seven chakras, the mastery of mind, body, and soul as well as your chosen course of study. By the time you graduate from the academy, you will be..."

He stops and looks to the teachers as if he's trying to come up with the right words. "You will be highly trained and therefore highly sought after."

Li's gaze settles on Ziana. "If you remember nothing else, self-control is achieved through the heart chakra, it brings us balance. You will meditate often because only through keen self-awareness and focus at a level you cannot yet possibly grasp, will you achieve greatness. Calm your inner fire. Control your sphere of influence. Be one with the universe."

He pauses for a moment, his expression peaceful as if he's staring at cherry blossoms shimmering in the breeze. "Ours is a world of secrets—of privileged information we are at *no time in our lives* at liberty to share with anyone beyond our walls. And when you are ready, you will be asked to pledge yourself to our principles. As white belts, you absolutely must prove your commitment to your coursework."

He stops and scans every face in the room. "Your contact with the outside world will be limited. Cell phones must be held in the office. There is no telephone service here aside from satellite phones. Students are allowed to make calls on Wednesdays and Saturdays."

Though Grace took my phone, I didn't realize there wasn't service. I wonder how Rex's vacation is going. He took my news a lot better than I thought.

My attention shifts to the arch.

I lean toward it, unable to stop staring. The air inside the gap shimmers and a sense of overwhelming dread makes a cold sweat bead my brow. It's like knowing something really bad is happening but not being able to do anything about it. A white light shoots through the gap. I squint, trying to make out the shapes of tiny shadows coming through it. Or are they in the distance behind it?

I can't shift my eyes away. Should I say something? But what? Maybe I'm just nervous because it's the first day.

The door opens and a man pops his head in. "Grand Master Li, you're needed, sir."

Li's obsidian gaze flickers straight to the arch. Then for a moment, he goes glassy-eyed.

I sense his unrest. Except I'm positive he knows *why* the air is so charged.

"Thank you," he says. "If you'll excuse me, class, Sensei Bashir will continue with your orientation and issue the white belt handbooks." He beckons Sensei Nakamura. Together they leave and he's moving a lot faster than when he arrived.

While Bashir talks, his words garble together like we're underwater. I can't stop watching out the window, itching to rush outside.

Until Sensei Okoye pushes a button and lowers the shades, blocking my view.

Ziana hands me a stack of booklets and I take one and pass on the others. Thumbing to the back, there's a campus map. As soon as I get some free time I'm going to climb up to the arch and have a good look. Except at the top of the map it says the Dragon's Arch is off limits.

How stupid is that?

Bashir raises his voice. "Everyone repeat after me, 'the Dragon's Arch is off limits to white belts.'"

We all comply.

"Why white belts?" Ziana asks.

The sensei grabs both sides of the podium and leans forward. "Because it's dangerous up there."

"Then why isn't it off limits to everyone?" I ask.

He glares at me. "Because those are the rules."

Ziana and I exchange expressions of silent indignation.

"*Obey?*" she mouths.

I shrug and widen my eyes.

"All right," says Bashir. "The schedule isn't easy, but it will turn you into a warrior. We wake at four a.m., followed by the first workout of the day—morning workouts are separated by belts. After breakfast you'll attend your scheduled classes. Lunch is at noon followed by weapons training, afternoon classes, and then your second workout is with your assigned group in which belts are intermixed. Dinner is at eight. Lights out by ten. Any questions?"

Just about everyone in the room raises their hands.

Sensei Bashir grins. "Good. You should all be inundated with questions at this stage. Believe me, you will find your answers in time. I'll see you at dinner."

Ziana hops to her feet. "You mean that's all?"

Bashir has nearly made it to the door when he stops and eyes her with a hard stare. "Sir. You always end a question with sir." With that, he walks out.

As the door shuts behind him and the rest of the staff, Ziana thrusts her fists to her hips and snorts. "I can't believe it."

"What?" I move to the window and find the button to raise the shades. Outside, Grace strides past with a group of blue belts and waves, but there's no sign of Grand Master Li or Sensei Nakamura. "I guess all we need to know is dinner isn't until eight and we have to be up every day at four o'clock."

"That's going to kill me," says Elias.

"Me, too," says Piper. I met her before orientation started.

I lead the way to the courtyard, at least I think everyone's following me, but they all seem to be more worried about what's next than the flickering light in the arch. Was I the only one who saw it? It didn't seem like a coincidence when Grand Master Li left orientation so abruptly.

I leave my classmates behind and make a beeline the admin building. There's a woman sitting behind a reception desk and, beyond, a stark corridor. "Yes?" she asks, looking over the top of her glasses.

"I was wondering, um..." What do I say? I can't exactly tell her I have a weird feeling and want to talk to Grand Master Li. Besides, I'm hard-wired to stay out of the principal's office. And he already told us there are secrets white belts cannot know.

"But what about the Qiang?" I hear Li's voice even though the receptionist doesn't seem to notice. And I don't exactly hear it as much as know the master is speaking. This is the second time he's mentioned the Qiang and the second time it's given me an uneasy chill.

"We got him," says a deep voice that I can't place.

"Just one?" asks Li.

"Yes, sir."

I blink and the receptionist's face comes back into focus.

Her eyebrows arc up. "What were you wondering?"

I'm just about to ask where I can find Grand Master Li when the sound of a helicopter whirrs in the distance.

"Never mind. I'm sorry to bother you."

Following my gut, I run outside and race toward the sound. There's a helo pad ahead and a dust cloud scatters as the chopper touches down.

Bending at the waist, Li and Nakamura head beneath the blades, followed by a tall guy carrying someone in his arms—a girl. And there's another, shorter, skinnier dude in his wake. The girl wipes a hand over her forehead. Oh, God, her fingers smear a swath of blood.

Li and Nakamura talk to someone on the chopper while the two boys help the girl inside. Then they all crouch and skitter away from the rotating blade.

As the chopper ascends, I catch Grand Master Li's eye. Stepping away from the others, he frowns and beckons me. "Why are you here?"

I purse my lips while my gaze shifts toward the arch. Weird. Blue sky shines through the gap just like any normal day. Should I tell him?

"Do not withhold the truth from me, Genesis."

He throws me off by using my name. I mean, we haven't exactly been introduced. If I tell him what I saw and how I felt, he's going to think I'm a nutcase and send me home. Gah! How can I resist him when his eyes are boring through me almost as if he can read my thoughts? Does he already know?

Freaking out, I grab the ends of my belt and yank on them to tighten the knot. "Um...when we were in orientation I thought I saw sparkles and a beam of light through the arch, circling sort of like a spiral. A-and it looked like shadows were approaching. But they weren't close, they were..." I stop, trying to figure out how to explain it.

"You saw glittering lights through the arch?" he asks with a hint of alarm in his voice—alarm or amazement, I'm not sure which.

"Yes. During orientation." I nod my head, smoothing a trembling hand over my hair. I should have kept my mouth shut. "Maybe I'm just hungry. I missed lunch."

"Hmm. There's something else you're not telling me." He leans on his cane and looks closer like he can see into my head. "What is it?"

I have no idea what he's talking about. "Uh...the...*feeling*?" I ask, my voice totally unsure while my entire body tenses, ready for him to tell me I'm expelled—after all, I was sent home for a week in the sixth grade after sticking up for Rex. Ever since, I've been paranoid when it comes to talking to the principal.

And Li is more than a principal. He's a *grand master*. I'll bet he can kill me with a tap of his fingernail. "Explain."

A lead weight sinks in my gut. Now I'm done for. I'll be shipped out on the next Greyhound tomorrow.

But this is driving me crazy. He's the source of the eerie sensations I've been having, isn't he? "There was a cold chill—*ah*—especially when you mentioned the Qiang."

With his sharp inhale, the master's eyes narrow.

"Who are they?" I ask, ignoring the voice at the back of my mind telling me to shut up.

Saying nothing, he starts off, his cane tapping the ground.

I take a step toward him. "What happened to the girl, sir?"

"She won't return," he says, but then stops as if he's thinking. "The Qiang is an ancient Tibetan order thought to be extinct."

"Thought to be?" I ask.

"Aye." He looks me in the eye like he did when I was in the ring. "I sense you already know they are not."

It's at least ninety degrees outside and I have goosebumps skimming up my arms. There's something about the Qiang that's really bad. "They're evil," I say and I know it as sure as I am breathing.

"Yes. And you will learn more in time." He claps a hand on my shoulder and squeezes, his grip like iron. "Let nothing stand in the way of your studies here and you will succeed."

I gape at him as he totters away, now I'm even more confused. The shorter of the two guys walks past and doesn't even glance at me. His face is covered with grime, a line on one cheek washed clean by the stream of a tear. He's not wearing a gi or belt. His clothes are rough-hewn—some sort of wool leggings, kind of a medieval-looking tunic, and thin, leather shoes with pointed toes. My heart twists in a hundred knots as if I can feel his pain.

Turning, I look to the second dude. The one who'd carried the girl. His shoulders slump and he's raking his fingers through his long brown hair and shaking his head. He's dressed in medieval attire as well. Have they attended some sort of reenactment?

In the middle of the high desert?

And something went terribly wrong?

This guy's aura is roiling with anger and grief. His vibes make me shudder.

I want to reach out to him, to say something to comfort him, but I just stand clenching my fists at my sides. To him I'm a stranger and he's obviously just been in an accident or something. He must be freaking.

The dude saunters toward me, his expression as hard as steel, his jaw square. There's a defensive edge to him from his cocky gait to the way he holds his chin. As he wipes a hand across his mouth, I notice a cross tattooed between his thumb and pointer finger.

He slows as I step into his path. His eyes flash with malice like he's more than mad, like he wants to kill somebody. He's a good head taller than me and his shoulders are buff as if he's wearing pads. A tic twitches in his jaw. Whoa, the dude's intensity takes my breath away.

My fingers splay, aching to reach out, to help calm the fire raging off him. "Are you okay?" I ask.

He stops and stares down at me with incredibly vivid eyes—transparent as glass and as intense as the lightest of blue diamonds. I'm instantly connected as if something unsaid passes between us, something that makes my entire body tingle with awareness.

This guy is obviously mega-tough with a savageness about him. For the love of God, he'd make a few of the Muddy Hollow's biker dudes quake in their pants.

His lips part and I think he's going to say something, but instead he steps closer, grabs the ends of my belt, and wraps them around his fists. He's so close, my mind reels. I should parry out, break his grip and back away, but I'm totally rooted where I stand. I've never been this attracted to anyone in my life and his face is only inches from mine. He smells like fresh earth and woodsmoke—as wild and feral as his tanned face.

My stomach flips. I can't breathe. He's not going to kiss me, is he?

He dips his chin, his mouth moving closer, but those full lips pass beyond my cheek and to my ear. "Go home white belt."

Chapter Five

"Worry not that no one knows you. Seek to be worth knowing." - Confucius

"No one ever told me we'd have to study Latin," says Ziana as we walk out of class.

I keep my mouth shut because I know she didn't get better than a sixty percent on her quiz. Sensei Okoye said that was the highest grade, and my paper came back with the top mark. Who knows, maybe we all got sixty? I really don't care. In my book, the entire class failed.

"My mom will kill me if she finds out I'm not acing everything."

"Then thank God she's not here," I mumble. Two weeks have passed since orientation and none of us have had much time to breathe, let alone perfect anything. And no wonder Ziana is so quick to tell me how superior she is—her mom has been pressuring the girl all her life. From what she's told me, her mother is like one of those hideous beauty pageant moms. It doesn't make Ziana's bragging any easier to take but at least I understand why she does it.

I'm struggling the same as everyone else, even the geniuses like Elias. Back home I was Sensei Soto's protégé, but here I'm just a plebe. Now I know why they assigned the first years with white belts.

There is so much to learn, I feel like I'm drowning in a sea of infinite data.

And sore. When we're not doing bookwork, we're toning our bodies. Strength training, flexibility, running, weapons, and karate on an immersive scale. There are new katas with intricate moves I can't even wrap my mind around. I think I'm executing something perfectly when the sensei stops, demonstrates, and makes me repeat the move a hundred times. I can honestly say from experience that repeating an intense karate move, twisting forearms and wrists in unnatural positions while leaping and spinning through the air, isn't only exhausting, it makes your arms and legs cramp in the middle of the night.

"Seriously, I'd crawl in a hole and die if my mom was here," Ziana continues.

I stop outside the gym, grab her shoulders, and give her a firm shake. I've heard enough about her darned mother. "Listen, the last thing you need to worry about is whether or not you're disappointing that woman. We are sworn to secrecy and your mama can't possibly know what goes on here unless she has some sort of silent drones in the sky."

Crouching, Ziana looks up. "They have those?"

"No, silly!" I release my grip. "Besides, you're a junior in high school. You're practically an adult. Your mommy doesn't control you and the sooner you realize it, the sooner you'll shed all your mom-fear baggage and be able to focus on what's really important." I'm amazed this comes out of my mouth because, only a few weeks ago, I was wishing for a crystal ball to tell me what to do when I grow up.

Anger flashes through Ziana's eyes. Then she snorts, the corners of her mouth turning up. Now that we've been roomies for a while, she's ratcheted down the snob-queen attitude—at least enough where I don't mind telling her what I think. "You're right. You're lucky your mom didn't badger you all the time."

"If only," I say. She has no idea what it was like to be twelve years old, lose my mother and try to hold it together while Dad fell to pieces. My throat closes as I reach for the door. But I can't let emotions get me down. Not with a sixty percent on my Latin test. I shake it off and strengthen my resolve. Li told me not to let anything get in the way of my studies. I'm going to earn my yellow belt, goddammit!

"Aren't you going back to the room?" Ziana asks. We have an hour to study before the final workout of the day. So far, the white belts have been confined in a solitary group, but tonight we'll get our assignments for new evening workout groups called waza class, not by belt rank, but by where the instructors believe we'll benefit most.

I incline my head toward the gym. "I need some workout time to myself."

Ziana holds up her books. "I'd better go practice my Latin."

"Then I'll see you back here in an hour."

Inside I hear kiais bellowing from the main karate gym, but that's not where I'm headed. Sensei Bashir has been giving an introduction to medieval weaponry and I want to prepare for his next test. The weapons gym has a section on the wall dedicated just for the Middle Ages. It's probably the coolest thing I've ever seen. And some of the weapons are heavy. Medieval warriors had to be brutishly strong. For starters, they wore chainmail, or plate armor in the later period. Not to mention, they swung hulking hammers, flails with chains and spiked iron balls, battle-axes, and pikes with rusted spearheads. Archery was critical. They had deadly crossbows and catapults that hurled rocks crashing into stone barbican walls. Some catapults threw fire onto roofs to burn them down.

It amazes me that anyone survived the era. But the brutal savagery grips my interest and I'm dying to know more.

I enter and the halogens automatically illuminate while I stride straight for the swords. We've been practicing with wooden wasters, but there's a Templar replica I've been dying to swing. I rub my fingertips together before I wrap my hand around the leather hilt, draw the weapon from its scabbard, and hold it up.

It's not as heavy as I would have thought—maybe three pounds. I slice the blade through the air a few times relishing the hiss, then I pick up the shield and slide my arm through the leather loops at the back. It's made of wood and heavier than the sword. I imagine when wearing eighty pounds of chainmail, just moving an arm takes effort, let alone fighting nonstop for an hour or more, defending with the shield, striking with the sword.

I go through the positions Bashir has been teaching. Templar training is different than the Samurai sword training I had with Sensei Soto. The weapon isn't balanced the same. Using a shield is awkward for me as well. I lunge and thrust against an imagined opponent. I raise the shield over my head in defense while I hack sideways, grunting with my clumsiness.

"You'd be better off using a two-handed great sword."

I'm startled by the deep voice and even more stunned when I see who it is.

"Noah Jones?" I say, unsure why *he's* here.

It's the guy with the crystal blue-diamond eyes I saw at the helo pad a couple weeks ago. The one who told me to go home and made me feel like a total idiot. I know his name because he's like the top martial artist in the school. *Everyone* knows him. But he's not dressed like a medieval sage anymore. He's wearing the standard uniform with a blue belt denoting he's a third year—a college freshman— probably eighteen, I guess. I've seen him in the cafeteria and he's glanced my way a couple of times, but I'm pretty sure he doesn't know I exist. Well, maybe he does now.

"Two handed?" I ask. "Doesn't the shield provide more protection?"

He saunters toward me those intense eyes checking me out. "Not if you're female and want to live."

I set the shield on the mat and balance the sword in front of me with both hands. It feels a lot better and far more like the Samurai sword I use at home. I swing through the pattern of positions we've been working on with Bashir, incredibly aware of Noah's scrutiny. He probably thinks I move like a sloth.

"So, Gen-e-sis," he says, drawing out my name. I'm floored that he even knows it. "I thought I told you to go home."

"Sorry." I present the sword in *en garde* position as a bit of a challenge. I even level my gaze. Feeling no fear, my mind homes on my target. "I guess I'm a glutton for punishment. Besides, I didn't realize you were the boss of me."

I don't like being bullied and I don't appreciate any guy who's rude to me regardless if he looks like Thor.

Even though I'm holding a weapon sharp enough to hack off his hand, he steps in and grabs my wrist. Applying only a hint of pressure to my ulnar nerve, he disarms me in a blink. He's close enough for his scent to envelop me. The earthy fragrance is gone, replaced by worn-in leather reminding me of the Harleys parked outside the Muddy Hollow. But most of all, the smell alerts me of danger and makes electric tingles fire across my skin. I'm not sure if I'm attracted or turned off. It doesn't matter. He's made it clear he doesn't give a rip about me and I'm not about to start acting like I'm thirsty for his attention.

Shifting my gaze to his face, I gulp. I'm five-foot nine, and he's towering over me like I'm some sort of petite waif.

"Where are you from?" he asks, his tone kinda friendlyish.

I wonder why he cares. "Nevada. You?"

"Chicago." He returns the sword to its place on the wall and retrieves two wooden wasters. "I guess it's time to show you why you shouldn't be here."

I take one of the wasters and swing the practice sword in a circle. "Only me?"

"Women in general—unless you want to be support." He backs away and assumes a medieval en garde position. "But something tells me you're not here for I.T. like my little brother."

I'm not, but I reckon he's already figured that out. I mirror Noah's stance. "You have a brother here?"

"Elias. He's a white belt."

Seriously? Noah and Elias are complete opposites, like Mutt and Jeff.

"He's smart," I say though I know Elias didn't get more than a 60% on today's Latin exam.

"Yeah."

My heartrate spikes when, with no notice, Noah bellows like a savage, heaves his waster over his head and attacks. I barely escape having my head cleaved in two by a wooden practice weapon when I manage to deflect. Darting aside, I regain my composure and circle. "Cheap shot, asshole."

He smirks. "What? Did you think I'd go easy on you?"

I leap back with an empty fade, faking him out and returning with a thrust. "We're sparring, right?"

Pivoting, he easily defends and passes back to my rear. "Are we?"

I hate having an opponent at my six. On full alert, I counter. "So, you want to kill me even though you hardly know me?"

"I want to show you why you shouldn't be a fighter." He's faster and levels the wooden blade at my neck. "You're dead."

A spike of anger inside me jolts through my blood. I hate being told I can't do something. With the pounding in my temples, I shift back to an en garde position—not holding the waster to the side like Bashir taught in medieval class, but forward as I learned from Sensei Soto. I take in a breath and relish the sensation of oxygen rushing through my blood. I don't know how it happened before, but I did it in the ring at the tournament and again in the parking lot. I turn myself over to chakra's subtle energy systems in the body. With my next six-count inhale, my mind goes to a place of utter tranquility.

Bring on the Zen.

"Are you ready?" Noah asks.

"Not going to blitz me?" My words come out breathless as if I'm half-asleep.

"Not with your eyes closed."

When did I close them? It doesn't matter. As I raise my lids, I see his attack in my mind's eye. I'm already moving to deflect when he lunges with a sideways slice. We spar back and forth almost evenly matched until he cranks up the tempo.

My heart pumps with exertion, though I'm fighting like this is a dance—if it weren't for the burning in my biceps from the brute strength required for every defense.

I can't allow myself to think. He's coming so fast, all I can do is sense his action and react, deflecting the brutal strikes of his waster. Swinging the wooden sword over his head, he hacks downward as I lunge aside and fend him off with an arcing umbrella defense. As our weapons connect, they both crack with deafening booms. The top half of my waster flies across the room while Noah's hangs by a splinter.

"Holy shit," he says, gaping at his mangled blade.

I pick up the broken piece of my sword and match it to the broken lower half. "I'll bet you weren't expecting that."

He glares at me, those crystal blues turning to ice. "No, but you're still no match for a man."

"All right," I agree. After all, I've never faced a man in competition. "Why do I need to be?"

"You don't want to know."

The whole mystery thing around here is getting to me. There are too many secrets. Why is Noah acting like a dick? Is he always this way? He has a good sixty pounds on me and I managed to hold my own against him, not to mention he also has two years of rigorous training at the academy beyond my newbie status.

"Is it because of the injured cadet?" I ask.

"Stacy." His forehead furrows as his tone softens. "Her name is Stacy and she was injured because I couldn't protect her."

"Protect her from what?" I shouldn't ask but the question just spills out of my mouth.

A white line forms between his lips. "You know that's classified and you damned-well better not ask again, white belt."

Oh great, pull the lowerclassman card and make me feel like a jackass. I know Grand Master Li told me to keep what I saw under wraps, but I'm dying to know more. It's eating at me like being in the midst of a crime and never knowing who, what, when, why, or how. I'm not going to rush out and blab about it. I need to ask why Noah was dressed like a medieval dude. I'm wracking my brain trying to figure out what happened to Stacy. How did she end up bloodied and where is she now?

"Is Amir as good a fighter as you?" I ask, skirting a little but still fishing for more. I've learned the second boy's name as well—he's a brown belt, a fifth year. He's probably twenty but he's not physically as impressive looking as Noah.

The big guy tosses his broken waster in the trash. "Amir can hold his own."

I make a mental note to watch the upper classmen spar—if I ever get the chance. Surely there must be a role for women martial artists here, otherwise why was I recruited or Ziana or any of the female cadets?

I throw my two halves away and head for the door.

"Genesis," Noah says as I reach for the latch, the sound of my name making goosebumps skitter up my arms.

I stop, but don't look at those icy eyes—eyes so intense I know they'll make me doubt myself all the more.

"If you're planning to stay, do me a favor and aim for a desk job," he says, not sounding edgy, but his tone is filled with concern. Does he really think I'm some kind of delicate flower?

No way. I head out while fury shoots through me. Little does he know he's just thrown down the gauntlet.

"I've never been one to resist a challenge," I say before the door closes behind me.

愛

I don't know why it comes as a surprise, but when I report to my first waza team class fifteen minutes later, Noah is standing in the center of the weapons gym. So are Grace, Amir, a purple belt named Sebastian, and some other cadets whose names I haven't yet committed to memory.

Noah's vivid gaze settles on me and he makes a show of shaking his head, groaning, and looking to the rafters.

I refuse to let him get under my skin.

Grace moves beside me. "Hi, Genesis. I'm so glad they put you with the Tigers."

"The Tigers?" I ask.

"It's our team name."

Before I can ask another question, Sensei Okoye comes in with a clipboard. "You'll all be happy to hear Sunday's challenge is seize the flag."

"Awesome," says Amir while the others agree, nodding their heads and giving each other high fives.

I lean toward Grace and whisper, "What's seize the flag?"

"I'm glad you asked," says Okoye, arching an eyebrow at me. "Class, welcome Genesis Mans."

My face flushes as all eyes shift my way. "Um...why is there just one white belt, sir?"

"Because our team only needed one more member." He pushes a pencil behind his ear. "I'd say waza class is a favorite of most cadets. The object is to work together on various tasks and exercises with the goal of winning Sunday morning's challenge."

I'm a bit confused. "Sunday's challenge, sir?"

"Ah, yes, you have not had the benefit of competing in one of Grand Master Li's contests. White belts are so busy in the first two weeks, we wait before we include them. Waza is structured to encourage teamwork, and Sunday's victorious team is rewarded with a private class with the Grand Master himself."

I roll up on the balls of my feet. Having a class with Li ought to be amazing.

"Today we're heading outside for some rock climbing."

"Rock climbing?" moans Grace, turning green.

Noah chuckles. "Yeah, you never know when you'll need to scale a stone wall."

Sensei Okoye gives him a look and Noah holds up his hands in surrender.

After Okoye leads us to the cliff face, I totally understand Grace's reluctance. We're going to climb a sheer wall that's about a hundred feet high.

"You queasy yet?" asks Noah.

"Not at all," I reply, testing a rope. Rex and I once spent a day at a rock-climbing gym in Las Vegas. That had to count for something.

"Don't worry about him," says Amir, smacking Noah's shoulder. The brown belt has dark brown eyes and could totally be a stunt double for Rami Malek. "This guy thinks if you can't beat him in sparring you have no business being here."

A stifle a snort in the back of my nose. "I've gathered."

Amir grips my shoulder and turns his lips toward my ear. "But the truth is no one beats him."

I level my gaze at the blue belt. "It would be awfully lonely around here with one student."

"Enough." Noah pulls on one of the ropes. "They've made it easy with these. In the real world you have to set in your cams and latch on your carabiners..." He shifts his gaze to Amir as if they've scaled hundreds of walls. "...unless there aren't any available."

"So, what's the object of today's lesson?" I ask.

Noah drops the rope. "Just climb up to the top as fast as you can."

"There are three lines. Three go at once," says Okoye, tossing a duffel bag on the ground. "Except there's a warrior at the top and each of you must take a piece of his equipment up with you. The game is not over until the warrior is fully outfitted."

"Is it a race?" I ask.

Amir gives me a nudge with his elbow. "Only when Noah's climbing."

"And on Sundays," adds Grace.

I pick up a medieval helmet and put it on my head. It's super loose, but I figure it's easy to carry. Noah puts on a white quilted shirt and has Sebastian help him into realistic-looking chainmail.

"How much does that weigh?" I ask.

"Everything in the kit is a true replica," says Okoye. "The coat of mail is roughly eighty pounds."

Noah straightens and jostles his shoulders. "You want to try it?"

I pretend to check out the ropes. I'll need some serious weight training if I'm going to carry an extra eighty pounds. "I'm good."

Noah places the middle rope into my hands. "We'll go first, Genesis."

"Why? So you can prove to me how much stronger you are?"

Amir takes the rope on the other side. "Don't bait him. It'll only bring out the angry beast."

Before I start, I tug on the rope, wondering what sort of beast Amir is referring to. The dude already tried to kill me with a wooden waster. Is the worst yet to come?

I'm not exactly a seasoned rock climber even though I figure a hundred feet isn't too overwhelming. Of course, the blue belt starts without giving me any warning and I'm already a length behind as I clench my stomach muscles and plant my feet.

Hand-over-hand I climb while the helmet wobbles precariously, blocking me from seeing the other two. I've been working with weights and I'm up to a hundred pushups, so it's not as hard as I thought. But just when I'm getting the hang of it, my foot slips and I crash face-first into hard stone. My nose throbs as the helmet cocks to one side and I nudge it back up with my shoulder. Next time, I'll use my belt to strap the thing in place.

Grunting, I hoist my feet back up and climb the rest of the way. Noah is already up. He thrusts a hand in front of my face. "I'll pull you up."

"Thanks," I say while his big fingers grip my hand. He yanks me up like I weigh nothing and I'm not little. Five-nine and muscular like my Dad, I'm not easy to throw around.

I glance over the edge and am psyched to see Amir about two-thirds of the way up. I beat the brown belt? That rocks.

Noah shifts his shoulders, adjusting his chainmail. "Give me a hand with this."

He bends at the waist, holding his arms up and I tug. Damn, it's worse than pulling of a wetsuit—way heavier, too. I plant my feet and after a few straining tugs, the thing comes off and the bottom edge drops to the dirt.

"Thanks," he says, taking it from my grasp with one hand and heading for a straw-filled mannequin.

"Help!" someone hollers from over the cliff face.

I race for the edge and find Grace dangling about five feet down with a flail swinging from her belt, the spiked ball smacking into her leg. "It's stabbing me!"

"Hold on!" I shout.

Sebastian hauls himself up the middle rope and I scramble down, while the stupid helmet falls off my head and crashes to the ground, landing beside Sensei Okoye. I can't worry about that now as I push away from the wall and swing toward Grace.

The side of her leg is bleeding through her white pants.

My body shudders as I hold myself against the tension of the rope and tug the flail from her belt. "Can you make it up?"

She's holding on with both hands and gives me a terrified nod. "I have to."

The flail weighs a ton, but I manage to jam it into my belt and pull the chain through so the spiked ball won't swing. Though it's poking my waist, I can tolerate the pain long enough to reach the top.

Amir gives me a hand while Sebastian and Noah help Grace.

I pull out the flail and start for the mannequin, but Amir nabs the weapon from my grasp. "I'll take that."

Noah thrusts his finger toward the cliff. "Back down, white belt. You lost something."

"But Grace is bleeding," I say. The bloodstain on her pants leg is spreading.

"It doesn't matter," she says, bending over and putting her hands on her knees. Her face is white as if she'd terrified of heights. "The exercise isn't over until the warrior has all his gear. If you drop something, you go get it, those are the rules."

I gape at them in disbelief.

"Sorry white belt." Noah takes my hand and leads me to the edge. "If you were on a mission—a real life-and-death mission that meant our warrior here would be killed without his helmet, you'd go without hesitation. That's how it works."

Mission? Sensei Bashir told my class that students aren't eligible for missions until they're orange belts, but it's one of the reasons why our training is so grueling. He said only the best of the best are assigned to them. And they're always top secret.

As chills spread over me, I understand. There was something seriously dangerous about the mission he and Amir had returned from. Though I can't know where they've been or why, I'll never forget the tragedy written on Amir's face, or the angry defeat on Noah's.

If these exercises are meant to prepare us to face unknown danger, then I'd better take them seriously, regardless of how much it's going to kill me to climb down and back up again.

To make it faster, I take off my belt, cinch it around the rope, and use it to rappel to the ground.

"Time, Genesis." Okoye taps his watch as I retrieve my helmet and start back up, taking a second to tie it to my head.

It has been a long day. This is my third workout and I'm exhausted. Halfway to the top, my biceps turn to burning fire as I drag myself upward. Sweat drains into my eyes. I'm dripping everywhere. Even my fingers slip on the rope. I try to hold on tighter as I fight. My labored breath sears my lungs as I suffer with every inch.

I can't fail. I can't let my team down but I want to scream with the agony. I should have paced myself the first time. I should have put my helmet on the mannequin before I helped Grace. And most of all, I shouldn't let Noah get to me.

Just when I think I can't make it much farther, fingers drop in front of my face.

"Take my hand," says Noah, heaving me over the edge with another show of brute strength.

"Thanks," I say, my palm tingling as I catch my breath, but I don't dare look him in the eye. I know what he's thinking and he's wrong. I was *born* to be part of the academy and he's not going to convince me to go home. "I won't let the Tigers down again."

Grace slips the helmet from under my belt and limps for our warrior. "Thanks for the rescue. That's what teams do. We help each other."

There are high-fives all around and everyone seems happy except for Noah. He brushes past me. "Too bad our warrior is dead."

My grin fades to a frown as I watch him head for a trail. "What's his problem?"

"I think he likes you," says Amir, beckoning for us to follow.

I slap our warrior's armor. "Hardly."

Chapter Six

"When it is obvious that the goals cannot be reached, don't adjust the goals, adjust the action steps." - Confucius

On Sunday it doesn't surprise me to discover Noah is our team captain for seize the flag. In fact, he's the captain of the Tiger team.

He gathers us around and reads from a sheet of paper. "Every team starts with sparring and are assigned tasks from there."

"Everyone or just the winners?" I ask.

"Winners move on to an easier task, losers more difficult."

"Let's huddle up." Noah extends his hand into the middle of the circle and everyone does the same, even me. "Who's gonna win?"

"The Tigers!" they shout while I go along with it.

"What do you say?" he bellows.

"Aye ya!"

Our fearless leader points to a purple belt. "Jarrod, you'll spar."

"Only one of us?" I ask.

Noah gives me a look like I've lost my mind. "No, white belt. Each of us does one thing. Jarrod is sparring because he's the best."

Would he cut me some slack? This is my first Sunday challenge. For chrissake, how does he expect me to know the rules? I flick my ponytail to the back. "I thought you were the best at everything."

Amir sniggers.

Noah ignores him because his eyes are still focused on me. He flicks the back of my ponytail. "Believe me, there will be something tougher than sparring."

I'd tell him he's an arrogant asshole, but that wouldn't exactly inspire the team spirit. Besides, he's probably right.

I sidle away and stand by Grace at the edge of the mat and we watch as Jarrod annihilates his opponent. Okay, so Noah knew what he was doing. The judge gives him our next task.

"Forms." Noah waves the paper. "Grace, you're up."

As she heads for the mat, I lean into Sebastian. "I thought this was a team."

"It is."

"Then why is Noah making all the decisions?"

"You need to understand how serious challenge days are. If we stand around and take a quorum, we lose valuable time. That's why we have a captain. This isn't just about being the best, it's about taking orders and executing them."

That makes it clearer.

"Commander Noah Jones," I mumble under my breath.

Grace's form is flawless and performed just like her namesake. The only critique I have for her is to put a bit more power behind it. The judges give her a score of 9.7, which I think is freaking awesome, until the next person beats us with a 9.75.

"Swords," says Noah after he gets another slip of paper. I rub my hands together, ready to take the mat, but he points to Amir. "You got this, man."

Amir is awesome but the match ends in a draw.

Noah receives another note and circles his hand over his head. "Outside. I'm jousting."

Grace loops her elbow through mine. "Come on."

"Is he serious?" I ask.

"Absolutely."

I can't believe my eyes when the commander not only mounts a horse, Amir hands him a lethal-looking jousting pole.

I gulp. "Is that real?"

Grace leans on the fence surrounding the field. "The pikes are of hard plastic, but they're covered with about three inches of painted foam-rubber so we don't kill anyone. They still hurt, believe me."

"Have you jousted in waza class before?"

"Only in medieval weapons class."

I glance over my shoulder and spot Sensei Bashir. "Then I have something to look forward to."

"As long as you don't get knocked off your horse."

I hadn't thought about that part. "Do you ride?"

"Enough to know I prefer to drive a car. You?"

"Only my dad's motorcycle, and not often."

"Horses are a lot more skittish." Grace thumps my arm. "But you and Noah ought to get along. He rides a Harley."

My stomach squeezes and I don't know if I like that I have anything in common with a guy who thinks I'd be better off baking cookies. "I drive a truck. It's a Ford. A red one," I say just to be clear. "My dad's the biker. He owns a biker bar."

"Oh my God, that's epic!"

Placing my foot on the bottom rung, I give her a pointed look. "Seriously?"

"Well, yeah. My dad's a computer programmer. Boring, huh?" She climbs the rails and sits on the top. "Hanging out at a biker bar would be so much more interesting."

I hoist myself up beside her. "Why? Do you have a thing for tough guys?"

Waggling her shoulders, she gives me a toothy grin. "Don't we all?"

A laugh snorts through my nose as a picture of Noah the first time I saw him flashes through my mind. No matter how much I want to resist him, those first seconds practically made my heart stop. "I grew up in the apartment above. I cleaned the place every morning after my mom passed away. It's a dive, though I have to admit the biker dudes would never let anything bad happen to me—they might be rough around the edges, but they're big teddy bears, you know?"

A dreamy expression fills Grace's eyes. "I'll have to visit you one of these days."

"Yeah, after I turn twenty-one."

"Oh, that's right. The darned issue with possessing legal I.D."

"I'd rather stay sober," I say as Noah kicks his heels into the barrel of a horse and gallops down a dirt track toward another insane cadet doing the same.

"Oof!" I cringe as our fearless team captain nails his opponent in the center of the chest, racing his horse to the end of the arena while dust billows behind him. Just like a stunt man, he reins it to a halt right before they crash into the fence.

"Show off," I mutter under my breath.

The jousters go at each other two more times before Noah is proclaimed the victor. He flashes a grin my way—maybe he's looking at Grace. I pretend not to notice. Though the next time jousting is part of the waza games, I hope he'll still be on my team.

The next task is relay racing and four more kids are picked. They lose and we're given a brass conical cypher, which Noah hands to Sebastian. "Here, mastermind, do your magic."

There are four clues, which Sebastian reads aloud. "You'll find the City of Temples there." Then he looks at the cypher. "City of Temples?"

I know this and I raise my hand. "Can I answer?"

"Today," says Noah, chopping his hand.

"Kathmandu."

"You'd better be right," warns the captain as Sebastian turns the dial to "K".

"Next clue: What Mesoamerican confederation established three city-states in 1427?"

I'm thinking Mayan, but it doesn't jive with the time period.

"Aztec," says Sebastian turning the dial to an "A". "Okay...Who were the Poor Fellow Soldiers of Christ?"

"Templars," blurts Amir without even having to think about it.

"Last clue: What country did Captain Cook claim to have discovered in 1770?"

Sebastian looks up, his eyes narrowing. "Australia."

"You got it," I say as he turns the fourth dial to "A" and the cylinder pops open. I knew it would. I already saw the word "kata" in my mind's eye.

Maybe next time I ought to just blurt it out and show the blue belt exactly why I was recruited—*I think*.

Noah reaches inside and removes a note containing the next test. "Genesis, it looks like you're up. Rock climbing."

Grace pulls me by the hand and heads off at a run. "And you're the last. That means the flag's at the top of the cliff."

I break into a sprint, passing her as I realize this whole game is up to me. Ahead, Ziana is starting her ascent with a good head start. I search for the other contenders. Though I don't spot anyone else, I'm not fooled into thinking they won't be coming. Worse, it's going to take a Herculean effort to pass my roommate.

I race to the wall and take a flying leap, grabbing the rope a good two feet above my natural reach.

"No way!" shouts Ziana, almost a third of the way up.

I bare my teeth, pulling myself hand-over-hand as fast as I can, keeping my feet moving and solid against the wall. There's no chance I'm going to lose my footing here—maybe the first time, but not today. I'm stronger from our practice round and I'm gaining on her.

Below, my teammates are shouting my name, drowning out Ziana's team who are doing the same. The Tigers' exuberance gives me strength and I push myself harder. I can see the top now...just a little higher.

Out of the corner of my eye, Ziana is dragging herself over the edge. I bear down with all my strength and launch myself over the top, flying through the air, defying death as I strain to catch my balance.

Grand Master Li is holding the flag above his head. Ziana surges forward, but I'm faster, my legs are longer. I see the wooden post and stretch for it. My fingers brush the shaft just as Ziana snatches it from my grasp.

The master presses his palms together and bows. "Winner, the Sharks. Well done, Ziana."

I stand in disbelief for a moment, breathing like I'd just run a marathon.

Li bows my way. "Impressive effort, Genesis."

"Thank you, sir," I say, while my heart sinks to my gut. Not because I lost, but because I don't want to face Noah and tell him I blew our chance at a class with the Grand Master.

Ziana waves the pennant under my nose. "Better luck next time."

Though I want to scream, I step back and bow. "Nice job." As I turn, under my breath I add, "But it won't happen again."

Of course, Noah is waiting for me at the bottom of the cliff with his arms crossed. "You nearly caught up to her."

My feet feel like lead. "I know."

He gives me a gentle punch on the shoulder. "You'll nail her next time, white belt."

My jaw drops and I stare at him in disbelief. I totally thought he was going to rip me a new one. "Hey." I figure that's earned me the right to ask a question. "Why do you only choose dudes for the tough stuff?"

He blinks right before those eyes drill into me. "Climbing the wall and catching up to an opponent with a head-start wasn't hard?"

"You know what I mean. Jarrod sparred. You gave Amir swords and Grace forms. *You* took jousting. Sebastian was the only dude who didn't fight."

A tic twitches at the back of his jaw. "I know my team."

"Is that why I was last? You don't know me?"

"I know you well enough." He crosses his arms, his gaze flickering to my mouth as he licks his lips. "You're just like all the other white belts who come here after winning a national title, thinking they're badasses."

Okay, now his animosity comes out.

"Well don't lump me in with a mob of arrogant a-holes like yourself. I'm here to learn." I shove him in the shoulder. "You have no idea what my life has been like or what I've been through. I imagine you grew up with the perfect parents in a perfect house in a perfect neighborhood. You probably turned down a scholarship to some Ivy League college. You're the type of guy who wouldn't know failure if it smashed you between the eyes with a nunchuck!"

I storm off. I don't want to hear his reply. Not if he thinks I'm on some sort of ego trip because I won the title.

Chapter Seven

"Study the past, if you would define the future."
- Confucius

For the next three weeks, I throw myself into my studies both physical and mental. Whenever I can steal a spare moment I focus on chakras, working toward meditating in a way that entirely sends my mind into a spiritual realm, relaxing into a state of weightlessness. Sometimes I even manage to hover like I'm having an out-of-body experience. But it only lasts a couple of seconds. It amazes me how difficult it is to meditate more than five or ten minutes while completely letting go. Sure, in a few seconds I can coax my mind into a trancelike state, but to truly unblock the seven chakras of the body takes time and that's one thing white belts don't have at the academy.

In Sensei Bashir's medieval studies class, I slide into my seat five minutes early, fold my hands on the desk and close my eyes, first focusing on my root and initiating my six-count breathing cadence. Almost instantly, a floating sensation envelops me.

My body is soaring like a feather carried by a breeze when my mind's eye sees Bashir open the door. In the next moment, there's a click, a slight whoosh of air, followed by heavy footsteps approaching the front of the room. Bashir doesn't greet me. I sense he knows what I'm doing and respects the silence.

The room soon fills with activity and idle chatter as my classmates arrive.

"Take your seats, cadets." Bashir's voice surrounds me, but I don't even twitch. "We have a lot to cover today."

Chairs screech over the waxed tiles to the rustling of my classmates' activity.

"Can anyone tell me what medieval document is still alive today and is referred to as the cornerstone of modern democracy?"

"The Magna Carta?" asks Elias.

I've been at the academy long enough now to know who's talking without opening my eyes.

"Correct," says Bashir. "Who wrote the Magna Carta?"

Silence.

I know the answer to this question, but don't have a mind to raise my hand or open my eyes, for that matter.

"Genesis?" asks Bashir.

I should have guessed interference was coming. With my next exhale, I slowly open my lids and focus on the sensei. He's frowning, arms crossed. If I could see his feet over Piper's head, I'd bet he's tapping his toe, as well. "Archbishop Langton is thought to have had an influence on the draft that was sealed at Runnymede. He and the coalition of the twenty-five," I say, trancelike.

"Who are the twenty-five?" Sensei persists.

"English Barons who were disgruntled with the extortionist and ruthless tyranny of King John." The feeling of weightlessness slowly ebbs. My answer is pretty good, though the chapter only touched on the

Magna Carta of 1215. In truth, the document proved to be an utter failure until after John's son, Henry III ascended to the throne at the age of nine. And if it weren't for the brilliance and steadfastness of William Marshal, Earl of Pembroke, the Magna Carta might have been lost to obscurity. Last night, Marshal caught my interest and I ended up awake far too late Googling him.

"Correct," says Bashir giving me a pointed stare. "Meditation is over, white belt. I expect complete attention in my class."

Even after I answered him correctly, he thinks I wasn't paying attention? I open my book as we skim over the history of the origins of Magna Carta and why it initially failed. I read along while Bashir changes tack, talking about Pope Innocent III and his obsession with the Crusades.

Of course, the mention of the Crusades grabs my interest especially since we have been practicing with medieval weapons. At the end of class, Bashir assignment is to write a three-page document comparing the Templars to the Knights Hospitallers. Everyone groans including me. Because until two minutes ago, I'd never heard of the Knights Hospitallers.

"Class dismissed," the sensei says, his gaze landing on me. "Except you, Genesis."

"Me? But I need to go to the gym like everyone else."

Ziana gives me a pat on the shoulder. "I'll tell Sensei Nakamura you'll be late."

Everyone files out and Bashir sits on the desk across from mine, eyeing me like he's a cop and I'm a suspect. "How did you feel when I approached you in the parking lot?"

Was this a trick question? I squirm in my seat and tuck a loose strand of hair behind my ear. "How does anyone feel when they're attacked out of the blue in a strange city by someone they don't know?"

"I sensed your fear at first."

"Sure, I was scared." To be honest, I was terrified—saw my life flashing before my eyes.

"But you recovered well. Always remember, we may study warfare, but our end goal is peace. If we can walk through life without ever raising a hand, defusing every situation peacefully, then we have truly mastered our body's seven centers of chakra."

"So...I should have let you hit me?"

"I did not say that. Always defend while keeping your emotions in check."

Does he think I was acting emotionally? If he wants to really see emotional he ought to go to the women's dorm first thing in the morning. Or talk to Ziana. She's one of the most emotional people I know.

I slide my book into my bag and stand. "Thank you for the advice, sir."

"Grand Master Li wants to see you," he blurts out of the blue.

I freeze. "Do you know why?"

"Yes," he says, leaving me standing there with my mouth open.

A gazillion things attack my mind as the receptionist leads me through the stark admin building to Grand Master Li's office. What did I do to screw up? I didn't have my score from the last Latin exam yet, but I don't think I did well. Did Noah complain about me? My failure in seize the flag was weeks ago and I've been pretty good about staying out of his hair, except for waza class because I can't ignore him there.

I also don't think I've done anything to piss off my instructors.

Yet.

By the time the receptionist announces me, I'm terrified I'm going to be expelled, even though I can't for the life of me figure out why. Maybe it's leftover anxiety from the sixth grade, but ever since, I've been allergic to the principal's office.

My palms are sweaty, my heart's racing and all the deep breathing while meditating in Bashir's class is a distant memory. I suppose I can always go back to Bunkerville—pick up where I left off, cleaning the Muddy Hollow. And since this is a year-round school, I haven't missed anything at Virgin Valley. Those lucky ducks are still on summer vacation, including Rex.

The only problem is the idea of going home isn't an option. I'm more driven now than I was when I arrived. I have to show Noah I'm just as worthy of my place here as any other student.

I step inside, placing my feet carefully. Li's office is like none I've seen before. It reminds me of a dojo with a bamboo floor and lattice screen doors. There's a small coffee table with two pillows on either side near the window. Beneath the pane are built-in drawers. A large crimson pillow sits alone in the center of the room upon which the Grand Master is kneeling with his back to me.

His hands are at his sides with his palms up and, as the receptionist slides the screen closed behind me, I chew my lip and wait quietly. Though I can't possibly know, I'm positive he spends a great deal of time meditating each day.

On the walls are scrolls of Mandarin writing and I recognize the symbols for destiny, energy, and fire.

With the release of his breath, his head raises a bit. "Hello, Genesis."

I tiptoe around him and bow. "You wanted to see me, Grand Master?"

"I did."

He opens his eyes and I'm reminded of how intensely black they are. In one fluid motion, he stands then moves to the window and opens the silk screen to an unobstructed view of the Dragon's Arch. "At every time of day, the sun brings out new shadows on the rock."

I step beside him, sensing he hasn't called me here to talk about the arch. But I also understand that it is impolite to immediately jump to the topic at hand before starting a conversation with some niceties. My mother and Sensei Soto were always good about prefacing their discussions with a story or observation as well.

I shift my gaze to the red rock beyond. The shadows come alive and I see a wave through the archway like a mirage in the desert. I'm sure it means nothing—after all, the academy *is* in the high desert. "It's beautiful. I could sit and stare at it all day if I had the time."

"Me as well." He turns his back to the window. "You have been at the academy over a month now."

It seems longer. "Only a month?"

"Has time dragged for you?"

"Not at all. I've been so busy and I have learned so much already, I feel like I've been here for a year."

"Interesting. Usually students say time flies rather than slows."

"I didn't mean—"

He holds up his hand. "There is no right or wrong answer. Yours is simply unique."

I nod, pursing my lips, afraid to blurt out anything else that will peg me as an oddball.

Pressing the palms of his hands together he cocks his head to the side and gives me a contemplative look. "Tell me, how well do you know your mother's ancestry?"

"My mother?" I cross my arms over my midriff at the pain her mention brings. It seems such an unusual question. "She was born in San Francisco—an only child. Her parents died way before I was born. I don't remember seeing any pictures of them, either."

I ought to order one of those DNA kits online 'cause I have no clue about my ancestry. I mean, when I look in the mirror I see wild hair, crazy amber eyes, and olive skin. I'm probably a Heinz fifty-seven like most Americans. "Do you know something about my ancestry?" I ask.

"Perhaps."

I hate vague responses and this one's killing me. What does he know? Why did he mention my mom? "Is that why you were at the tournament in Los Angeles?"

"I was there to observe."

Another vague answer. Regardless if he's the big boss, I'm compelled to know more. "What did you do to me when you were standing beside the mat?"

"Not a thing." A single eyebrow flicks up. "You felt...*peculiar*?"

"That's an understatement. I totally embraced peace with the universe. It was the strangest thing I've ever experience of my life." Though lately it seems as I've entered the strange-uverse permanently.

"Interesting. Tell me more," he urged.

Taking a step back, I hold up my palms. "You're gonna think I'm a total nutcase."

"Not at all." His eyes pin me. "We all are here for our special *talents*."

And mine's sparring. Maybe weapons. Maybe something else? I bite my lip and wait while the clock on the wall ticks. When Li doesn't budge, I know I'm cornered and I'd better spill it. "Um...well, at first I thought you threw me out of my zone. But when I returned my attention to Ziana, it was as if I knew what she was planning before she attacked. I saw her moves in my mind's eye. Everything happened in slow motion but I wasn't hyped up like before. I mean, I was in the midst of the most important match of my life and I felt calm like in an open state of chakra."

"Very interesting, indeed." Li gestures to the red cushion in the center of the room. "Kneel."

"There? Do you want me to meditate?"

"I do. But this time I want you to look into my eyes."

I take my position with my legs crossed and rest my hands on my knees. It isn't easy to stare into this man's eyes. They still remind me of obsidian arrowheads, but once our gazes are connected, I can't pull away.

"*Breathe*," he says, except he doesn't speak it aloud. I just know that's what he wants me to do.

The feeling of weightlessness buoys me as he lets me transform my nervousness into a calm state.

"Tell me what you see," he speaks without blinking.

Weird. I have no idea if the command was verbal or in my head.

"Cherry blossoms. Hundreds of them...they're being scattered by a gentle breeze." Is he thinking this? Is he transferring his thoughts? "Oh...there's a pond, and a bridge, and lotus flowers..."

The master blinks, and for a moment I see only his face. "Now close your eyes."

Footsteps move, no more discernable than a whisper. An open-handed chop slices toward my neck and I parry outward, deflecting a strike. A second comes to my left, then a stab to the face, a jab to the right, all of which I easily defend. I raise an upward block over my head, preventing a hacking chop from braining me.

"Open your eyes, Genesis."

Li is standing about a foot away. With his hands in prayer position, he looks like a Buddhist monk. "You have a great deal of potential."

"Thank you." I chew the corner of my lip. I need to know so much more—like how did I just do that? And exactly what does he know about my mother? I gulp, trying to decide what to ask first. "Do...ah...am I maybe a little strange?"

His eyebrows slant inward at my question. "How so?"

"You just threw strikes at me with my eyes closed and I defended them. Can all the students here do that?"

"They cannot."

"May I ask another question, sir?"

"You may."

"Did you know my mom?"

"Yes."

I suck in a huge gasp. "Why—"

"Did I not tell you before today?"

"Uh-huh."

"Because until you had been a student for a time and I've received evaluations from your instructors, I was not at liberty to say."

"How did you know her?"

"She was a student. Long ago."

Oh, my God. "Why didn't anybody tell me before? Did my father know? Is that where I got this weird sixth sense?"

Grand Master Li held up his hand. "So many questions, I'm sure you have. But you must be patient."

What the heck? Why? Doesn't he know I'd do anything to learn more about her?

I crack my thumbs. "Then why did you ask me about her...about my ancestry?" Now I'm not going to be able to sleep until I get that DNA kit. "Is there something in my pedigree that has made you curious?"

He presses the tips of his fingers together while he studies me. "I may tell you this: You are one of the thousands of descendants of Sun Tzu—*that* I can confirm without question. However, most of Sun Tzu's descendants do not have his gift of second sight. You, Genesis Mans, inherited it on some level, as have I."

Holy freaking apocalypse!

That is the absolute last thing I expected him to say. I mean my head's about to explode! I'm not Asian. At least I never thought I was, but then again, doesn't everyone have all kinds of whacky stuff in their ancestry if they go back far enough? "Y-y-you mean we're related?"

"Very, very distantly. I'm afraid our session has come to an end." Grand Master Li glides toward the door, slides it open, and bows. "Do not bother sending for a DNA kit because it will mention nothing of what I've told you."

I stand and follow him. How does he know what I'm planning? Can he see into my mind? "Why not, sir?"

"Because Sun Tzu was born in 544 B.C. The methods presently used to track DNA are not sophisticated enough to go back that far in time. And you would be amazed to learn the number of blonde-haired descendants he has in the world." He gestures into the hallway. "I trust you to keep our sessions confidential, please."

"Of course," I say, giving a respectful bow before heading for my next class and wondering what the heck just happened. I'm a descendant of the brilliant war strategist Sun Tzu, and that makes me see things? But not always? My head fills with questions, like how can I hone my skill? What can I do with it? Will it be useful at the academy? Will being a seer help me secure my yellow belt? Will it help my grades? Is there anyone else here who is like me? And what did Grand Master Li mean by "our sessions"?

Chapter Eight

"Imagination is more important than knowledge." - Confucius

Ziana leans close to the mirror and applies purple lipstick while we're getting ready for the Independence Day dance. "The first place I'm going during our break is an Ulta store. Moab doesn't have any of the makeup I wear."

Since it's a holiday, this morning a group of us were given leave to do some shopping in Moab and I couldn't resist—at the very least I had to restock my supply of protein bars. I even caved and bought a packet of peanut M&M's. Of course, they were gone before we climbed into the Jeeps to head back to campus. I even got to use my cell phone. I called Dad and Rex and told them how much I miss them. I was careful not to say anything about my session with Grand Master Li, no matter how much I wanted to ask Dad if he knew Mom had been a student at the academy.

I nudge my roommate aside just enough to see my reflection in a corner of the mirror and pull the top off my lip gloss. "I can't believe Moab doesn't have a Walmart. Even Mesquite has one."

Ziana smacked her lips. "I thought you said you were from Bunkerville."

"I am—but it's a stone's throw from Mesquite where I go...*went* to school. It's not exactly a mecca, but they do have a Walmart."

Ziana taps me with her elbow. "Woo-hoo, who knew how citified you are?"

"Hey, at least I've been to an Ulta store."

"Good Lord." Ziana snorts. "Next you'll be telling me you shop exclusively on Rodeo Drive."

"Never." I pull my hair back into a sloppy ponytail. "Even if I was too rich to care what things cost, I'd rather give my money to the poor than buy a...a..." I wrack my brain trying to think of something that's outlandish.

"A twenty-five hundred-dollar Prada purse?"

My jaw drops. Who on Planet Earth would blow $2500 on a purse? No one I've ever met, that's for sure—unless my roomie has. "Exactly!" I give her a once-over. "Do you have a Prada purse?"

"Only one."

"Seriously?"

"Dad gave it to me for my sixteenth birthday." Ziana tosses her lipstick tube into her make-up bag and faces me with her arms crossed, her hip akimbo. "Don't tell me you're going to the dance with your hair like that."

I turn my head from side to side, checking to see if I have any flyaways. There's not a lot I can do with the mop. "I think it looks okay. If only Rex were here. I don't know how he does it, but the dude can work magic."

Ziana grabs a long-toothed comb and holds it up. "Mind if I have a go?"

"Why not?" I settle into a chair and glance back. "There's no need to go overboard. I won't be dancing." For obvious reasons, no fireworks are allowed at the academy, so some brilliant mind decided we ought to have a dance instead.

My head drops back as my roommate drags the comb through it. "So say you."

I rub my lips to even out the gloss. "I'm not a dancer—unless they want me to perform a kata."

"Didn't you dance at school? Rex sounds like he's quite the social butterfly."

"In hicksville Mesquite?" I dare to peek in the mirror. Just as I feared, Ziana has my hair looking like something out of the 1980s. I slide a hand over my eyes and cringe. "He's as much of an outcast as me."

Ziana doesn't seem to notice my aversion to her hairdressing skills. "Do you miss him?"

"Yeah. He knows how to make me laugh, that's for sure." Honestly, I don't know who I miss more, Dad, Rex, or Sensei Soto. But I do know it has been nice not to have to clean the bar or cook or worry so much about Dad's drinking.

"I miss my friends, too. God, I'm so looking forward to midterm break."

"I can't believe it's coming so fast." I peek at my hair again. It's not any better. "Do you worry about making yellow?"

"Only every waking moment."

"Yeah, me too."

"You're an ace. You'll make it for sure."

I grin and give her a wink in the mirror. "We both will. Know why?"

"Why?" she asks pushing in some pins.

"Because we're both fighters."

"You got that right."

"Have you thought about what's next—you know, declaring our majors?"

"Sensei Nakamura says we won't need to decide until the end of our purple belt year."

"Yeah, but what are you thinking?"

"Definitely intelligence."

"CIA, huh?"

"Absolutely." Ziana gives my hair a pat and stands back. "How about you?"

She'll need to work on her poker face if she wants to be a spy. But at least she's been thinking about her future. On the other hand, I haven't thought beyond making it through the first six months. "Not sure yet...um...a spy sounds interesting, though."

She gestures toward the mirror. "What do you think?"

Standing, I stare for a moment before I dare to reach up and touch it. She's pulled the curls to the top of my head in a super voluminous bun thing with a few corkscrew wisps framing my face. Now that she's finished, it doesn't look half-bad—not my style, but it's cuteish.

"It's gorgeous," she says, flicking a wisp.

I guess it's growing on me. "I like it—though I'd never be able to get my hair to look like this if I tried for hours."

"I'll show you next time. You won't believe how easy it is."

"Where'd you learn to work with curly hair?"

"*YouTube*...duh."

Okay, I must have been too busy at the dojo or cleaning the bar or fixing dinner for Dad. Besides, I had Rex to help me with hair, makeup, and stuff.

Ziana moves beside me and waggles her eyebrows in the mirror. "Look at us. We're two smokin' hot babes."

We do look good. Of course, she always looks good with her asymmetrical bob, still bleached. Together with her strikingly dark brows, the combination brings out the blue of her eyes. And I'm sure that's no coincidence. Everything about Ziana is planned and perfected. Even her Latin is improving.

"Are you sure you don't want to borrow a dress?" Ziana's wearing a strapless thing that clings to her body as if it's painted on. I'm not the shyest person on the planet, but I wouldn't be caught dead in something that skimpy. Call me a prude, but I've owned about five dresses in my entire life and none of them were close to being that *revealing*.

I gesture to my three-quarter leggings and white blouse—it's frilly. Sort of. At least it has a scooped neck and puffy sleeves. "I'm good, thanks. Besides, you're the hottie."

"Are you kidding?" Ziana grabs my hand and pulls me toward to the door. "I work hard to look like this. Not everyone can make no effort and manage to look like a dime."

"What, are you buttering me up so I'll do your homework?"

Rolling her eyes, she grabs me by the wrist and pulls me to the door. "Shut up."

It's still daylight—it will be until about ten o'clock—yet the courtyard is decorated with glittery lights while Calvin Harris blares from the sound system. If I'm ever going to start dancing, this soundtrack might move me to it, but instead I stand there among my group of white belts and feel awkward, just like at a typical school dance. Everyone's gathered in their little cliques and we're all staring at each other with our proverbial thumbs in our pockets.

I don't have pockets, so I hold a glass of ice water and twirl one of my corkscrews around my finger. As soon as I realize I'm acting like a junior high schooler, I drop the hair.

A few groups along, Grace is wearing a blue dress with a handkerchief hem. Her hair's down and she looks awesome. She waves and I give her a thumb's up in return.

I try not to let my gaze wander to the other side of the courtyard because Noah is over there standing with Amir and Jarrod and I don't want to appear like I'm a complete loser, thirsty for him or anybody else to ask me to dance.

In truth, I'm mortified one of them might.

I don't have to worry, though because when the music morphs to *Shut up and Dance*, the three dudes run for the floor and Noah pulls an aerial butterfly twist kick while Amir and Jarrod flank him with five-forty spinning hooks. Holy effing hell, all of them jump so high they clear the ground by at least five feet. And they've obviously planned this performance because they're freaking awesome.

The crowd eggs them on while they execute a modern synchronized kata which is more off the ground than on. Every strike is intensified with lightning fast power. The best part? All their kicks are like something out of a *Spiderman* movie.

"Woo-hoo!" I shout, probably clapping louder than anyone else. If you ask me, this is real dancing, and the guys are nailing it.

The song ends and the floor is mobbed. A redheaded blue belt makes a beeline for Noah. I step sideways for a better view. Though she's not in my waza class, I've seen her on campus. She's pretty and wearing a dress.

Crapola. I should have borrowed something from Ziana.

When Noah brushes a lock of hair away from the girl's face my gut tightens. So does my jaw as if I'm jealous or something. And now they're laughing.

I clench my fists. *So what if he has a girlfriend?*

But I can't shift my gaze away. I don't even like Noah Jones. Why on earth would I be attracted to a guy like him? He takes alpha male to an obscene level. Amir is more my type—contemplative, smart, and deadly if he wants to be. We all might not be as skilled as Noah, but each one of us are forces to be reckoned with in our own rights, or else we wouldn't be here. Anyway, Amir is a wide-eyed geeky type and he's about an inch shorter than me—definitely not intimidating.

Noah looks up and I quickly turn my back. There's no way I want him to know I was staring. I put my glass on the table, feeling like a clod in my sandals and leggings. When I go home for midterm break, I'm asking Rex to take me shopping. After all, I am a girl. I ought to have at least one dress.

As I stand at the edge of the courtyard, the arch catches my eye. In the evening sun, it looks like a watercolor with distorted shadows. When I first arrived, I wanted to climb up there, then Bashir hit us with the "off limits to white belts" bull. I check the time—there's still two hours of daylight left.

Surely there's not a rule against hiking up to the general vicinity. Maybe the rule is for climbing on the arch because of the desert patina or something. Then I glance over my shoulder at the crowd—almost everyone is dancing now. I may as well let the party animals live it up. No one will miss me, that's for sure.

It takes about a half-hour to hike to the base of the arch and by the time I get there, I'm sweating and covered in red dust.

I run my hand over the ancient rock and wonder how long it has been since the arch was formed. It's still warm from the day's sunshine and, as I look out over the campus, I can hear the faint sound of music coming from the dance. It's peaceful up here, but it's more than that. As my hand rests on the rock, a spark of energy swells inside me. I wonder why I like being alone so much, but then as soon as the thought passes through my head, I know it's more. This place is ethereal, I'm convinced of it. The dragon in the arch called to me. He wants me here.

But why?

Ahead is a narrow trail leading behind the arch and I follow it, finding a wall of petroglyphs, but they don't look anything like the Anasazi glyphs near Bunkerville. They're almost Asian, but not Chinese. At least I don't think they're Chinese. I reach out to brush my fingers over them, but quickly snap my hand away. I know better than to touch ancient art and contaminate it with the oil from my prints.

In the center of a myriad of etchings is a stream flowing downward and ending in a large spiral. As I study it, I'm wondering if it's a stream or a path. I take a step back and narrow my gaze when the etchings grow more vivid. There are trees, and tiger-like cats, and...is that an elephant? These animals are all wrong for this part of the country.

How did they get here?

I blink and a scene from an Indian temple darts through my brain, complete with the trumpeting of elephants. I smell curry and something like game roasting over an open fire.

"Whoa," I say, shaking my head. "I've been working too hard."

I skirt around to the back of the arch and gasp. I've seen the blue mirage-like, glittering waves before, but it's a gazillion times more vivid up here. Maybe I was right about working too hard, but I'm convinced I'm not imagining things now. After all, my eyes are wide open.

Stretching out my hands, I inch toward the gap while the sandy dirt crumbles away from beneath my sandals. My fingers skim the shimmering blue, making me tingle all over. I lean forward reaching farther and my fingers completely disappear. A rush fills my ears followed by men shouting and women screaming.

Suddenly the collar of my shirt strains against my chest as I'm hurtled into the air. "Aaaaaaaa!" I shriek, while the rubble gives way beneath my feet. My entire body jolts, giving me whiplash as I'm yanked back to the trail with Herculean strength.

"What the hell do you think you're doing?" booms Noah, slamming me against the petroglyph wall and pinning me there with a hand planted on either side of my head.

"Ow!" A sharp pain shoots through my shoulder and down through my elbow. I glare up into his face and his crystalline eyes drill through me, filled with anger as if I'd made off with his prized Harley. But there's something else I hadn't seen before.

Fear.

He stares at me, his lips parted with his quick inhales. His gaze shifts to my mouth, and I suddenly realize he's trapped me with his body, and though he's wearing a shirt and jeans, his personal heat is searing my skin. An explosion of butterflies erupts inside me, and I'm either going to grab his face and give him the biggest, most tonsil-probing kiss of his life or I'm going to issue a heel palm to his snout.

By the fire burning low in my gut, kissing is way too tempting—especially with the leader of my waza class and a guy who challenges me at every turn. Not to mention he's just shoved me against a rock wall and my shoulder is going to be purple come morning. Hot moisture oozes from my elbow, streams down my forearm and drips from my finger.

"I'm bleeding," I say, trying to sound like he hasn't affected me in the slightest.

He immediately eases the pressure away and I'm suddenly cold, missing his warmth, needing the connection between us...even though he's so damned intense.

"What?" The ice in his eyes is replaced by concern. "You're hurt?"

I push up my bloody sleeve and get a good look at the knot that's forming beneath the broken skin. "It's nothing."

"No. It's bad," he says, ripping off the lower half of his shirt.

My jaw drops at his ripped abs. God. I'm dead.

He doesn't notice I'm staring as he ties the bandage around my elbow. "I'm sorry, I didn't mean to be so rough."

Heat is blasting to my face and I turn my head away. It would be too awkward if he sees me blush. "I can take it."

"I've gathered." He pats my arm, the tips of his fingers lingering on my skin. "Even so, you shouldn't be up here."

"Why not?"

"Didn't you know the Dragon's Arch is off limits to white belts? Besides, it's too dangerous."

"Right." Groaning, I look to the arch without an iota of guilt. The blue mirage is gone and I see only the setting sun. "That's so weird."

"What?"

I let out a long breath and slide down the wall, landing on my butt. "You're going to think I've lost my mind."

He sits beside me with one knee up, draping his arm casually on top. How do guys like Noah do it? They can be sweaty, grungy, hair mussed, and they're totally sexy. I scoop a handful of sandy dirt and watch it run through my fingers. At least it's a lot better than watching him.

He brushes a knuckle over my cheek. "Hey, anyone who puts up with this place is out of their minds. So, tell me, what's so weird?"

I want to avoid his question and ask why he's being so nice. I even hesitate for a second before I blurt, "The arch. Before you came up, it seemed wavy—like a mirage, but now all I see through it is the sky."

"Holy freaking hell." Groaning, he drops the back of his head against the wall. "Well, white belt, you should have turned your talented ass around and headed for home the first day." He stands and pulls me up. "Now I'm afraid you're gonna have to pay a visit to Grand Master Li."

Wonderful. So much for the nice guy act.

Chapter Nine

"I slept and dreamt life is beauty, I woke and found life is duty." - Confucius

"I don't see what's so earth-shakingly important to make us rush to see the Grand Master of all people." For the love of God, we could explain what happened to one of the senseis or anyone besides Li.

Noah completely ignores me as he tightens his grip around my wrist and hauls me into the admin building. The muscles flex in his jaw like he's on the brink of putting me in a rear naked choke and squeezing the life out of me. "White belts don't need to understand, they just must obey."

Can I kick him? A roundhouse to his twitching jaw ought to do. I'd take a shot if he weren't walking so fast. I'm practically running to keep him from dragging me. "Will you let go? You're cutting off the circulation in my fingers," I say as we stop outside Li's door.

Releasing his grip, Noah gives me another one of those "you stole my Harley" leery-eyed stares. "Sorry," he whispers before he knocks.

He's sorry? I rub my aching wrist and pray the Grand Master isn't there. I mean really, why would Li be in his office at this hour especially when there's a dance going on?

"Enter."

"Damn," I curse under my breath. Why in God's name do I feel like I'm in trouble? I'd at least like the enjoyment of being bad before I'm hauled to the "principal's" office.

Li turns away from the window and wipes his forehead with a cloth. His face is blanched and I wonder if he's not feeling well. "Noah? Genesis? Why are you not at the party?"

"Because she..." Noah thrusts his upturned palm at me. "Decided to take a hike up to the arch. By herself," he growls as if I'm a toddler who needs a babysitter. "And it's a good thing I followed because she was inches away from falling in—and you know what I mean, sir."

I swear, Li's face grows paler as his eyes shift to me. "Is this true?"

I throw out my hands. "I don't dance, okay? And we haven't had much time to ourselves. I-I didn't think there was any harm in going for a walk."

"Tell him what happened," Noah demands.

I run my fingers over the makeshift bandage he tied on my elbow and give him a stink eye. "I am *not* crazy."

"Of course you're not," says Li. "But it is very important you tell me exactly what you experienced."

My stomach jolts like there's a swarm of ginormous honeybees trying to escape up my esophagus. "Um...I noticed the arch on the first day—you know, who wouldn't? Remember? We talked about it. Sometimes there seems to be a mirage in the gap." I told them about the petroglyphs and the odd sensation of being in India, then went on to admit curiosity made me push my fingers through the sparkling blueness. "It reminds me of a rippling shallow pool, but instead of water, the air oscillates like in a science fiction movie or something."

Li turns and paces, stroking his fingers down his thin beard. "This is providential."

"This is a disaster," Noah says.

Obviously, they both know something I don't.

"Please, tell me I haven't lost my mind," I groan.

"Do not be so hasty," says the Grand Master, stopping in front of Noah as if I hadn't spoken. "There has been a disturbance."

Noah clenches his fists. "Again? So soon?"

"Are you not ready?"

"Ready for what?" I ask.

The blue belt doesn't even glance my way. "I'm always ready, sir."

"Go. Find Amir. He's still your choice?"

Noah throws his shoulders back. "He is."

As Jones leaves, Li shifts his attention back to me. "There's little time to spare. The window can close as fast as it opens."

"Window?"

Li clasps his palms in a gable grip. "You have not yet been put through the required curriculum. But judging by our sessions and what you have described, I have no doubt you have your mother's gift. It is very rare."

"Wait." My head is about to explode. "Tell me about her."

"I will, but not now. I have never sent a white belt on a mission, but this time it cannot be helped."

Did he say white belt and mission in the same sentence? While I'm grappling with this, he urges me to kneel on one of the red pillows.

"The world as we know it is in peril." He kneels across from me and grasps my shoulders, digging in his fingers until it hurts. "You must swear to utmost secrecy."

I nod dumbly. "I swear."

"This is a risk. You need another year of training, but there is no other option." I start to interject, but Li stops me with the thrust of his palm. "What you saw in the arch is a gateway."

My breath catches in my chest. I knew it had to be something strange, maybe even supernatural. "Leading to...?"

"Wherever the Qiang are wreaking havoc."

A violent chill spreads from the center of my back all the way through the tips of my fingers and toes, I shudder and clutch my arms over my chest. "Why is it every time I hear that name, I'm filled with dread?"

Li clasps his hands again, his expression intensely serious—and honest. I sense whatever comes out of his mouth next will be the unadulterated gospel. "Because you have a gift."

I shake my head, not comprehending. I expected him to say something like we're guarding the gateway to protect America from invasion.

"Gift?" I whisper.

"Not everyone can see the window. In fact, only a handful of people on this earth are able."

Wonderful, so I'm not crazy. I'm *special*. "Who are the Qiang? Didn't you say they were an ancient people? I Googled them and found zilch...except they're an ancient tribe of Tibeto-Burman origin who existed something like five thousand years ago. But they're extinct. Other dynasties have descended from them like the Yuan. At least that's what I could find."

"Partially correct. But as I've said before, they are not extinct. They are a Tibetan order that has survived the centuries only through elusiveness and cunning."

I shudder again. "And they're evil."

Li gives a sober nod, his eyes blacker than black. "Think of the evilest person who has ever lived then multiply it by ten."

My mind immediately goes to Hitler, then Genghis Khan, then Nero and a hollow chasm fills my chest. "Oh my God."

"This is why we do not instantly reveal our purpose to white belts. They must first prove they are not only trustworthy, but that they will be valuable contributors to the Alliance before we can burden them with such enormous responsibility."

My lips quiver with the innumerable questions dancing on them. "Alliance?" I blurt.

"A coalition of governments, over the centuries has become...joined together to prevent the Qiang from changing the past and inflicting their will upon us all. And it's our job to find them and prevent them from altering the past."

Now I'm completely blown away, my jaw dropping as I wonder if *I am* the psycho person in the room. "The past?" I ask, flashing back to the day the helicopter took Stacy away. "Is that why Noah and Amir looked like they were dressed for a Renaissance faire?"

"Daylight is fading and we haven't much time. Ask no questions. Listen and commit what I say to memory." Li takes a deep breath. "Sun Tzu attended The School of Military with his good friend Whang

Due who, through treachery, became China's greatest adversary."

I open my mouth to ask how when the Grand Master holds up a finger. "After the two men entered service to King Helu, Whang Due stole the Jade Goddess from the king's treasury—a most valued relic from the Hongshan culture, said to be over five-thousand years old."

I gasp.

"Sun Tzu pursued Whang Due relentlessly but was never able to find the Jade Goddess, a life-sized skull hewn from a solid piece of jade."

"And it is in the hands of the Qiang?" I ask, unable to quash my burning desire to ask questions.

"To whom legend states Whang Due fled—up to the far reaches of the Himalayas."

"But why is a missing jade skull a problem now?"

"Because the Jade Goddess is no mere relic. It has the power to enable the enemy to control the destination."

"Huh?"

"The most important thing for you to know is the Qiang pose the greatest threat to civilization as we know it. They are and have always been bent on world domination and it is our duty to see they do not succeed—both in the past and in the present. To my chagrin, only youth can travel through time to the past. Settling occurs around the age of twenty-two, after which our students join with forces to protect the world from the Qiang in present-day."

My head spins as Li pulls me to my feet. "Only descendants of Sun Tzu can travel through time and only three at once." He opens a drawer of the chest beneath the window and pulls out something that looks like a tiny shell and holds it up. "No metal can pass through the gateway—no cell phones, no guns, knives, metal jewelry, nothing any larger than a tooth filling. Our lab has designed this translator. It is invaluable. Put it in your ear."

I take the piece. "Does it come out?"

"With tweezers. Worry not. It is very safe and proven."

I raise the device to my lobe but stop before I insert it. "Why are you giving this to me now?"

"Because the Qiang are on the move. Without the Jade Goddess we know not where they're headed, only that the window will take you where you must go to stop them."

"Even though I'm a white belt?"

"True, it is a grave risk. However, you have shown more of a sixth sense than anyone I have met in a very long time."

"Like my mom?" I ask.

"It appears so."

"Do I focus on the chakra energy systems?"

"Meditation is a way to harness your gift, but you can and must call upon it at will. Have you done this?"

"I think so. At the tournament I didn't meditate before my winning strike when I was in the ring with Ziana, and it happened again in the parking lot when Sensei Bashir attacked. I sensed him coming, but there was no time to stop and meditate." I look Li in the eye. "But that was right after I saw you."

He shoves a booklet into my hands. "Memorize page fifty-two before you go. It might keep you alive."

The door slides open and Noah leads Amir inside. They're both wearing canvas pants, soft leather shoes, linen shirts, and capes.

"Who's our seer?" asks Noah.

"Genesis will be traveling with you. Take her to wardrobe, but hurry."

"Wait." Noah crosses his arms. "We can't take a white belt."

Li stands square, leaning on his staff and, though he's not a large man, his presence is the most powerful in the room. "You can and you will."

Noah exchanges an exasperated glance with Amir. "Are you serious? She'll get us killed."

Li doesn't even blink. "No. She is more likely to save your lives."

"But—"

The Grand Master bangs his staff on the bamboo floor. "I have been the head of the academy for a very long time. If Genesis has seen the window, then she must go."

Growling under his breath, Noah's gaze cuts my way as he beckons. "Come."

"We'd better hurry," says Amir.

While I turn to page fifty-two, they take me to a room lined with racks of garments in earthy tones. I stare at a gargantuan list of countries and places like natural monuments—like Egypt and the sphynx in Gisa. "How am I going to memorize this in two minutes?"

Noah grabs a shapeless smock, a brown skirt, a linen shirt, and tosses them at me. "Put these on." He grabs the booklet, tears out the page and shoves it in my hand. "No one will ever be able to figure out what this means. Put it somewhere secure while I find you a cloak."

I duck behind a bamboo screen. Cloak? *Note to self, cloak sounds more authentic than cape.* "Do you have any clue where we're going?"

"No," says Noah. He's such a charmer when we're racing against time.

"Somewhere in the past," Amir's calm voice comes through the screen. "It can be World War II, Rome, Egypt, anywhere. Only the Qiang know because they control the Jade Goddess."

A cloak appears over the screen while I pull the smock thing over my head and realize it must be a chemise—and I shouldn't be wearing a bra. Hesitating for a moment, I reach back for the hook. Nah. Surely I don't have to be that realistic. Besides, it's a great hiding place for my list. "Then why are we dressing like medieval peasants?"

"Because plain clothes like these fit in anywhere—they're even fine for present day," says Noah.

"Yeah." I pull the shirt over my head. "If you're Amish."

"You wouldn't want to show up in the Dark Ages wearing a pair of jeans and a karate t-shirt." Amir explains things so much more pragmatically. By the way Noah talks, the blue belt would rather plant a jab between my eyes than answer questions. "There are many places in history where it's life-threatening to be dressed suspiciously."

Tying the skirt around my waist—ties, no buttons or zippers—I snort. "I suppose a white shirt and brown skirt wouldn't be out of place in 1945 either."

"Everything is out of place in 1945," Noah says while a pair of plain leather shoes come over the top of the screen. "Size eight?"

I take them. "How'd you guess?"

"Let's go, it's almost dark."

As I step around the screen, he folds his arms, one eyebrow arching as he looks me from head to toe. "You need to cover all that hair."

I run my hands over my head—last I checked, it still looked pretty good—better than usual anyway.

Amir hands me a long ecru scarf. "Lose the puffy bun, then drape this over your head—you know like the portraits of the Virgin Mother." I comply, removing the bobby pins and shifting my ponytail lower while he hands me a canvas satchel, same as the roughhewn bags they each have slung across their shoulders. "This is your first aid kit."

Taking it, I peek inside. There are four crepe rolled bandages and three stoppered glass bottles. I hold the first one up. It has an "I" stamped into the cork. "What's this?"

"Iodine solution," Amir explains. "The other two are 'A' for aspirin powder and 'AB' for antibiotic powder."

"Why powder?"

A cavern forms between Noah's eyebrows as if he's had enough of answering my questions. "Because pills might not exist where we're going."

"Come on," says Amir.

I don't even have time to tie the strings to close the satchel as Noah pulls me outside. The two dudes head for the arch at a run. Following like a lemming racing for certain death, I try to wrap my mind around what's happened in the past hour.

"Do you guys have the sight thing?" I shout.

"No," Noah barks over his shoulder.

"Stacy did," says Amir. "Sometimes."

Is that why Grand Master Li insisted I go? And they're both descendants of Sun Tzu. They have to be.

This whole thing seems surreal. I'm half-panicked, running uphill, and wondering what the hell I'm doing.

All I know is we need to stop some evil maniacs called the Qiang from an ancient Tibetan order thought to be extinct. What do they look like? How do we find them? Is my life in jeopardy?

My gut squeezes with the last question. If it weren't dangerous, they'd send anyone, not three highly trained martial artists. I'd rather have a sidearm if I'm going to need to fight. After all, Noah already warned me this is no job for a female.

No metal can pass through time.

Before I perseverate on all the warnings I've had from Noah since my arrival, we reach the arch. Grand Master Li is there, leaning on his staff as always, though he had to move pretty fast to beat us. I wonder what else I don't know and figure it's plenty.

He beckons me forward and cups my cheek with his palm. This close, his skin seems like old leather, his eyes wizened and filled with concern. "Listen to your inner voice. Noah knows how to keep you safe. And I pray one day Amir will become a history professor, because his mind is brilliant and full of facts." Li's gaze shifts between us all. "Be stealthy, be astute, and aware. Stay together and stay alive. I do not have to tell the boys that one misstep can mean doom."

I freeze in place, my blood rushing through my veins like ice. Doom? It sounds so final.

Noah grabs my wrist and guides me toward the arch—toward the mirage. "We have to go now!"

He starts to run, leaving my heart about five paces behind.

"Wait!" I shout.

But it's too late.

Chapter Ten

"The essence of knowledge is, having it, to use it." - Confucius

My throat burns from endless screams as I flail, frantically reaching for anything to slow my descent. I've never skydived before, but this must be what it feels like. Except without a parachute.

I can't breathe.

I can't see.

I'm going to die!

The drop is never-ending as my body hurls through a psychedelic abyss, shooting through some kind of wicked cosmic worm hole. My face is stretching from the force of the wind, my lips curl away from my teeth and the saliva in my mouth has turned to goo. I'm about to pass out, terrified to meet my end.

Faintly, I hear howls from my companions as I somersault, no more in control than a rock tumbling down a mountain.

Suddenly, I begin to slow. An acrid stench burns my nostrils. It's layered—the smell of a sewer, of farm animals, of mold. Dank air envelops me as my feet collide with pavement. I try to balance, but the ground is uneven and cobbled. Stumbling, I fall and jar my shoulder.

With a thud, Amir lands beside me and grunts.

Noah is already here.

I stand and balance myself by thrusting my hand against a stone wall while my head spins as if I've been in one of those g-force acceleration units they use to train astronauts—the ones that make the best of the best pass out.

"Easy, Genesis," whispers Noah. "It always takes a minute to unwind."

It's colder than Utah—damp, too. Clouds swirl above like it's about to rain. The breeze brings a myriad of smells, some good, most unpleasant. The rush of water isn't far away—but it's not the sound of the surf I hear.

"Where are we?" I ask.

"Good question," says Amir turning in a circle.

Upward, the stone wall I'm leaning against is the foundation of an enormous tower maybe five stories high. And straight ahead, the cobbles slope down to a giant river the color of coffee with cream. Stone and wooden buildings with thatched roofs surround us, their chimneys belching black smoke.

"It sure isn't 1945," I say, giving my head a shake to stop the whir.

Amir walks over to a post and studies something like a placard or notice with a scrolling border. "Not even close. This is in Latin—says there's a jousting tournament."

I crowd behind him, craning my neck to see over his shoulder. "Is there a date?"

"It's hard to read—the ink is streaked like it must have rained."

"Head's up," says Noah. No sooner are the words out of his mouth when footsteps slap the cobblestones.

Oh God, a half-dozen chainmail-clad, pike-wielding guards are running straight for us and, by the scowls on their faces, they're not going to ask us where we're from before they attack.

"Spies!" shouts the man in the lead.

"Crap," Noah grumbles under his breath. "Why can it never be easy?"

Amir grabs my wrist and sprints toward the river. "This way."

I have no idea what he sees, but at least we're heading in the opposite direction of the bloodthirsty soldiers. I'm guessing they don't believe in innocent until proven guilty around here.

The cobbles are uneven and challenging to negotiate with the thin soles of my new shoes. Amir is more surefooted as he leads us to a stone wall overlooking the river. To our left there's a set of stairs leading down to the water which is speckled with boats with single masts and rectangular sails.

Some sort of horn blasts behind us and I picture images of Vikings repelling down the walls in their bloodlust to pillage and plunder. Judging by the shouts, there's no mistaking it, the horn is sounding some sort of alarm.

I'm not an expert, but wherever we are, it's before the time of galleons and tall ships with three masts and loads of sails. Amir starts down the stairs, but a line of soldiers with pikes are running up from below.

I nearly crash into the brown belt as he stops and turns. "Reverse!"

I swear we're going to die before our mission even begins. Guards approach from everywhere. The only escape is the pathway along the wall.

Noah surges into the lead and beckons us. "Let's head for the bridge!"

Ahead it's like no bridge I've ever seen—yes, it crosses the river, but there are buildings side-by-side all along the expanse of it.

We're gaining ground when a wheelbarrow appears from behind a building. Unable to stop, I leap over it while Noah pulls an aerial somersault. The far edge of the barrow catches his heel and he stumbles. Amir doesn't clear the jump and plows into the mound of hay face-first.

"Halt!" booms the guard.

Noah grabs my elbow and squeezes. "Rule number one. We *always* stay together."

The first question I want to ask is why does he think I'd run off and leave Amir? But as soon as the thought flashes through my mind, my attention is drawn by an iron pike pointed at my face. Instinctively, I raise my hands.

I count ten snarling guards, each one with murder in his eyes, armed with a spear at least six feet long.

My heart races as I try to catch my breath. Are they going to kill us right now?

"How dids't thou cometh to be within these curtain walls?" demands one of the men as my earpiece translates, "*How did ye get inside the city walls?*"

I glance to Amir who's on his feet with straws of hay sticking out of his black hair. The look on his face confirms it, they're speaking English—but if I didn't have the earpiece the man would barely be discernable. Okay, that's the easy part, but how should we respond? One misspoken word and I have no doubt the pike I'm facing will impale my eyeball.

Hoping Amir has a good explanation, I plan my counter. If the bastard so much as bares his teeth, I'm bobbing under the spear, grabbing the shaft, and shoving the blunt end in into his solar plexus as hard as I can. Then I'll twist it from his grasp and hurl the pointy end at his throat.

"We are here for the tournament," says Noah as if he knows exactly what he's talking about.

And he sounds kinda like them, as if the earpiece translates our speech as well. I almost contemplate the mechanics of how that might work until the blade in front of my face inches a little closer.

The guard who seems to be in charge narrows his eyes, looking Noah from head to toe. "Whose champion are ye?"

Amir cringes as his brown eyes shift between our captors. "You see...ah...that's a bit of a problem. We've fallen on unfavorable circumstances, and—"

"Liars!" one of the guards bellows, poking Noah in the ribs with his pike.

"No!" I shout, then bite my lip. Damn, damn, damn, why did he have to jab his weapon? And why did Noah allow it? All heads turn my way as if I'd shouted a curse. And by the way they're studying me, I should have kept my mouth shut.

But I can't zip my lips now. I try not to look the guard in the eye and soften my tone. "Sir Noah is renowned throughout Christendom."

God, did I just say that? I sound medieval.

The leader upends his pike and struts toward the blue belt. "A knight are ye? Where is yer mail? Where is yer sword?"

"Um..." Noah gives me a scowl. "Our ship capsized. We were fortunate to make it ashore with our lives."

"Harold, ye ought to take them to Lord FitzWalter," says the guard holding his pike in my face. "He'll decide what is to be done with them."

I exhale as the pointed weapon lowers. At least we've gotten this far and I haven't had to kill anyone—yet. Not that I was expecting to kill anyone, it's just not every day I'm chased through a medieval city by pike-wielding guards wearing chainmail and helmets. God, they're practically frothing at the mouth.

How did we get into this mess? And in less than five minutes? We're supposed to be looking for the Qiang and figuring out who we need to prevent them from killing.

Right?

Now we're being marshaled to the tower, Noah has suddenly become a knight and, after our boat capsized, we've been washed ashore with nothing but our lives. If we continue to conjure tall tales, I'm never going to be able to keep it all straight.

I'm wondering how much Amir has been able to piece together—though there's no way I can ask. I figure we must be in England sometime in the Middle Ages. The river could be the Thames but I'm not sure. The only thing I know right now is it was an understatement when Noah said jumping through the gateway was dangerous.

"*She'll get us killed,*" he'd said. Now I know why. Except I may not be the cause of our deaths.

From what I learned from Sensei Bashir, human life is very expendable in this era. People are suspicious—of *everything*. And it doesn't take a soothsayer to know those guards were looking at us with distrust. Worse, I doubt neither Amir nor I have a drop of English blood running through our veins. We'd fit in far better in India, or any of the Arab states for that matter. Jerusalem would work. Maybe southern Europe. But England? What if they torture me because my eyes are the most unique color on the planet?

None of us utters a word because if Noah and Amir are remotely as terrified as me, their instincts are screaming to keep their mouths shut. I swear, asking something as simple as what year it is can send us to a torture chamber. As we walk through the tower's enormous door with sharp iron teeth of a portcullis staring down as us, I have no doubt every torture device imaginable exists in the dungeon of this place. I'm petrified. I mean I'm shuddering as if it's twenty below outside with a foot of snow on the ground.

I wrack my mind but can't place Lord FitzWalter anywhere in history. They lead us through an enormous hall filled with benches and tables. At the far end is a raised dais with a table covered by a scarlet cloth and an enormous silver candelabra in the center. Ornately carved wooden chairs with velvet cushions surround the table. It must be the place where the lord feasts. Gargantuan tapestries hang on the walls that must cost a fortune. This FitzWalter dude is someone super important for sure.

Is he the one we've come to protect? I have no idea, no sensations whatsoever, aside from being scared out of my mind.

Come to think of it, I haven't had a premonition since we arrived. Why not? Didn't Grand Master Li say I'd sense the Qiang's presence? Do students ever get sent on a mission and never find the Qiang? I practically go cross-eyed holding in all my questions.

They lead us into a stairwell and start up a narrow, winding climb. It's dimly lit by the sun and, every so often, I pass a long, narrow window not more than three inches wide—the perfect size for arrows. I stub my toe on an uneven step, flinging out my hand for the banister...but there isn't one. My palm meets with cold stone as I'm rewarded with a prod in the back.

"Continue," growls the guard behind me.

We exit into a pie-shaped room where a ruddy man sits on an uncomfortable-looking wooden throne. He's surrounded by more soldiers, mostly dressed in mail and tunics as if they're ready to march into battle. Even the man on the throne is wearing a shirt and coif of mail and with an orange tunic over the top bearing a coat of arms. Aside from a long, dark-wood trunk, there is no other furniture in the room which is lit by two six-foot standing candelabras and a wall sconce that reeks of burning fat. There's a window behind the throne, but it's covered with fur and, as it gently billows, I realize there's no pane.

Beside me, Amir nudges my arm and taps his lips, indicating silence as if he thinks I'll open my mouth. I'm just praying he has a plan that doesn't include our imminent execution.

"Good day, my lord," says Harold, bowing and addressing the man who must be FitzWalter. "We found these three miscreants outside the tower. They claim to have come for the tournament yet carry no weapons."

Another guard steps forward and bows. "Nor have they a destrier or palfrey that I've seen."

"No horse?" FitzWalter regards us with a booming belly laugh. "Are ye certain ye're not court jesters? Tell me, where do ye hail from?"

Amir bows. "Rome herself, my lord." He gestures to Noah. "Allow me to introduce my champion, Sir Noah Jones, fierce tournament contender."

"With no weapons, no horse, no mail?"

Amir turns a tad green. "Ah...we were capsized off the rocks of Dover and scarcely made it ashore with our lives."

"Who is yer patron?" asks FitzWalter.

"Was, my lord," says Noah.

"Cardinal Benedict, I'm afraid," Amir continues. "As a result of his unfortunate passing, Sir Noah is seeking sponsorship."

FitzWalter leans back in his throne. "Without a mount or means to defend yerself?"

Sliding a foot forward, Noah bows with a flourish of his cloak. Where on earth did he learn that? "Lend me a beast and I'll prove I'm worth your favor, my lord."

His Lordship plucks a dagger from a sheathe on his belt and starts cleaning his fingernails. "And what if ye do not win, what then?"

"As you suggested, I shall play the jester for all to humiliate."

I almost snort at the idea of Noah as a jester. It's nearly as absurd as me being a seer and traveling to medieval England to stop the Qiang from altering the past. I pinch myself. Is this real or am I in the midst of a nightmare?

Please be a nightmare!

"What if he's one of John's spies?" asks Harold.

Is he referring to King John? Or am I jumping on that because we've just been studying the era in Bashir's class.

FitzWatlter pretends to run his knife across his throat. "Then we will ensure the king receives no report." He stands and saunters up to Noah, craning his neck. Good heavens, the man cannot be more than five foot four and almost as wide. He wraps his fingers around the blue belt's arm and grunts but I can't tell if the man is impressed or if he has indigestion. I'd be impressed. Aside from my dad, Noah's stronger than any dude I know, and that's saying something.

FitzWalter saunters over to me. "Is he as good as he says?"

I return the man's gaze with a thin-lipped nod. "None better." What the heck do I know? He can out-joust anyone at the academy, but in the midst of an era where knights grow up jousting?

He's gonna get killed.

"Very well," says His Lordship. "If ye reckon ye are man enough to prove yer worth, ye and yer comrades will be held in the tower until the morrow. I will grant ye use of a destrier and should ye win the purse, I will take a quarter."

Noah nods. "Fair enough."

"However." FitzWalter waves his nail-cleaning dagger beneath Noah's nose. "If ye should fail, ye will be thrown into the pit to rot for the rest of your miserable days and your woman will become my whore."

Me? I frantically shake my head, looking between my two companions. Being used as a whore is not and will never be part of the bargain.

A white line forms between Amir's pursed lips telling me to keep quiet. Easy for him.

"I'll wager she's a wild one," says one of the guards with an ugly chuckle.

I think I'm going to puke.

After meeting with Lord FitzWalter, our satchels are taken and searched before we are escorted up the narrow steps of a dank tower. The stone walls are filthy and cold. Shadows cut through the corridor like unhappy ghosts. An iron prison door swings open and I'm pushed inside with the blunt end of a guard's pike.

"Knock it off," I shout, stumbling into the small cell ahead of Noah and Amir.

"Yer speech is odd, wench," says the guard. "Anyone with eyes like a cat's is an outlander for certain and I don't trust ye."

"What is the date?" asks Amir, stepping between me and the guard.

"The first day of June, ye simpleton—a sennight afore the festival of Whitsun."

"And the year?"

"Are ye completely daft?"

Amir bows for what seems like the hundredth time. "Things are different in...ah...where we hail from. Please, humor me."

"`Tis the year of our Lord twelve hundred and fifteen."

"My God," Noah whispers under his breath.

I move beside Amir and the three of us stand shoulder to shoulder while the man slams the door. He pats a whip coiled at his hip and eyes Noah through the iron grillwork. "Ye may be as tall as

Goliath, but ye're no champion, mark me. I reckon ye're one of John's back-biting spies and I aim to make ye pay in flesh and blood. I give ye my oath I will."

I clutch my cloak closed and shiver. It's damp and dank in here and the only light is from a tiny window with iron bars. Noah stands frozen like a doomed warrior, his glare unflinching while the guards march away. His only movement is the muscles clenching in his jaw, his fists balled at his sides. As the footsteps fade, he turns to Amir. "Cardinal Benedict? He was a pope. What were you thinking?"

"It was the first name that popped into my head." Amir slumps down the wall, landing on his ass. "At least they didn't question me. If it's 1215, then Pope Innocent III is in power."

"Who cares about the damned cardinal or the pope?" I ask, shoving Noah in the shoulder. "You just agreed to compete in a medieval tournament...with real medieval knights. Men who are trained from birth to *kill* you. Are you insane?"

He slaps the wall. "What should I have done? You're the one who told them I'm a knight."

"You're the one who said we were here for the tournament. Regardless, that didn't mean you should have volunteered to sacrifice yourself."

"How else were we supposed to worm our way out of FitzWalter's grasp?" asks Amir.

"He's right." Noah grabs the bars and tests them with a powerful shake. "If I didn't throw my name in for the tournament, that medieval baron would have convicted us as spies and we'd be marched to the gallows with nooses around our necks rather than enjoying his hospitality in this cushy chamber."

I move over to Amir, slide down the cold stone, and sit beside him. On the far side, water trickles down the wall through green algae. There's a wooden bucket in the corner and there's no doubt in my mind what it's used for. I cross my legs. Tightly.

My heels scrape over some old, disgusting hay on the floor which hasn't been swept in forever. We're stuck in here for the night and there's not so much as a stool to sit on. Thoughts of rats scurrying in the shadows make my skin crawl. And thank God we're about a hundred years too early for the black plague.

"Cushy?" I ask, not hiding my sarcasm.

Amir gestures downward with his thumb. "Doubtless there's a dungeon below that we definitely do not want to see."

I gulp. "You mean it gets worse?"

The brown belt smirks. "Much worse."

"So, what are we going to do?" I ask.

Noah joins us on the floor. "I'd better win the tournament, hadn't I?"

Okay, maybe *everyone* at the academy is insane. "How?"

"Let me worry about that." He rests his elbows on his knees. "Amir will be my squire, and you...ah...you'll be a lot safer if you pose as my wife."

He doesn't look happy about it but my stomach flips all the same. Biting my lip, I decide my reaction is unpleasant. "Wonderful. I'll be a widow by sunset tomorrow."

"Thanks for the encouragement." He nudges me with his elbow. "More importantly, have you felt anything—you know—the reason why we're here?"

I shake my head, then take a deep breath and close my eyes. I go through my meditation protocol, but the only thing I can sense is Noah's driving intensity and Amir's overpowering curiosity.

I open an eye and glance between them. "Breathe with me, dammit."

After a few minutes of group meditation, Noah pushes to his feet. "Anything?"

"Nothing."

"I knew it." Again, he rattles the iron door, making the lock clank. "You're too green. You don't have a clue what to zone in on."

"And you do?" I challenge, following and shaking the bars with all my strength. "You ought to be helping me, not telling me how much I suck."

He slams his fist against the door. "I don't blame *you*, dammit."

His anger makes every muscle in my body tense.

Amir stands and joins us. "Grand Master Li wouldn't have sent her if he wasn't sure."

"Right," Noah says, those crystal eyes glaring at me. "Is he ever completely sure about anything?"

"He is about me." I just my chin upward and scowl, yeah my poker face is definitely better than Ziana's. Maybe I am quaking in my boots but I'm not about to let the blue belt think he can intimidate me. "I know what it will feel like. Every time the Grand Master mentions the Qiang, I get chilled. I mean my veins start pumping ice like nothing I've experienced before. It's as if my body is allergic to evil—to *them*. He told me I'd have the same sensations when the Qiang are near."

Gah, I cross my arms, hoping I'm not blowing wind.

"That sounds about right." Amir moves to the window. "Besides, we've never gone on a mission, immediately found the Qiang, stopped them, and headed for home. Whatever the forces there are in the universe decide we need to go on an adventure first."

"How many missions have you been on?" I ask.

"Three," says Noah. "Amir's the old hand at this."

The room grows deadly silent and uncomfortable. It reminds me of talking to a veteran who's been in a war. They don't want to remember.

Even Amir slumps. "Missions are never the same. And they're never easy."

I chew my lip thinking of a clever reply and finally say, "None of us signed up for easy, did we?"

Noah splays his fingers. "You have no idea."

True. I don't. But I'm about to find out.

Turning his attention out the window, Amir stretches up on his toes. "I can see the river."

"Do you know where we are?" I ask.

"My best guess? We're in London."

"Wait a minute." I snap my fingers. I just took Sensei Bashir's exam on the 1200s. Why didn't I think of it sooner? "If it's June first, 1215, then the barons have sacked London."

"That's right." Amir smacks his forehead with the heel of his hand. "And FitzWalter is their leader—calls his men the Army of God."

Noah goes glassy eyed. "It's the Magna Carta."

"That it!" Amir snaps his fingers. "We need to get to Runnymede. That's where they gather to sign the document."

"Maybe Runnymede, but how can we be sure?" Noah asks, tapping his temple with his pointer finger. "After the barons sacked London, they started negotiating. That should be about now, right? And all the knights in England are either here or with King John. I'll bet that's why there's a jousting tournament."

Amir throws out his hands. "We need to come up with a list of the Qiang's possible targets and find them. You know, the big players during the Magna Carta negotiations."

"There's King John, of course," I say. "And Archbishop Langton. He advised on both sides of the argument."

"There's FitzWalter and the rebel barons but aren't most of them here?" asks Noah.

"Yeah. It could be any one of them." Amir pulls a piece of straw out of his hair. "And don't forget Pope Innocent excommunicated them all—rescinded the Magna Carta almost as soon as it was written. But it's not the pope, he's in Rome trying to organize the Fifth Crusade."

I pace, drumming my fingers against my lips and suddenly stop, my mind clicking. "William Marshal, Earl of Pembroke, needs to be on the list."

"Now you're talking." Noah falls into step beside me. "From what I remember from Bashir's class, Marshal is the only man in this era with some principles."

Amir moves in front of Noah and shoves him in the shoulder. "Yeah, but it's King John's seal on the Magna Carta."

"So, we have our list," I say, counting on my fingers. "The king, Marshal, Langton, and the barons with FitzWalter at the top since he's the first one we saw. We check them off until we find the Qiang."

"Agreed," says Noah.

My mouth drops open. Did our fearless knight just agree with me on something? "But it can't be FitzWalter."

"Because you would know? Right? You would have had the ice in your blood?" asks Amir.

"Yes," I say with more conviction than I feel.

The brown belt claps my shoulder. "Makes sense."

"Good." I glance between them, pretty sure we're on the right track. "Now that we know our goal, I don't think I had ten minutes with Grand Master Li. He told me about Sun Tzu, Whang Due, and the Jade Goddess, but there are about a gazillion holes in all this. I need some answers."

"Like what?" asks Noah.

"Well, who are the Qiang? How many do we need to find?"

"In modern day, they can be anybody—usually militant extremists, though." Amir leans against the wall and crosses his ankles. "And they can't send more than three. They're restricted by the same rules we are."

Noah shakes the bars again. They don't budge. "Did Li tell you not to intervene?"

"You mean with the Qiang?" I ask.

"No. In this time. You know, when you're in the past."

Amir places his hands on my shoulders and kneads with his fingers. God, I knew I was tense, but I had no idea how tight my muscles are. "Whenever we travel we see things that mess with our ways of thinking—you know, modern ways. Like women's rights, and corporal punishment. What Noah is telling you is we have to turn a blind eye, no matter how much we want to intercede."

I can only shake my head, wondering how much I don't know about that can completely mess things up. "I feel like I'm totally not ready to be here."

Noah snorts. "Now you understand what I've been trying to tell you, white belt."

Chapter Eleven

"Our greatest glory is not in never falling, but in rising every time we fall." - Confucius

After a meager breakfast of stale bread and bitter ale, my head swims as our satchels are returned and we're marshaled down the spiral staircase. A person can get dizzy enough using these worn and uneven steps but try it on a mostly empty stomach topped by a pint. Even Noah admitted the brew was potent. I figure they're trying to put him at a disadvantage, or else they've all built up their tolerances, which makes sense. If the water in the Thames is an indication, I wouldn't chance drinking anything that hasn't been brewed or boiled—not in the city anyway.

When we step outside, it's drizzling and I pull my scarf lower on my brow. There's a retinue of mounted guards and foot soldiers waiting for us. Beside them, Harold is holding the reins of an enormous horse.

"We're providing an armed escort—a diamond formation," says Harold. "Yer woman and squire will walk beside ye and if anyone tries to run, they'll be the first to die."

Taking the reins, Noah lets the horse sniff the back of his hand. "I'd like Lady Jones to ride with me."

I nearly spit out my teeth. No one has ever called me the lady of anything.

Harold gives me a good once-over, one that blares his doubt loud and clear, one that tells me he has absolutely no qualms about running me through with the mammoth sword hanging from his belt. "She walks. His Lordship's orders."

"Not to worry, my love," I say, patting Noah's arm and trying to look wifely, though I'd really prefer to take out one of Harold's knees. "I always enjoy a brisk stroll."

Londoners line the street, watching our impromptu parade while we march toward the Thames. I can't help but gawk at everything. The stone buildings are cruder than I imagined, making the Tower of London look as if it's the work of a masonry genius. For the most part, people are plainly dressed. Aside from the red shields embroidered on the guards' tunics, there are no vibrant colors and all heads are covered by caps or veils.

The stench of farm animals fills the air as we approach the bridge. To the north, there's a fenced yard packed with sheep, mud, and I can't see a blade of grass. Chickens wander everywhere, ignoring the procession as they peck for scraps of food. No one seems to be bothered by the manure—chicken, horse, and Lord knows what else. I'm stepping around landmines as best I can.

The odors grow worse as we march under the gateway to the bridge. Now it wreaks more like a sewer. My eyes sting and I pull my veil over my nose.

The bridge spanning the great river is like another city with only glimpses of the Thames between the two and three-story buildings.

Hundreds of small boats dot the river—well, small by my standards. The only time I've been on a boat was when I went on a cruise to Mexico with my parents. I was ten. The ship was gargantuan with twelve floors and a rock-climbing wall.

I'd give away my red Ford to be there now.

As we proceed, merchants offer their wares to the soldiers. Raw chickens, cloth, casks of wine, woven horse blankets. At the far end, a woman is selling pigeon pies. They smell delicious and, for the first time since we arrived, my mouth waters. Worse, my stomach growls and I feel a little shaky.

"I'm starving," I mumble.

Sitting the enormous steed, Noah leans down and whispers, "Don't swipe anything. You might end up with your hand cut off."

I have no intention of stealing but then that makes me wonder how we'll find our next meal. I certainly can't survive an entire day on a crust of bread and a pint of ale. Are the free-roaming chickens for anyone who's hungry? I doubt it. At this time in England, poaching a deer from the king's forest comes with severe punishment. I learned that in Bashir's class. According to the history books, King John was the worst of the Plantagenets, claiming vast quantities of forest for himself while his people starved.

When we pass the fish shop with eels hanging from the awning my stomach definitely stops growling. I long for Mexican food in Mesquite or a bowl of almond granola. Maybe a piece of toast? With peanut butter?

Before we cross under the enormous archway at the end of the bridge, I glance back. The buildings form a tunnel leading to London. A fog of black smoke mingles with the clouds above. Despite its crude smells, farm animals, and bad-tempered soldiers, I find it captivating, fascinating, and I'm drawn to learn more. I want to wander her streets and discover everything to know—if I can manage it without being arrested.

Once we cross into Southwark, it's like another world. Sure, there are shops near the Thames, but beyond is a field with white tents displaying colorful pennants. It has the look and feel of a Renaissance faire—sort of. As the tension from the city fades, I step lighter as if someone is pulling a heavy backpack off my shoulders. Over the withers of Noah's horse, Amir catches my eye and grins. He senses the ease of tension, too.

Now all I have to do is sense the Qiang. I'm frustrated that Noah thinks I'm a loser because I don't feel anything yet. If I am useless, then why did Grand Master Li send me? It's not like I can will the feelings to come. Besides, most of the people on our list aren't even here.

How the heck are we going to find them?

If Noah wins, we will be free to go and continue with the mission.

But what if he loses? What then?

There's no way I'm ever going to let FitzWalter lay a finger on me. Besides, we're supposed to stay together—and here we are marching toward doom. This is a disaster of humongous proportions. If Noah loses, he's headed for the bowels of hell, unless the three of us can take on FitzWalter's army.

Not.

I try not to think about dungeons and medieval torture as we march past the jousting arena. A wooden fence runs down the middle just like the one at the academy. On one side are the spectator stands. There's even a covered area where the important people will sit. My stomach turns over as I imagine the carnage. It isn't much different from gladiator sport, though I suppose using blunted weapons no one dies in the end. Usually.

When I get a glimpse of the other knights all the doubts I'm having mushroom like a cloud from an atomic bomb. Every one of them can pass for heavyweight MMA fighters dressed in chainmail. Some are flashy, wearing bucket helmets and bright tunics matching the caparisons on their horses and their shields. Their beards are long and bushy, and their faces are contorted with deadly scowls like they just murdered their mothers and are looking for their next victims.

Harold leads us to the far end and gestures to a couple of nicked up jousting poles. "Since you are destitute, Lord FitzWalter has agreed to supply ye with lances."

"Only lances?" asks Noah.

"God's bones, His Lordship has already given ye the lend of a horse. If it were me, I'd have booted yer arse into the Thames by now. If ye're as good as ye say, a lance is all ye will require."

I consider sticking my foot out while Harold marches past but manage to restrain myself.

Amir holds the horse while Noah dismounts. "You're number three, so that means you'll joust second."

Brushing himself off, Noah looks like a pauper compared to the rest of the knights in their pomp. Thank God he doesn't seem to care. "It's better than first."

"You need armor," I say.

"Yeah, just like I need to be on my Harley on a cross-country cruise about now." He gives me a lopsided grin as he tucks an errant curl under my veil. "There are hundreds of things I need, babe, but the only one that matters is winning."

"It would be nice if you had a shield," says Amir, turning in a circle.

I search the grounds, hoping to find a friendly face. The crowd has grown and the stands are full of people in medieval costume. Jesters tumble into the arena to the beat of a drum and tambourine. A man dances in, playing a wooden flute and a crowd gathers to watch, but none of them has a shield.

"Do you think we could borrow one?" I ask.

Amir throws his thumb over his shoulder, pointing to one of the competitors. "No self-respecting knight will let anyone borrow a piece of his equipment. The only way Noah will get ahold of a shield is to win his first round. Then he'll claim the 'spoils of combat', send me in as his kipper and I'll have to fight him for the privilege of taking his weapons."

My mouth drops open. "That's how it's done? Seriously?"

"That's how it's done. And don't even think about 'borrowing' a shield without permission. We'll all be skewered."

I want to scream. "This stuff wasn't covered in Bashir's class. How the hell do you know it?"

"My first mission was during a crusade—"

The blare of trumpets cut him off while the jesters are replaced by a master of ceremonies of sorts. I can't hear what the man's saying because his back is to the jousters and ground crew. The people in the stands applaud as the knights are introduced.

There are clearly favorites with Sir Geoffrey receiving the loudest applause. Noah is introduced as Noah the Terrible and the crowd boos while he canters his horse in front of the stands.

Sir Geoffrey takes a kerchief from the lady sitting with Lord FitzWalter and makes a show of holding it to his nose, then waves it above his head. "I will carry this with pride, my lady."

Squires are positioned on each end of the ring along with their assistants. Not surprisingly, their arsenals of weapons have pikemen guarding them. Harold and FitzWalter's men move to the edge of the arena and lean on the fence.

I grit my teeth and approach the guard wearing a shield on his back while a new plan forms in my mind. Amir's a good fighter, but why risk it if there's another way?

Medieval people put the church before everything, at least that's what the books say. Maybe I can pour on some guilt. I politely bow my head and smile at the man. "FitzWalter has given Sir Noah a horse and lance, but no shield or armor."

The guard's eyebrows slash downward. "Has he sent his woman to beg?"

"He would never do that, though I am not above making a request. As a God-fearing Christian, surely you would not deny a man the chance to protect himself. What harm is there in lending him your shield?"

"Are ye daft? A soldier's targe and sword are his tools of trade. They're nay for barter."

I point to the stands. "What if Sir Noah wins the purse? What if he guaranteed you payment?"

"And what will the miserable beggar pay if he loses, which is far more likely? What odds then?" He grabs my cloak in his fist and yanks me to within an inch of his face. This close, the man reeks, his breath is sour, his teeth black. "Will a night with ye be his collateral?"

Gulping back the bile burning my esophagus, I place a hand on his wrist and apply just enough pressure to his ulnar nerve to make him release me. Then I glare across the faces of the guards. "Is there not a decent Christian man among you? The lending of a shield for a...a shilling." Surely there ought to be a host of shillings in the purse. "And if Sir Noah loses, he'll, he'll—"

"He won't lose," says Amir, his voice dead serious.

"Bleeding hell," says the guard, pulling the shield off his back. "It'll be good sport to watch the bastard fall. But if he damages this, he'll have me to answer to, for certain. And if I have to, I'll take me payment out of his hide."

"Thank you, sir," I say, with an awkward curtsy before I take the shield. "Your kindness will be rewarded on Judgment Day."

Amir gives me a wink as I let out a long breath, relieved I didn't have to agree to have sex with any of those smelly beasts.

"Quick thinking with the Judgment Day," he whispers, sliding the targe from my fingers and slinging it over his shoulder.

"It just came to me. It was probably mentioned in history class."

"I don't doubt it."

"So, why are you so smart?" I ask as we head around the ring.

"Genetics, I guess. I'm a product of a test tube."

"Seriously?"

"Nah. It's my parents' little joke." He chuckles. "They're both physicists."

After the parade, we join Noah while the first two jousters take their places.

The judge drops the flag and they barrel toward each other. Sir Geoffrey knocks Sir Randolph from his horse. By some miracle Sir Randolph manages to get back on his horse and they go at it again like a pair of muskoxen during the rut.

To the crowd's joy, Sir Geoffrey wins. But there's a bigger problem.

Noah is next.

Before he enters the arena I grab the horse's bridle and look up at Mr. Fearless. "Are you sure you want to do this?"

Our jouster just gives me a narrow-eyed smirk and shakes his head. "If I win, pretend it's not a miracle. If I lose, be ready to run."

"Run?" asks Amir.

Noah pats the destrier's neck, then takes the guard's shield from Amir. "This fella is sturdy enough to hold all three of us, plus I'm not wearing armor to weigh him down."

"What if you're knocked off?" I ask.

"Then as squire, Amir will run after the beast. Dammit, Genesis, stop worrying about me. You just need to make sure you're ready for anything. I have no intention of stalling the mission with a lengthy stay in the Tower. Got it?"

I will never be able to explain why, but Noah beat his opponent and the next. Maybe he was faster because he wasn't wearing armor. Maybe his eyesight is keener. All I know is he pulled two miracles out of his ass.

But can he make it three?

They've narrowed the field to the final two jousters and it's winner takes all. I'm not deluding myself this time. Noah is facing Sir Geoffery who has annihilated every single one of his challengers. If this were modern day, they all would have been sent to the hospital for concussion protocol.

Before the blue belt mounts his horse, he signals for us to come. "Remember what I said. No matter what happens, we're out of here. We've already wasted too much time. Don't forget there's a mission to accomplish."

Amir runs his hand down the destrier's nose. "If you win we'll need the purse. I'm already lightheaded from going without food."

The mere mention of a meal makes knives of hunger stab my stomach. I step in and grab the front of Noah's tunic. "You've come this far, you can win."

His gaze drills into mine and he gives me a thin-lipped nod.

I move my hands to his cheeks and hold his stare. A zing of energy makes my heart race, my breath catch. I didn't expect the rough stubble beneath my fingertips or to feel the thrumming of his pulse against my little finger. Why is it now I admit he's gorgeous? Even more so, he's human— not the tough guy on the outside, but I sense he hides a ton of feelings inside.

I have about a half of a second before the moment is over and I do the only thing I can think of. Rising on my toes, I kiss him. On the mouth. It's not a juicy romantic kiss, but a kiss I hope shows him how much I care.

"For luck," I say, stepping back. "Though you don't need it."

He stares at me like he's stunned.

Amir smacks his shoulder. "It's time, dude."

Noah licks his lips and blinks. "Right."

He mounts and rides off. My throat grows thick when he doesn't look back. Maybe kissing him was a bad idea.

Yeah.

It was really stupid—could have thrown him out of his zone.

I stand alone while Amir follows with the lance. So, we're fleeing to Runnymede when this is over? If only I weren't wearing a skirt, I'd be able to run faster.

A whisper of a warning prickles the back of my neck. I almost think I'm getting one of my ESP feelings until Harold's stench invades my nostrils. I spin with my elbow aimed at his face, but there are three pikes pointed at my back, making me stop mid-turn.

"That's right, Yer Ladyship." He chuckles with an ugly sneer. "If yer man is thinking of giving us the slip, he won't be leaving the grounds with his pretty wife."

Chapter Twelve

"Wisdom, compassion, and courage are the three universally recognized moral qualities of men." - Confucius

My every nerve endings fire on red alert while Amir helps Noah prepare to joust. His horse shakes his head and strikes at the dirt with his front hoof while the judge moves to the center of the ring and raises his flag.

The skin across my back needles with awareness. They've taken me to the far end of the arena and the three guards standing behind my back aren't paying attention to the games. They're watching me, pikes poised to pierce my flesh. I close my eyes and splay my fingers, rehearsing my defense in my mind. The man on the right is the smallest. He's my first target. Once I seize his weapon, I'll deal with the others.

If they don't kill me first.

I've made eye contact with Amir so at least he knows I'm not going to be able to make a mad dash for salvation.

My nerves are frayed like exposed electrodes because I can't do anything but wait.

The flag drops and Noah slams his heels into the destrier's barrel with a resounding, "Ha!"

I was nervous in the last two rounds, but this one tops the charts. Is he galloping faster? Is it because the stakes are higher? Or is it because my life is hanging by a precipice, in the hands of these barbaric guardsmen?

The ground thunders beneath my feet as the knights race toward each other and level their lances. Noah's face is hard, his stare fixed on Sir Geoffrey. The wind whips his hair back and I wish I'd found him a helmet. A length to impact, he gnashes his teeth and shifts his shield right. As they collide, my heart lurches into my throat.

Geoffrey's lance slams into the shield, crushing it against Noah's chest. The force of the strike lifts him a good foot out of the saddle while the horse continues galloping down the tilt. Noah's arms fling wide as he sails backward toward the ground, the lance flying from his grasp.

A woman screams and my throat burns as I realize the blood-curdling noise came from me. I dart forward. "Noah!"

Iron fingers wrap around my wrist and stop my forward progress. "He'll be tended by his squire," growls Harold.

I wrench my hand away. "He might be hurt."

"Look there," says the guard on my right—the smallish one I'm planning to take out first. "Sir Noah is already up."

Amir is brushing him off while a boy is jogging toward them leading the destrier. It seems Noah the Terrible has won over someone if not the crowd.

Taking a deep breath, I calm my nerves as I watch the blue belt lumber to the steed. He's sore, but I don't think he's broken anything. He probably landed on his skull, which would save the thick-headed dude every time. I wipe the smile off my face. This isn't funny and I shouldn't be joking. Not even with myself.

On the second round, Noah's lance slams Sir Geoffrey's shield first, but doesn't knock the knight from his horse. Nonetheless, the judges award a point to Noah and, if he wins the next round, the purse is ours.

I'm so excited I'm about to pee myself.

As the jousters take their places, Noah's mount is frothing at the mouth and there's white foam leeching from his neck.

I turn to Harold. "What's wrong with FitzWalter's horse?"

The animal starts shaking his head, his nostrils flaring.

"Worried are ye?"

"God, yes, I'm worried. It's hard enough to win with a healthy steed." I look for the boy and can't find him anywhere. Did he poison the poor destrier?

"Not to worry," says Harold. "The beast is fatigued is all. Look at him strike the ground. He has the heart of a lion, that one."

Is this normal? I drive a truck. I don't know anything about horses.

The flag drops.

The destrier rears, then takes off like he's been shot out of a cannon. Okay, he hasn't been poisoned but Noah slips sideways as he struggles to steady his lance. The two jousters are speeding for impact even faster than before. Sir Geoffrey is steady as a freight train.

I hold my breath and clench my fists over my mouth. *Please, please, please!* My entire body tenses. Grimacing, I squint but don't quite close my eyes.

"Nooooooo!" I scream as Noah takes a deathly hit to the chest. The wooden targe shatters around him as he's hurled to the dirt, hitting with an unforgiving thud. Without thinking, I take a step forward.

Before Harold's fingers seize my arm, I squat and weave to the right. Spinning outward, I grab small-man's pike with both hands and wrench it downward. He's stronger than he looks and gives resistance.

But I have a gazillion more moves in my arsenal.

As the crowd goes wild, shouting cheers for Geoffrey, I shift my far foot backward and use the momentum to flip small-man over my hip. Flung to his back, the bastard manages to keep hold of his weapon as if it's a part of his anatomy. I leap on to his chest and pin him beneath me.

Using my knee, I'm about to crush his larynx with the pole when Noah bellows over the pandemonium, "Stop in the name of His Holiness, Pope Innocent!"

What? My mind scrambles until I realize the pope has more power than the king. In addition, at the moment King John's popularity is at the bottom of the murky Thames. Silence spreads across the arena.

As I look up, the two other pikemen are about to cut my throat.

The man beneath me stares up with a mixture of fear and shock in his eyes, but I've got him in a chokehold no one can escape. I might die with my next breath but I don't let up—not until I hear what Noah has to say.

The cocky blue belt struts in a circle like he owns all of Southwark.

He moves in beside Sir Geoffrey and faces the stands. "Congratulations to the victor," He says not so convincingly. "I am a newcomer and an outlander to you. But I have fought with no armor on a borrowed horse with a borrowed lance and shield...and yet I succeeded to the final round. As a man of honor, I challenge all knights of this joust to a passage of arms! Right here, right now, before the good people of London, I proclaim that I will fight them all, without arms, without armor, without squires or interference of any kind."

Across the arena, Amir catches my eye, nods, then folds his arms. With his gesture, I understand. Noah might not have been able to win on the back of a horse, but I'd be surprised if any medieval Englishman could beat the Harley-riding badass in a brawl...unless they gang up on him.

Which could happen. Hey, it's 1215 and I don't think chivalry has been invented yet. At least not among the people we've seen.

Sir Geoffrey removes his helm and accepts the challenge by shaking Noah's hand. Okay. I'll admit chivalry has been invented but, as far as I'm concerned, it's mighty scarce.

I eye the guard beneath me. His face is blue and his eyes are bulging. "Sorry," I say, easing off while the other men's pikes remain pointed at my eyeballs. "My mistake."

They back off enough to let me push to my feet. But I have no choice but to let small-man have his pike back. "Just watch where you're aiming the pointy end next time."

I hope a little humor helps, but he rips the weapon from my hand and jabs it at my throat. I can't help but parry the damned spear away. This time I look him in the eye like I mean business. "Mess with me and I'll mess you up. Got it, asshole?"

I don't care if I'm talking trash. I guess living above a bar has given me some rough edges. Besides, it might be better if the jerk doesn't know what I'm saying. Still, I must have made an impression because he allows me a little room. I glance over each shoulder. The guards are watching Noah, but I have no illusions that their attention will shift to their duty if I make one wrong move. Worse, now I've shown my hand and need to come up with another plan. Fast.

I grin with my own bit of satisfaction when the hilt of Harold's mammoth sword taps my hip. But my concentration is pulled back to the action. All eight jousters have entered the ring without arms and they've formed a circle around Noah. Good Lord, talk about ganging up. He's their target.

Three judges run around waving flags while the master of ceremonies holds forth. "This will be a spectator's sport like none other! Sir Noah the Terrible has thrown out a challenge no knight can refuse. No weapons of any kind are allowed—no daggers, no flails, no whips, no chains. You must fight with the hands God gave you. If anyone breaks these rules, he will forfeit the purse. The last man who remains standing will be our victor!"

The trumpets blare and it's on. That miserable sinking feeling drops in my gut again. Seven knights creep toward Noah as he crouches, his arms out to the sides. Sir Connor is the burliest and he attacks first, grappling for Noah's neck. But the best fighter at the academy leaps in the air, throws a lightning fast split kick, nailing not only Sir Conner in the snout, but smacks Sir Geoffrey as well.

As soon as Noah lands, he jumps again, this time pulling an aerial somersault over Sir Randolph's head, landing outside the circle.

For a second they all stand dumbfounded. Sir Conner is out cold and Sir Geoffrey is on his knees with blood coming from his mouth. The crowd goes wild, screaming for more.

And it's coming.

Within my next heartbeat, the arena erupts in pandemonium. The brawl morphs into a free-for-all with knight fighting knight, fists swinging savagely.

As Sir Geoffrey wobbles to his feet, Sir Randolph grabs him by the collar and headbutts him, followed by a triumphant bellow.

Noah holds his own against three while two on the far side of the ring are grappling on the ground. Throwing a spinning hook, Noah decks another. "Stay down," he barks, dancing in place, his guard up.

It's like a Roman gladiator riot. Noah's bleeding from the corner of his eye and there's blood splattered on his tunic but he doesn't flinch as he throws a jab and a hook at the next opponent.

My attention is yanked away as Sir Geoffrey and Sir Randolph are bellowing curses, pummeling each other with punch after punch, each staggering like they're drunk.

Noah takes out the third man with a jumping roundhouse to the head, but Sir Robert and Sir Gerard barrel straight for him on opposite sides. Thinking quickly, the blue belt pulls a backward flip while the two knights collide. But when he lands, fists fly in a furor of brutal combat.

Geoffrey is decked by Randolph and the true winner of the joust crawls to the sidelines, bloodied and spent.

Randolph joins the final four, but Noah looks like he's only getting started. Without being weighed down by armor, he's faster than every man, nimbler with deadly kicks. The knights of this era have definitely been trained with their fists but are lacking when it comes to kicking anywhere above the knee.

After repeated blows to the face and solar plexus, Noah's last three combatants fall one by one.

My heart soars and I clap...until Sir Geoffrey returns to the arena with a great sword in his fist. "I won this joust fair, and ye took it from me, ye bloody swindler."

Noah backs, raising his hands. "I challenged and you accepted. So did the others."

Geoffrey lunges, hacking across with his blade. "But ye said nothing about being a bleating sorcerer!"

Noah hops away and the two men circle. "I'm a flesh and blood man, just like you. But I've trained with the Mongols. Have you heard of them?"

"Ye're one of them!" Geoffrey attacks with a fake, a fade, and a lunge. He's skilled—and wields the big sword like it's as light as a waster. "Come to take our lands."

"I've come to save them," Noah shouts, spinning into the knight, grabbing his sword wrist and shoulder.

I clench my teeth, clutching my arms across myself, praying the warrior with the ice-blue eyes doesn't slip and end up dead.

Gah!

Noah swings up and grabs ahold of the weapon.

"Kill him!" Geoffrey shouts to the others as he pulls a dagger from his boot.

Bellowing cries erupt from the sidelines as knights, guards, and squires rush the ring.

God no! I search for Amir, but I can't find him in the mayhem.

I grab Harold's hilt and shove the douche to the ground while pulling the sword from its scabbard. A pikeman reaches for me, but his fingers only manage to brush my cloak as I leap over the fence and rush into the melee.

The damned guards are on my heels and I spin in place, panning the sword across them. "Stay back!"

"Seize her, the wench has my bloody sword!" shouts Harold.

The clang of iron striking iron resounds behind me as I slowly back away. A guard lunges in, jabbing his pike. I hack downward, breaking the shaft. And then it's on. Moving too fast to think, I breathe with the hiss of the sword while air fills my limbs with strength.

Before they happen, I sense the three strikes aimed my way and defend, the blade hacking through each pike as the men attack. Harold comes at me with a dagger. Spinning outward, I slam the hilt of his sword into the vile man's temple.

As he drops to his knees, I seize my chance and dash around the edge of the arena, wielding my blade and battling off men crazed with bloodlust.

Amir and Noah are fighting back-to-back in front of the stands, both of them defending with brute strength like nothing I've ever seen.

A knight rushes in on their flank, swinging a flail over his head. I reach him just as his arms hurl forward. With an upward strike, I stop the ball and chain.

A warning in my mind fires and I see a crossbow behind me. I snatch the knight's dagger, whip around and throw the knife, hitting the archer in the shoulder. His arrow releases, but shoots toward the stands.

Screams erupt from the crowd and the people scatter.

"Now, Genesis!" shouts Noah, as he and Amir break away, but they're running separate directions. As I make up my mind, Noah hurdles over the fence and swings himself into the stands to where FitzWalter is cowering. He grabs the leather purse from the terrified lord's grasp. "I reckon I've won this fair and square."

"Over here!" Amir beckons me toward the destrier while he lunges, grabbing the reins of a runaway horse.

As I arrive, he tosses me the destrier's reins. "Climb up."

There's no time to ask what Noah will ride—and there's definitely no chance I'll ask anyone still standing to hold the beast while I mount.

"Nice horsey," I say, shoving my foot into a stirrup and swing my leg over. The animal sidesteps, making me tighten my knees. Snorting, the enormous beast rears.

"Ease up on your seat!" hollers Amir as Noah takes a flying leap and lands behind me.

"How the hell do I do that?" I shout as the horse takes off with every bit as much speed as he showed in the arena.

Noah's fingers grip my hands as I squeeze my knees tighter. Holy crap, I'm going to die on the back of this animal.

"After them!" bellows someone as we gallop past.

"Faster!" Noah shouts.

Ahead, Amir slaps his horse's rump and leads us to Lord only knows where.

We've been riding at top speed for a mile or two and Amir's horse suddenly slows.

Noah moves his hands forward, reaching in front of my fingers and securing the reins. "Relax your legs or this big fella won't stop until his heart gives out."

I immediately let my knees flop. As if by magic, the horse settles into a trot. "I don't want to hurt him."

"He's a prey animal," Noah's deep voice in my ear, "If he senses your fear, he'll be afraid, too."

I let myself breathe. "Where are we going?" I shout, praying Amir has put together a plan.

"Away from here—as fast as we can."

I steal a backward glance and don't see anyone following. "They're not on our tails."

"You'd better believe they are. We just got a head start." Noah says, his tone anything but reassuring.

Chapter Thirteen

*"Roads were made for journeys, not
destinations." - Confucius*

The coins clink in Amir's pile as he tallies our
winnings while I use one of the bandages to dab
iodine solution on the cut beside Noah's eye. After
about an hour on the run, the destrier slowed to a
walk. We rode into a town with a cobbled street and
before we got to the other end, Amir led us into a
stream so FitzWalter's men wouldn't be able to track
us. Before dark, we found a farmer not far from the
Thames who took us in. Well, not into his decrepit
cottage. We're camping in the stable with the
animals.

At least it's dry and reasonably warm. Better yet,
we're not behind bars. There's even enough hay to
make a bed, or a pallet as the farmer called it. No
matter what, it's an improvement over spending last
night sleeping on cold stone. And I'm becoming
accustomed to the odors.

Sort of.

I blow on the wound—not sure why. I guess it's
something my mother would have done. My body
tingles as I realize how close I am. He really is the
hottest guy I've ever seen even if he never looks
twice at me.

Realizing I'm way to close to his face, I lean away. "You ought to have this stitched."

Noah gives me his trademark "not happening" look, except it's not as convincing with his eye red and swollen half-shut. "I've endured worse. It'll be fine."

I stopper the iodine bottle and return it to my satchel. "Well, at least it's clean."

He brushes a wisp of hair away from my face. God, every time he does that it makes me all tingly and gooey on the inside. "Thanks."

The skimming of his fingers on my cheek turns my tingles into a gasp and a full-body quiver, but I ignore my stupid reaction. He's just trying to be nice, and I'm being a total idiot because my lizard brain has decided he's hot.

I glance to Amir, dutifully counting the coins and wish I could be more attracted to him. He's the type of guy a girl ought to set her sights on—super smart and grounded with no chips on his shoulder. At least none I can see. And why am I even thinking about these two guys as anything but teammates? I ought to find a corner and meditate.

But I'm too hungry.

"This is a fortune," Amir says, spreading his hands over the piles of coins—they're odd shaped— sort of round but not uniform. Most are bent, some are cut in quarters, but they were all forged of silver.

"Enough to keep us alive for a week or two?" Noah asks.

My attention piques. We may end up enduring two weeks of this? After the terrors of the tournament and racing away with our lives, I've just about had enough of this century. I've only been here a couple of days and already long for a hot shower, a big juicy steak, and my cozy closet-bed back at the academy.

Amir flips a coin and catches it. "There's five marks, forty shillings, and fifty-six pennies—nearly double a year's salary for a common laborer."

Stretching forward, Noah picks up one of the largest ones—a mark. "I think we ought to divide the booty between us. If we each take a third, then we won't lose it all if one of us is robbed."

I take one of the pennies and turn it over in my palm. It's stamped with a goofy-looking head with curly hair and some sort of elven-looking writing around the edge. I'm sure it's supposed to be a rendering of a king, but the art looks juvenile compared to modern-day coins bearing realistic profiles. On the back is a square cross embellished with more writing and clumps of circles.

"I think that's a great idea," I say, agreeing with Noah. "Amir, why don't you portion it out?"

We all take our cut and I slip a couple of the larger coins in my bra. If we happen to get captured together and searched, that's one place they won't look. I pray. At least they didn't pat me down at the tower.

The door of the stable swings open and I smell food before anyone steps inside. The farmer comes in carrying a cast-iron pot followed by his wife who's toting a wooden cask and a basket. Amir paid them five pennies for room and board. And now that I know what a laborer makes, I'm thinking we overpaid.

We're each given a wooden bowl, cup, and spoon. "The pottage has chicken in it today," says the farmer, ladling a dollop into my bowl. It looks like broth and I stir it around a bit finding a couple measly pieces of chicken. The prospect of watered chicken soup nearly makes me cry. Is this all?

But the woman gives us each a hard roll of sorts. I'm guessing it's unleavened bread. At least it's calories. Our cups are filled from the cask and one is placed in front of me. "What's this?" I ask.

The woman doesn't look me in the eye. "Watered wine."

I almost ask if they have milk, but don't want to be rude. Besides, milk in this century is probably always on the verge of spoiling. I taste the wine. It's red and fruity and warms my throat all the way down to my empty stomach where it sloshes. In about two seconds I go lightheaded. Noah is already digging into his pottage, so I follow suit. I'm definitely not sipping any more wine until I eat.

The food is bland but I'm so ravenous, my bowl is empty in a flash. The farmer gives the boys a second helping, but when I hold up my bowl the couple exchange purse-lipped looks before he gives me half of what the boys were given. No surprise I suppose. They're men. They're bigger, though Amir is a little shorter. I imagine under normal circumstances the guys eat more than me, but right now I could devour a whole chicken by myself.

"Can you tell us how to reach the meadow they call Runnymede?" Amir asks.

"Runnymede, aye?" The farmer rests the ladle in the pot and I strain to see if there's anything left. "Word is, the king's knights are gathering there to make peace with the barons. What would the three of ye have to do with the royal party?"

"We carry messages for…" Noah looks to me and I give him a nod. "For William Marshal, Earl of Pembroke."

"Marshal, aye? Are ye messengers from the Holy Land?"

"Yes, we are and it is very important that we find him," says Amir, tearing off a bite of bread with his teeth.

"Very well." The farmer picks up the pot and takes a step toward the door. "Ye would have been better off if ye'd stayed on the London side of the river, but ye're here now. And as such, ye ought to ride west until ye come to Richmond. There ye'll need to pay for a ferry to take ye across the Thames. Once ye're there, ride north until ye cross with London Road. She ought to take ye near enough."

Amir gulps down his bite, his Adam's apple bobbing. "How will we know when we reach the London Road? Is it marked?"

"By the ruts of course. I've only been that far north once in me life, but all travelers say she's one of the heaviest traveled byways in the kingdom."

I spoon a bite of pottage and look at my bowl, trying not to laugh. Why should I be floored? Of course it's obvious when a person comes across a well-traveled road because of the ruts. I should have thought of that myself. *Not*.

Taking his wife's elbow, the farmer leads her toward the door. "We'll leave ye be for the night. Sleep well."

"Thank you," I say, shifting my attention to Noah's bowl. He's left a bite and I reach across with my spoon and scoop it up. "Are you going to eat this?"

"I was." His eyebrows draw together as he glances down. "You're hurt."

I stuff the bite into my mouth and feel the sting on the underside my forearm. I push up my sleeve and examine a six-inch cut on my arm. Of course, my sleeve is stained with blood—all our clothes are. "What the? I never even felt it."

Noah points to his eye. "I didn't feel this when it happened either."

"But you'll both feel it in the morning." Amir stands and refills his cup. "They left the cask. You ought to have some aspirin powder mixed with wine so you're not miserable on the ride tomorrow."

"Except I don't drink," I say. "Ale this morning, and now wine? I'm going to be hung over."

"Two cups won't kill you. Besides, it's what they drink here—even children—and it's watered down." Grabbing his satchel, Noah pulls out the iodine and a bandage. "I need to see to that arm, Genesis. What were you cut with?"

"Hmm..." I drum my fingers against my lips. "It could have been one of the pikes that was pointing at me throughout the joust. Or any number of swords as I fought my way toward you after Sir Geoffrey decided to break the rules and charge into the arena brandishing his blade. Or maybe it was the flail I stopped from crushing both of your heads."

Noah takes my wrist in his meaty palm and brushes his fingers over my hand ever so lightly. I draw in a shaky breath nearly telling him to stop, but wishing he'd continue. He blows on the gash and the whisper of warm air makes goosebumps rise all the way up to the back of my neck. God, he shifts his eyes and our gazes collide. The corner of his mouth ticks up as he licks his bottom lip.

Is he thinking about our kiss? Well, me kissing him, not the other way around.

My face burns hot. The last thing I need is for the blue belt to think I like him.

He rests my hand on his thigh and douses a bandage with iodine. "You fought like a true waza Tiger today. When Harold and the guards surrounded you, I was afraid Amir and I would have to mount a rescue, but you proved me wrong."

"What?" I snorted like his compliment didn't just make my heart zing. "You doubted I could escape a half-dozen pikemen?"

"We both did," says Amir. "Couldn't believe it when you stopped that flail. You'd better watch it. My man here might decide you're a badass."

Noah snorts. "Bite me."

My mood picks up though I hiss when Noah pours the iodine directly onto my cut. "Well," I say, baring my teeth while my eyes water with the sting. "You both were pretty awesome yourselves. Fighting is a hell of a lot different when your life is on the line. I still don't know how you hung in there with the joust, though. That was nothing short of amazing."

Noah shrugs, using quick flicks of the gauze to clean the wound. "That's why we work so hard at the academy."

Amir stretches his hands behind his head and leans against the wall. "Yeah, and that's why we're usually the ones who are sent on missions."

"But you're descendants, right?" I ask.

"Yep," Noah secures a bandage around my arm and tie the ends in a knot. "But that doesn't mean we're better. All of us train to battle the Qiang, some just have to wait until they graduate to get the honor."

"And others learn cyber warfare," Amir adds.

I examine his handiwork. "What's that?"

"The desk jobs," says Noah. "The Alliance monitors internet chatter and it's gotten a lot more sophisticated in the past five years or so. From the intel they feed to the school, our senseis adjust the curriculums so that we're studying things and places where they expect the Qiang will attack next."

Whoa, the pieces are starting to fit together. "That's why white belts are studying the Magna Carta?"

Amir tosses up his last morsel of bread and catches it with his mouth. "Yep, browns even reviewed it."

I take another sip of wine. My head's not so light now I have a little food in my stomach. "Are missions always like this?"

Noah pushes the hair away from his face. "At best they're unpredictable."

"But perilous?" I ask.

"You can count on it." He traces his finger around the blood stain on my bandage, his light touch taking away the sting. For a moment his expression is lost in some memory. "On the last mission we were sent to the sixth century B.C. to the Chinese court of Wu. I lost count of the number of times we were almost killed. And it took us three weeks to figure out the Qiang were there trying to prevent the murder of King Dao."

My breath hitches when his gaze meets mine. I think the dim light makes his eyes even more vivid. "You know we're going to figure this out," he says.

I wish I did know, but how could I? I didn't pick up on any premonitions in London and tomorrow we're heading to find the other people on our list. But what if I don't ever sense anything?

"You got that right. She-Ra slayed them today," Amir says. He's resting his head back and his eyes are closed.

I smile to myself as I tap Noah's shoulder. "Your last mission took three weeks?"

"Stacy figured it out. Well, more or less. We stopped them from intervening in the course of history, but she was almost killed." Noah places my arm over my midriff then gives it a pat.

An uncomfortable silence spreads through the stable. "Oh," I whisper. No wonder Noah is averse to women going on missions. Was she his girlfriend? Maybe I'll ask Amir later. "Do the Qiang ever find you first?"

Noah nods.

I finish the last of my wine and suddenly I'm exhausted. "Maybe that's why we never land right in front of them. If we did, we'd stick out too much. I'm thinking we need time to acclimate."

Noah yawns and stretches his arms. "Right, and splatter ourselves with blood and dirt before we walk into the line of fire."

"Though I could have done without spending last night in the tower," says Amir, opening one eye.

The blue belt lumbers to his feet and kicks a bunch of hay into a pile. "Maybe the next time someone will be nice to us when we arrive."

"If they were, I might not be so anxious to leave." I start gathering some hay of my own. "Ah...have you heard from Stacy?"

God, I'm lame, but I asked and I can't take it back. Chewing the corner of my mouth, I pay diligent attention to making sure my pallet will be comfortable. At least I hope it's what the dudes think because I know I'm blushing.

Noah plops down and pulls his cloak over him, then rolls to his side. "After she got out of the hospital, she transferred to a state school. Emailed me that she was done with fighting."

"That's too bad," I say.

"What is too bad is that she entered the academy in the first place. She wasn't cut out for this stuff."

"Or any woman?" I ask with an edge. I don't think I'll ever forget his first words to me—*"Go home white belt"*.

He bunches the hay beneath his head. "Going back in time isn't easy for anyone. Women are weaker."

"Physically weaker," Amir interjects.

I glance between them. "But surely they can be useful in given situations. Besides, I might not be as strong as you but I can hold my own."

Noah closes his eyes and settles a bit. "Whatever you say, white belt."

At least he didn't try to tell me I shouldn't be there.

"My man doesn't like to see a girl get hurt," says Amir.

"I don't like to see anybody get hurt." I sit on my pallet and test the hay for comfort. "Too bad none of us have superpowers."

The blue belt opens one eye. "God, Genesis, you're a seer. What else do you want?"

"Lightning from my fingertips might be nice. How about you, Amir? What powers would you have?"

"I'm partial to Brainiac."

"He's a superhero?" I ask.

"In my book, he's the smartest character out there."

I tap Noah's shoulder. "How about you, Jones?"

"Batman all the way, baby."

"Ha. My friend Rex calls me Batgirl."

"Rex, huh?" Noah pushes up. "Is he your boyfriend?"

"Best friend, but not *boyfriend*." I scrape my teeth over my bottom lip wondering why Noah even asked. "Rex...well, he has way better fashion sense than me and after high school he wants to be a highflying hairdresser in New York."

As I curl up on my own pallet, I wonder if Stacy is happy now. I can't imagine being done with fighting—karate anyway. It's not the fighting that I love as much as the way of life. Karate has been a foundation that has grounded me, helped me make sound decisions in times of crisis. I don't think I can ever walk away from it.

My mind wanders and I think about home. About Dad. About Sensei Soto and how all my dreams dramatically changed after the tournament. "Before the academy offered me a scholarship, I'd planned to graduate from high school and then pursue a business degree online so I could help my dad with his bar."

"Your dad owns a bar?" Amir asks.

"Yeah." I glance across to Noah—the guy who rides a Harley. "A biker bar. Can you believe it?"

I have no idea how a dude can grin and make a girl's stomach zing with hundreds of butterflies, but there's no question in my mind that Noah Jones has aced the grinning-eye-shift thing.

Damn him.

愛

Outside, a squawking noise rouses me and I peer through tired, slitted eyes. There's a small, paneless window above Amir and, by the glint of cobalt in the sky, it isn't quite daylight. A cool breeze is blowing through the gap and caressing my face though I'm toasty warm and comfortable. The noise comes again—a rooster. Not ready to be awake, I shift a little against something warm and soft.

Noah emits a sleepy sigh behind me. A big arm drops across my waist.

My eyes snap open.

Oh. My. God.

He's spooning me. All thoughts of sleepiness flee as I totally freak. How did we end up like this? Did I slide back? Did he creep forward? Crap! What if Amir sees us?

Something tickles my cheek and I brush it off only to watch a black spider scurry off my arm—right toward a mouse burrowing its way into my pallet. Double crap! Noah behind and a mouse wheedling its way toward my toes? My skin crawls along with instant panic.

"Get off!" I scream, leaping to my feet, brushing away the hay and any other vermin that may have crawled into my clothing. Hopping around, I shake, scratch, and claw at everything. Is my hair infested? I bend over and scrub my fingers through the tangle.

By the time I straighten, both men are on their feet, swords in hand.

"What happened?" Noah demands, his face deadly in the shadowy light, not to mention the bruising around his eye makes him look like a mass murderer.

My gaze shoots to the hay and I swear it's crawling. "There was a spider on my face and a mouse gnawing on my feet!" It wasn't exactly gnawing but if I hadn't moved quickly, the varmint would have been.

"A mouse?" asks Amir, snorting and lowering his sword.

"Shut up. I was asleep. And don't tell me you cuddle with spiders and mice in your cozy dorm bed."

The rooster interrupts and Amir looks out the window. "The sun's coming up. And look there, our hosts are heading this way with breakfast."

Noah kicks the hay around, then sweeps his hand downward, giving me an exaggerated bow. "All free of critters, my lady."

I grab his hand and tug him down, making him sit beside me. I might be a national campion but, evidently, I can be bested by a mouse. There's no way I'm going to sit on this floor without Noah keeping watch beside me.

"Thank you." I give him a cursory once-over. "Your eye isn't as swollen today."

Amir sniggers. "Right. If you ask me, it looks as if you went a few rounds with Conor McGregor and lost."

"Cool," Noah snorts. He's such a renegade.

Breakfast consists of boiled eggs and porridge. The farmer and his wife leave a wooden bowl full of oats, so I'm able to eat my fill of carbs for the first time since arriving. They also give us a leather-wrapped parcel with cheese and more unleavened bread rolls for our journey. After their generosity this morning I suppose I'm not so annoyed about paying five cents to sleep in their mice-infested barn.

It's a day of hard riding and rain drizzles on and off. Finding the ferry in Richmond is easy enough.

So is locating the London Road with the ruts. Carts mostly pulled by oxen pass us and everyone offers a greeting. There are wagons laden with all kinds of goods from leather pelts to hay to pigs and chickens.

Still, after the first few hours the journey grows tedious. My butt is falling asleep and, no matter how romantic my lizard brain might think it is to ride double with Noah, it's just plain uncomfortable.

"We ought to buy a horse I can ride," I say, craning my neck to look at him.

His beard is darker today—longer. Unfortunately, it makes him more attractive and when he shifts his gaze to me, the dark stubble contrasting with the icy blue of his eyes is downright heart-stopping. "Maybe we'll reach Runnymede, find the Qiang and head for home."

"How do we get home?"

"It's in the manual. The one yellow belts memorize."

Oh, right. I forgot about that. I pull the ripped-out page from my bra and read the title, "portals". They're listed by country and generally comprise natural wonders. I find the United Kingdom. "The White Cliffs of Dover, the Giant's Causeway in Northern Ireland, Faery Glen, and Fingals Cave in Scotland. Oh look here, there's something manmade. Stonehenge."

Beside us, Amir is swaying with the gait of his horse. "If we keep heading west, Stonehenge is most likely our best bet."

I shake the page at him. "If only we could stop the Qiang and instantly beam back home."

"Too easy," Noah grumbles.

I set my mind to memorizing...until the whisper of a chill comes over me—faint, but I'm positive it's the exact same feeling I had when Grand Master Li mentioned the Qiang.

Chapter Fourteen

*"The will to win, the desire to succeed, the urge
to reach your full potential...these are the keys that
will unlock the door to personal excellence."* -
Confucius

"Stop!" I shout, jumping down from the destrier and
sprinting through the muck. But there's no one
there. I run toward a copse of trees, then spin and
face an open pasture where there's nothing but
sheep grazing. Flinging my arms wide, my gaze
shifts between my colleagues. "I felt something. I
know it."

Amir dismounts. "Do you feel it now?"

Closing my eyes, I steady my breathing and
focus. Breathe in, two, three, four, five, six, out...

"Well?" Noah presses.

Not letting him get to me, I exhale and slowly
open my eyes. "It's gone."

Still sitting his horse, he looks to the skies. "This
is freaking nuts."

My chest feels like he just threw a punch,
striking right over my heart. I turn away and rub my
aching backside. Noah has a valid point and that fact
chaps me to no end. I had no more than five minutes
of training with the Grand Master and here I am
blindly bumbling around medieval England trying to

tune into some insane extrasensory perception skills I may not even have.

Shaking my head, my chin drops to my chest. "Maybe I'm not cut out for this."

"You're the only chance we have, sweetness. Know what else? The mere fact that you're on this mission speaks volumes about Grand Master Li's trust in your abilities." Amir pats my shoulder. "I swear, even he gets quirky sensations."

I bite my bottom lip and look up. "Does he ever sense a disturbance when nothing is really happening?"

"Maybe. Do you remember when I said my first mission was during a crusade?"

"Yeah."

"Well, we arrived in the Holy Land a month before the Qiang showed up." Amir brushes his fingers along his horse's mane. "And Noah here was still a white belt barely out of diapers."

The hulk scowls. "I was a yellow belt."

"Not much difference. And you hadn't gone on a mission yet, so bite me." Amir slings his arm around my shoulder. "Think of this as an academic adventure like none other—the mother lode of all history lessons mixed together with a mystery we absolutely must solve. We have everything we need. Noah's our muscle, I'm our brains, and you're our leader."

My breath stops, making my head spin. "Leader?" I ask, my voice cracking.

"Believe it or not. Let's just say you're our guiding light, our torch. I've been on six missions and it always takes time for the seer to figure out where to lead us."

I manage to inhale. "So, do you think we're on the right track?"

"We have a solid plan. Our logic is sound. We need to find the people on our list, starting with the most important and check them off one by one. But we have to stick with our plan no matter how much Noah wants to bust heads."

"Agreed, we follow our leads one at a time," Noah says, though he's scowling. "I hate to admit it, but we have never gone in, gotten out, bada boom. The Qiang don't give a rip about what I want, or what any of us want for that matter."

I can't look him in the eye. Sure, I get that he's irritated with my reaction—the way I leapt down from the horse and sort of panicked. But that's what I'm supposed to do.

I think.

At least I'm supposed to be on red alert. Regardless of what Amir says, I'm not the leader here. No way. Maybe after a few missions I might take the reins, but I'm having a hard enough time trying to hold it together. I mean, I freaked this morning because a mouse was in my bed.

I rub the back of my neck. Spending so much time this close to Noah isn't helping either. Dudes only think they're unemotional, but Noah's a bag of muscles packed with emotions running the gamut. One minute our gazes connect with breath-stopping intensity and the next he's doubting my ineptitude.

Does he like me or not?

Honestly, I'm better off if it's not. And I need to cool my stupid jets, too. We're a team here. Three students sent on a mission critical to the civilization as we know it. How daunting is that? I don't think the magnitude of the importance of our mission has totally hit me yet. But one thing's for sure, romance has absolutely no place in this scenario.

Gah!

It's no wonder Noah's so damned uptight. When it gets right down to it, there's a hell of a lot resting on our shoulders. *Like world peace or something.*

He taps his heels, urging the destrier to step beside me and offers his hand. "Come on, Genesis. We need to keep going."

No matter how much I like hearing him say my name, I ignore him and set off at a jog. "My butt's too sore to get back up there."

By the time we reach Runnymede, I'm back on the horse with Noah. A lush, green meadow stretches before us, spotted by two collections of tents with a larger one erected halfway between the clusters. Trees line the riverside. Opposite, the ground slopes upward to a picturesque hilltop.

There aren't as many people here as I'd imagined. Near the Thames there's a handful of men sparring with swords. And by the center tent, there are a few knights in conversation.

"So, this is where the deed happens?" Noah says, his breath warm against my hair.

Remembering that I am a girl in a male grossly over-dominated society, I pull my veil over my head and point to the hill. "If I were the king, I'd prefer to meet up there."

"I'm sure King John would, too." Amir stops his horse beside us. "But the meadow is considered a liminal space. Tradition has it that two disputing sides come together to settle their differences and pursue peace for the kingdom on neutral ground, hence the marshy meadow."

Noah lowers the reins and grips my hand as he's been doing when he helps me dismount. "Seriously, bro? Where do you fit all that stuff in that pointed head of yours?"

"If I read something once, it usually sticks."

"Halt!" bellows a guard, dressed in a tunic, mail and helm, carrying a pike and marching beside another who could be his twin. "These lands are sanctioned as off limits by the king and the barons."

"It's showtime," I whisper under my breath as I slide down to my feet.

Noah follows, landing beside me. "We come bearing a message for the king."

The guard chuckles. "If ye thought ye'd find His Grace here, ye're sorely mistaken."

"Have the barons not gathered with letters of safe conduct?" asks Amir.

"Some have. Most are waiting until after the Feast of Whitsun."

"But negotiations have started, have they not?" Good Lord, Amir is sounding more like a medieval person every time he opens his mouth.

"Negotiations have been going on for some time, though the king hadn't paid much attention until FitzWalter and the rebel barons captured London."

"And where might we find the king?" asks Noah.

"Last we heard he was hiding behind the walls of Winchester Castle. Though the three of ye haven't a chance of gaining an audience with him." The guard looks me from head to toe. "Not unless ye're looking for positions in the kitchen. This wench has a pair of devil's eyes like I've never before seen."

Noah steps forward, reaching for his sword, but I stay his hand. "It's all right," I whisper, imagining my hair is sticking every which way out from under my veil. That combined with the smattering of dried blood on my clothes, I wonder if I've ever looked this grungy.

Grumbling under his breath, he relaxes his hand. Nonetheless, he throws his shoulders back as he moves uncomfortably close to the guard. "She's part of our message."

"Well then, bloody good luck to ye. Heed me, if John is true to form, he'd sooner hang ye than entertain a chat." Then man pounds the butt of his pike on the ground. "Now ye'd best be on yer way, else we'll have to take ye to the prison at Basingstoke for causing a public disturbance."

I can't believe it. "But we haven't—"

"A moment," Amir interrupts, scratching the black stubble growing along the lower edge of his jaw. He's definitely more suited to the clean-cut look. "Where might we find Archbishop Langton and Earl Marshal?"

"Langton left this morn. He'll be spending Whitsun at Canterbury Cathedral. And The Marshal?" The man blubbers a raspberry. "He rarely leaves the king's side, though Lord knows how he can bear the abuse."

We watch them retreat, then gather in a circle.

"Langton's gone to Canterbury?" I ask. "That makes no sense."

Amir pushes a lock of my hair under my veil but it immediately slides out again. "Honestly, it does. He's the Archbishop of Canterbury, after all, and the Feast of Whitsun is an important religious holiday."

I shove the stupid curl far enough back to make it stay hidden. "I've never heard of it."

Noah eases the reins to let the horse graze. "It marks the festival of Pentecost. Christ's disciples receive the Holy Spirit."

And he's the brawn in this motley team. I roll my hand under his nose. "And you know this because?"

"Hey, I'm a Chicago boy, remember? Catholic middle school. Sister Mary Albert."

"So what next?" asks Amir.

Both guys shift their gazes to me, their eyebrows raised.

I draw in a heavy breath, shaking the jitters out of my fingers. But suddenly a sense of calm fills me and I have the answer. I think. "If Langton is killed, it's likely he'll be replaced by another bishop, and ordained Catholics take a vow of celibacy, so they don't have children, which means his lineage will end with his death."

Amir snorts. "No legitimate children, anyway."

"True." I run a hand across my mouth, while the seed of doubt takes root in my gut. If I'm wrong, we may end up going home to an unrecognizable world—if we return at all. "Look guys, I can't promise anything, but I really think we need to head for Winchester. Besides, with the king and William Marshal there. The odds are in its favor two to one."

Noah extends his hand with his palm facing the grass. "Agreed."

"Agreed." Amir puts his hand on top of Noah's, and I follow. It's just like the kiai we use before a waza competition. "Aye ya!"

愛

We ride until dusk when we arrive in the small village of Basingstoke. There's not exactly an inn, though the sign says it's an inn. The Boar's Head is more like a tavern with a raucous clientele of men that would put the Muddy Hollow to shame. Fortunately, the proprietor rents rooms above. But with all the people traveling for the holiday, there's only one.

"Ye're in luck. 'Tis market day on the morrow," the innkeeper says as he shows us to a room about the size of Dad's storeroom—I'm talking a square about seven by seven feet. The only furniture is a narrow bed shoved up against the wall with a dingy woolen blanket. But at least the fireplace has been cleaned.

"Apologies, but no fires are allowed after Easter. Meals are in the tavern. The bell will ring for supper, when 'tis time to break yer fast, and again if ye're here at the noon hour—actually the church bell rings for that." The tavernkeeper turns to me and knits his brows. "Ah...er...ye'll take the bed, mistress."

I curtsy and bow my head, hoping my action is appropriate in this situation. "Thank you."

He lights a wall sconce with his candle, closes the door, and leaves the three of us alone.

We all stand there staring at each other. My legs ache from riding so much it was hard to climb the stairs. With his black eye, Noah looks like he's about to blow a gasket. On top of that, Amir's hair is sticking out like a porcupine and his face is drawn.

No surprises, the brown belt is the one who moves first, removing his satchel and sitting on the bed. "Since we left Runnymede, I've been thinking..."

We look at him expectantly, but my legs are wobbling so I sit on the floor and start stretching.

Noah plants his palms against the wall and works his calves. "What were you thinking, bro?"

"Well." He hesitates. "You might not like it, Genesis, but the guard gave me the idea when he looked at you as if you'd descended from Mars."

With my legs in a side split, I stretch my arm to my toes and ease my stomach to the floor. "He's a jerk."

"Yeah, he's an ignorant bastard." Amir pulls a handful of coins out of his satchel. "But it's market day tomorrow and we have plenty of money. And don't forget that our not-so-friendly jerk told us we we're more likely to be hanged than be granted an audience with the king."

Noah pushes off from the wall and touches his toes, palms flat. "The three of us are good, but I doubt we can fend off King John's army."

Letting the coins slide back into his satchel, Amir grins. "Which is why I've been formulating a plan."

"Then out with it," I say, drawing my legs together and stretching forward.

"If you pair would stop interrupting." Amir takes a deep breath and hesitates, his brown eyes wide. "We need an angle. We've made up the story about bearing messages from the Holy Land, but King John's clerics will see through that in a heartbeat. And thank God the rebel barons are at war with him. At least I can bet our entire fortune that no one from London will be at Winchester. So, if Genesis looks like a foreigner to these people, then why not pass her off as an Egyptian princess sent from Sultan Al-Adil?"

"Oh that's brilliant," I say, rolling my eyes. "Isn't he the reason Pope Innocent is organizing the Fifth Crusade?"

Amir points at my forehead. "Exactly. And King John knows it."

"Hmm." Noah slides down to the floor beside me, one corner of his mouth turned up in a sly grin. "If Genesis shows up with two knights, say, the Knights Templar, she can tell the king she's bringing a message of peace from her father and is traveling with the Templars to prove her message is genuine."

With a smug grin, Amir drums his fingertips together. "Yes."

I flick out my hair. "Except I'm not an Egyptian. You look way more Egyptian, Amir."

"They won't know the difference," says the brown belt. "Besides, you have black hair and amber eyes."

Noah taps my forearm. "And you still have a Utah tan."

Have they both lost their minds? "You guys are going to be the death of me."

"Got a better idea?" asks Amir.

I assume the lotus position, close my eyes, and try to think. How does someone manage to get introduced to the king in this century? After wracking my brain, I realize I have absolutely no idea. "Okay, let's just say we do this. What sort of message am I bearing?" I ask. After all, Amir is the mastermind. I should trust his judgment, right? "And shouldn't we have some sort of gift for the king—a fancy gift, mind you."

"What about a ring?" asks Noah. "Genesis can say she's worn it throughout the duration of the journey. As my man said, it's market day *on the morrow*. We ought to be able find one with a polished stone or something that looks expensive."

"We'll all need clothes, too. Especially you, Genesis. If we're going to convince them you're a princess, you're really going to have to look the part." Amir pushes to his feet and paces. "I need a pen, or a quill and some vellum."

I move my leg right before the brown belt trips over it.

Noah flops onto the bed and drapes an arm over his head. "The tavern owner said there's a church. Isn't that where all the educated dudes hang out in these times?"

"Sure is." Amir snaps his fingers. "First thing in the morning, we head to the church."

Chapter Fifteen

*"A lion chased me up a tree and I greatly
enjoyed the view from the top." - Confucius*

After the third night, my neck is stiff and I've never
needed a shower so much in my life. With all the
other things we need to do today, I swear I'm not
going to sleep tonight before I bathe.

But first we have to attack the items on our list.

We head out after a breakfast of porridge and
beer and it doesn't take us long to end up in the
doorway of Saint Michael of the Mount church. The
odd thing is this particular parish is sitting on
completely flat ground.

"Saint Michael of the Mount wannabe," snarks
Noah under his breath.

I snort, holding in my laugh as Amir opens the
door. It's dark and cave-like inside and, as we step
into the church, I blink to adjust my eyes. The
vestibule has a bell tower right above us and the
nave extends in a narrow tunnel toward an ornately
carved rood screen. Through the gaps, I can barely
make out the altar.

"May I help you?" asks a man wearing a brown
habit. He's slight with a bald head encircled by a ring
of dark hair.

"Good morning, Father," says Amir, bowing his
head.

"Friar."

"Pardon?"

"Father Martin Beasley is tending the sick at the Hospital of Saint John the Baptist. I am merely a friar, Friar James. My vows of poverty are in service of society." His smile is genuine though his brow furrows when his gaze stops at Noah. "How may I assist ye?"

Amir bows his head. "My companions and I need to write a missive."

"Ah, yes, come with me. Are ye able to contribute to the church?"

"We are. I require two sheets of vellum, ink, and quill."

Friar James stops and looks Amir from head to toe. "Ye?"

"Uh, yes," says the brown belt.

"Ye are educated?"

"Well educated. My companions and I were capsized off the eastern coast." Amir takes in a deep breath, drawing down the corners of his mouth. I can tell he hates lying, especially to a holy man, but it can't be helped "This is Princess...ah...Genesis from Egypt. Sir Noah and I are Knights of the Templar Order, escorting Her Ladyship to King John."

"Knights, aye? I suppose that explains this one's blackened eye." Adjusting the rope tied around his waist, the friar turns his attention to me and frowns. "A princess? From Egypt? I find that difficult to believe."

Crap, if we can't convince a friar that I'm Egyptian, we'll never be able to convince a king. "I know we look as ragged as street urchins," I say, easing my veil enough for him to see my mop of black hair. Then I look him in the eye. May as well give him the whole treatment, amber eyes and all. "We have faced many setbacks on the journey to bring a message of peace from my father."

"Please, friar, the velum and quill," says Amir, reminding me to keep my mouth shut. The less we tell anyone the better.

The man's expression softens. "Of course. Please follow me."

He leads us into a side room with a large, worn table. "Here ye will find vellum and quill. Have ye a seal?"

"No, Friar," Amir explains. "I'm afraid all was lost. Though if you have a blank, I can fashion one in the wax."

Noah waggles his eyebrows at me. Then he affects a serious expression and clears his throat. "Friar, would you know where we can purchase a coat of mail and Templar tunics as well as a gown fitting a princess?"

"Hmm." The monk scratches his thick beard and regards Noah's chest. "There aren't any warrior monks living in Basingstoke, though our tanner is one of the best ye'll find. He might be able to fashion ye a leather doublet, one thick enough to stop a blade."

"Where can I find him?"

"I reckon Master Tanner will be in his shop in the market square." The little man opens the lid of a trunk. "I've some old white vestments here. Ye might ask the tailor to remove the sleeves and stitch on a red cross."

"Perfect," says Amir, sitting and dipping a quill in a silver inkpot.

Noah takes the neatly folded garments. "Thank you."

I tiptoe over to the trunk and peer inside. "You wouldn't have anything in there for me? Something purple and velvet, perhaps?"

"Apologies, my lady, but knights take an oath of obedience, poverty, and chastity to God. It would be heresy for ye to don holy vestments."

Ah ha. There was the heresy word I've been waiting to hear and it makes me quake in my shoes. With luck, it won't come up again. I purse my lips and nod.

"I'm sure the tailor will have something for you," says Amir. "I'm drawing a picture of what you'll need now."

I peer over his shoulder. He has drawn a long veil topped by a circlet, a cloak covering a gown with a wide, cummerbund-type belt. He glances up. "We'll need the finest fabrics, of course. In the richest colors he has available."

"And the missive?" I ask.

"That's next."

"We also need to replace the ring." I glance to the friar's fingers. Unfortunately, they are bare.

"Give me the drawing," says Noah, holding out his hand. "While you write the missive, I'll take Princess Genesis and visit the tailor and the blacksmith. Meet us at the tanner's or else your armor won't fit."

The tailor arches an eyebrow as we enter his shop. Since we look like gutter rats, I'm not surprised. The room is small and stark without a single rack of clothes. Judging by the bolts of fabric piled along the back wall, this guy makes garments from scratch.

"Sir." Noah hands the man the drawing. "My lady needs a veil, cloak, and gown in the finest, most vibrant fabric you have available."

The man studies the drawing and frowns. "Have you the coin to pay for such extravagance?"

The blue belt dug in his satchel and pulled out a handful of change. "We do."

Licking his lips at the sight of a small fortune, the tailor tugs the measuring ribbon from around his neck. "I believe I have enough wool and silk dyed with saffron for the veil and cloak. Perhaps blue for the gown?"

"Do you have silk damask?" I ask.

"I beg yer pardon?" asks the man, looking baffled.

"I must have misspoken," I say wracking my brain. I don't know what kind of fabric they have in the thirteenth century—wool and silk he'd mentioned. "Ah...velvet?"

"Velvet?" he spits as if the word is a curse. "'Tis too dear for me to keep in my shop. Do ye not know only royalty and the clergy of the highest order wear velvet?"

"I beg your pardon, sir," says Noah. "Her Ladyship is a princess."

Thank God he didn't say an Egyptian, or else we might end up with sackcloth. I know it in my bones. But still, the man gawks at my filthy dress in horror. "Princess of what, pray tell?"

Oh, no. Here it comes. "A far away land," I quickly say.

Noah gives him the white vestments and explains about being capsized. "We must have proper attire, fine enough to gain an audience with the king. What's more, we're pressured for time."

"Time, sir?"

"We need everything by tomorrow."

"The morrow?" The tailor asks, nearly spitting out his teeth. "I know not what ye are thinking, but I do have other patrons."

Noah pats the bulging coins in his satchel. "I understand, and I will pay double if you can promise to have our garments ready. Tomorrow."

"Please, sir," I add. "It is a matter of utmost importance."

"Double did ye say?"

Noah nods. "Yes."

Pursing his lips, the man holds out the measuring ribbon and eyes me. "As I was saying, I have some very fine blue wool for yer gown, my lady."

"Wouldn't crimson compliment saffron better?" I ask, trying to come off as meek, which seems disingenuous. Not that I dislike blue, but I've noticed a lot of women wearing blue. Heck, if I'm going to pull off the princess act, I need to make a bold statement.

"Very well. Red, though it will be from the same dye lot as the crosses for the knights' tunics."

"I think we can live with that."

"And my lady's belt," says Noah. "How can you help us there? It must be spectacular."

"Spectacular?" The man whips his ribbon through the air. "By the morrow? I will already have my wife, my children, and two laborers stitching into the wee hours."

"Do you have something ready-made?" I ask.

His face lights up. "A moment," he says before he runs through a door at the rear of the shop and returns with a long strip of blue cloth embroidered with gold thread. "Does this resemble what you have in mind?"

I run the piece through my fingers, admiring the exquisite detail of a scrolling leaf pattern. "This is beautiful."

"We'll take it," says Noah, paying the man and ushering me out the door.

Thank goodness we finally walk past a vendor who's selling soap. I grab the blue belt's hand and practically drag him to the table.

I pick a bar up, sniff it and then another. None of the cakes are uniform and most smell like urine. But on my fifth try I find a bar with lavender and minty overtones and hold it to Noah's nose. "How about this?"

As he inhales, his eyes grow darker, making my stomach flutter. Judging by the heat in my cheeks, I'm probably blushing, too. Why the heck do I let him affect me?

"Nice," he says. "Let's buy that one and go. Time's wasting."

I smile at the vendor. She has a pleasant face, square, sturdy, with kind eyes. Wisps of dark blonde hair peek from beneath her veil. Behind the table, a child of about three clings to her skirts as he watches me, an expression of amazement on the wide eyes peering over the tabletop.

I hold out the soap. "This one please."

"'Tis a fine choice. My husband collects the mint along the river and we grow the lavender right here in Basingstoke. 'Tisn't always in season, and I'll have to charge ye two fourthings."

I'm not quite sure what a fourthing is until I give her a penny and she returns two pie-shaped coin pieces which have been cut into quarters.

Amazing.

"Thank you," I say, giving the toddler a wink and slipping the bar into my satchel.

Next we visit the blacksmith's shack. Though Noah and I stand several feet away, the heat from the smithy's fire warms my face. Sword and knife blanks, horseshoes, and strips of iron line the rickety shelves.

"Are you able to make a circlet for a princess and a ring for a king?" asks Noah.

The smith rests his hand on an enormous set of bellows suspended from the roof by chains. "Princesses and kings? It seems ye have set yer sights on lofty targets, friend."

My companion inclines his head toward me. "Her Ladyship requires a circlet to match a veil of saffron. Do you have anything ready-made?"

"Nay, but it will not take me long unless ye require embellishment."

"It can't be plain," says Noah. "It must be fitting for royalty."

"Then it will cost ye, and it will take time."

"We must have it by tomorrow."

The beefy man scratches his bush of a beard. "Two pounds and I'll not haggle."

"Very well." Noah points to a wooden strongbox. "We also need a ring with a sizeable stone. Do you have anything in there to suffice?"

"Perhaps." The smithy pulls a skeleton key from a pouch on his belt and opens the lock. He holds up a ring with a pink quartz stone about the size of a dime. "Made this for Bishop Turner but he passed away afore he claimed it."

"It's perfect," I say. "Do you often make jewelry?"

The smithy takes a ribbon and wraps it around the circumference of my pointer finger. "Not often, but a request like yers gives me a respite from swinging the hammer." He compares the ribbon to the ring. "I'll need to take a bit off this."

"That shouldn't be necessary," I say. "It is a gift and will most likely need to be altered by the recipient. Maybe if we can wrap a bit of leather or string around the band, so the ring won't fall off my finger in the interim."

"Very well, I'll have the circlet for ye on the morrow, then." The blacksmith hesitates and peers at me. "You have most unusual eyes."

Noah wraps an arm around my shoulders. "They're beautiful, aren't they?"

Before the blacksmith answers, Noah leads me back out into the milling crowd which has grown since we set out this morning. I pat my veil to ensure it covers all of my hair. Nonetheless, people are giving us sideways glances and it's making me paranoid. "I think the sooner we leave this town, the better."

Noah's jaw tenses. "The sooner we leave this century the better."

"Yeah." I chew the corner of my lip. "Hopefully after we find the king. I'll tap into the zone."

Those icy eyes slant my way and there's an awkward pause like a brick wall has suddenly been thrown up between us. I immediately want to apologize for not immediately leading us to the Qiang, but then that would make me look incompetent and the last thing I want is to appear useless to Noah Jones.

I'm trying not to look at him when he places his palm in the small of my back and inclines his lips toward my ear. "When we get to Winchester just remember to let Amir and me do the talking. All you need to do is look gorgeous."

I stop and shove his shoulder, the gorgeous remark not quite sinking in. "Why? Because you're a freshman in college and I'm still in high school?"

"Because you're a woman."

I plant my fists on my hips. "Really? I'm surprised you noticed."

He glances over the top of my head before his gaze drills back into mine. "Do you want to draw attention to us? Because you're doing a good job of it right now."

Refusing to let him make me feel small, I peer over his shoulder and lower my hands to my sides. People are looking, their heads close together, obviously gossiping about the newcomers.

"Just don't bait me," I whisper with an edge.

"I didn't."

"Oh?" I ask as I roll my eyes. What is it with him? Women are supposed to be seen and not heard? Yeah, like before we earned the right to vote. "I've never looked gorgeous in my life. I'm not the type. And keeping my mouth shut? I'll say something if something needs to be said."

"Maybe you're right." He smirks and urges me to continue toward the tanner's shop. Even without the sign, it's easy to find by the stench. "At least on the mouthy part," Noah adds, chuckling to himself.

I subtly jab his arm with my elbow. "See? You're baiting me."

"Hmm. So, you mean to tell me Genesis Mans doesn't like being told she's fine as hell?"

My mouth drops open. "You didn't say—"

Grabbing my hand, Noah tugs me behind a tall hedge. He's looking at me like he's starved and I'm a juicy steak. I'm totally speechless as he pulls me into his arms. "You clearly need a demonstration, Shera."

"Wha—"

Before I can utter another word, his lips clamp over mine while his hand cradles the back of my head.

My body launches into total hyperdrive like nothing I've ever experienced. My heart races. My boobs grow a mind of their own and ache to press against his chest. I want to focus. I want to be angry. But my knees are turning to jelly while an explosion of unrelenting desire floods my senses.

My head spins.

I can't think.

Hot, wild steam pulses through my blood, taking over my judgment. It's terrifying and electrifying all at once. I go limp.

I want this.

But don't.

God, he's totally ambushed me. I've lost control and I have to get a grip.

Soon.

Whoa!

But kissing him feels so damned good.

Noah's tongue sweeps into my mouth, his hands hard against my back, finally drawing my boobs flush with his rock-hard chest. A guttural moan erupts from my throat as I match his fervor, thrusting my fingers into his tangle of thick hair, inhaling his scent. And he smells totally feral.

Dipping his chin, he attacks my throat with sweet, warm, deliciously soft licks of his tongue. As my head drops back my pelvis collides with his.

God.

I'm shaking.

But as soon as I stop arguing with myself, Noah grasps my shoulders and steps away, his face iron hard and recklessly tempting. "That's how hot you are. Got it? I never want to hear you deny it again."

He walks around the bush, leaving me alone.

What the hell just happened? I'm trembling, panting, and my lips are buzzing. If only my legs would move I'd run after him and tell him what I think.

What do I think?

I swipe my hand across my lips to stop the tingling. Was Noah just making a point? Did he feel anything? Does he *like* me? I mean, *really* like me. This is danger to the max. I can't, absolutely cannot like him—not that way.

No chance.

Zilch!

It's way better if I think he was goading me.

Adjusting my veil, I take a deep breath. Noah must not like me, not as a girlfriend anyway. We cannot possibly be romantic and anything that may have occurred—*like kissing*—is purely coincidental.

I brush my hands down my skirt and square my shoulders.

The only logical thing to do is pretend nothing ever happened, join him and Amir at the tanner's, and I'd darned-well better not say a self-deprecating word about my appearance ever again.

Chapter Sixteen

"Act with kindness but do not expect gratitude."
- Confucius

"Come on, Genesis," Amir's voice booms through the door of our room at the inn. "Even if you are female, it doesn't take all day to have a bath."

"Say that when your hair is as long as mine, you don't have a comb, and you're trying to bathe in a bucket the size of a five-gallon paint can." I didn't get my bath last night but this morning the innkeeper gave me a wooden pail, a sea sponge, an ewer of cold water, and an ewer of scalding. It took me five minutes to get the temperature right. And then I couldn't resist washing out my undies. Except without a fire, I swear hell will freeze over before they dry.

Giving in, I use my dirty shirt to towel off and comb my hair with my fingers while the umpteenth rap pounds on the door. "If you don't open up now, I'm going to kick it in." Even if I didn't recognize Noah's voice, I'd know this came from him because he's never subtle.

I step into my skirt and tie it closed over my breasts. At least it hangs down to my knees. "Okay, I'm decent."

The door swings open but Noah doesn't storm in like an angry bear. His arms are piled with our new outfits or costumes or whatever we ought to call our disguises. He stops in his tracks, gaping at me like he's never seen a half-drenched girl before. I glance down to make sure the skirt hasn't slipped or something. Whew. Why he makes me feel like I'm totally naked, I have no idea.

And how many times do I have to remind myself to stop letting him get to me?

Licking the corner of his mouth, he heads for the bed, followed by Amir carrying two steaming ewers of water.

"It's a half-day's ride to Winchester," Amir says. Even the mastermind gives me a gape-mouthed stare as he sets the ewers on the floor and picks up the bucket. "I'll go empty this and see if I can find a comb."

Noah shakes out my new red dress. To me, it looks like a smock, but the thirteenth-century women's clothing I've seen here isn't exactly flattering. "Put this on."

I collect my bra and panties from the sconce where I've hung them. "Turn your back."

With an exaggerated bow, he rolls his hand through the air. "If it pleases Your Ladyship."

"It does, smartass."

He shrugs and faces the wall. "You're not so romantic, are you?"

Me? What about him? He's the one who speaks in monosyllables. And I hardly slept last night because of that stupid kiss. Every time I closed my eyes I relived it. There's nothing worse than being hot and bothered while the object of your desire is sound asleep on the floor right beside your bed.

"I'm romantic when I want to be." It's just now is definitely not the time. And Noah Jones can't be the guy.

I struggle to tug the damp panties over my thighs. Not only are they sticking to me like wet rubber, the elastic rolls up on my skin. I wriggle, forcing them higher, my skin chafing. Once they're more-or-less in place, it takes me ages to straighten them out.

"Can I turn around now?" Noah asks.

"No!" I drop the skirt and cringe as I tug up my bra, the cold cups clamping over my boobs. I was clean two minutes ago, but now I feel gross.

"You shouldn't kiss me, you know," I say, pulling the dress over my head.

Just as the hem brushes the floor, Noah turns. Of course he takes a long look. "Why not?" he drawls.

He had to ask, didn't he?

I grab my skirt from the floor and busy myself with folding it. "I know you were just teasing but it throws me off. The last thing I need is a major distraction. It knocks me out of my zone."

"You have a zone?" He saunters toward me, coming way too close and breaking into my personal space. "You think I was teasing?"

I gasp. Not a shrill inhalation, but a quick, heart-spiking gasp. Doesn't he realize I like him more than he likes me? And how can I possibly tell him that? I lick my lips while his predatory gaze shifts from my eyes to my mouth.

"W-w-we need to keep our minds on the mission," I say, sounding as lame as I feel.

He brushes his knuckle over my cheek. It's rough and masculine and it makes my head woozy.

"Right. The mission." His voice comes out low and raspy and his Adam's apple bobs beneath his whiskered throat. Why do I find a mere swallow sexy? No lie, this guy could be covered with mud and look sexy.

Amir bursts inside. "Oh, good, it fits."

Noah whips around and snaps his hand to his side. Yeah, he knows he's being bad.

Still, I'm mortified that the rising heat in my face is turning the color of my dress. "I-I'll go downstairs and let the two of you clean up."

"Are you kidding?" Noah looks at me as though I've lost my mind which isn't a bad guess where he's concerned. "You can't go anywhere in public by yourself."

"Correct, *Princess*." Amir holds up a comb and two leather thongs about shoelace size. "These are for you."

I grab them and plop down on the bed. "Thanks. I guess I'll face the wall then."

"Do what you like," says Noah. God, his confidence borders on arrogance. What am I thinking? *Borders* on arrogance? He personifies the word. I suppose it would be difficult not to be egotistical when you're a badass martial artist who can take on medieval knights in a joust, not to mention a brawl.

Does he want me to stare and gawk at his naked butt? Probably. He'd probably enjoy some sort of sick satisfaction from the attention.

Fortunately, the snarls in my hair keep me busy as I work them out with the comb and flounce my curls, trying to air-dry them. Behind me, the water rushes and trickles.

"Is there a towel?" asks Amir.

Before I think, I turn. "I used the cleanest part of my di...*ah*...dirty clothes." Oh God, now I *am* staring and gawking at Noah's naked butt, and a kick-ass dragon tattoo on his back.

Clutching his hands over his privates, Amir clears his throat and I quickly snap my gaze back to the wall. Rubbing my eyes, the image of Noah Jones' nude backside is burned on my retinas. If I had any doubt, I certainly don't now. His butt looks like smooth, chiseled, caramel marble with dimples plunging into each cheek. Of course, the size of his shoulders didn't escape me or the way the fierce-looking dragon tapers down to...

I rub my eyes again. I am not doing this, dammit. I'll fall for him and as soon as we get home, he'll pretend I don't exist.

"Amir," I say, holding up the thongs. "What should I do with these?"

"Just a minute."

After some rustling, he steps beside me and reaches for the comb. "Braids. I've noticed most of the women are wearing braids under their headgear." He runs the comb through my hair and parts it down the middle.

I reach out with an upturned palm. "I can do it."

"Nah, I have a sister."

Amir wields the comb almost as expertly as Rex. I look at his nails—nope, no pink polish. And then by the gruff way he whips together two braids, I decide Amir probably isn't gay. Not that it matters.

When he's done I glance at his legs. "What are you wearing?"

He's bare chested and his bottom half is covered by something that looks like knee-length elephant pants.

"They're braies. The thirteenth century man's version of underwear."

They look a lot more comfortable than this scratchy woolen dress. "Did you get me a pair?"

A wicked grin spreads across his lips. "Women don't wear braies. Actually, they go bare."

"Eew." I shift my seat, possibly a bit happier with my damp panties. "How do you know this?"

"Six missions, remember."

The water trickles. "If he sees it, he knows it," Noah adds.

I don't dare ask what Amir saw or how. Instead, I incline my ear toward the cocky blue belt rather than gawk this time. "Did you know about women's undergarments?"

"In this century?" Noah chuckles. "Not as much as Amir. But I'm guessing going commando sure does make things easy."

"Stop," I say, laughing with them. But several unpleasant thoughts sift through my mind, like what do women do during that time of the month? Good Lord, what will I do? Use rags? How do they stay put? With luck, we'll be home before I have to worry about it.

Amir shakes out the saffron veil. "This silk is soft."

"You mind putting that on my head?" I ask. Without a mirror, he'll probably make it look a lot better.

Amir helps me with the veil, the circlet, and the belt, paying extra attention to tying it. "English women don't usually cinch their waists, but it's an important part of the Middle Eastern medieval costume."

"I hope you're right."

He stands back. "I am. And you look like a total dime."

"See?" says Noah. "What did I tell you?"

I just shake my head. In the time it took to braid my hair, he'd donned a pair of woolen chausses and a linen tunic beneath the new leather armor. It even smells like new leather and looks totally inflexible.

Rising from the bed, I run my fingers down the armor's buckles. "This is amazing. I can't believe the tanner made it so quickly. Too bad you have to cover it with the Templar tunic."

"It's great, though I would have preferred chainmail." Amir moves in beside me, assessing Noah with a critical eye. "But if we explain that our things were lost at sea and how we had to improvise, I think we'll pass muster."

"That or we'll end up in the torture chamber of Winchester's dungeon."

I shiver, fully aware of how close to the truth Noah may be.

Today my backside tolerates the saddle far better than my heart handles riding double with the guy who kissed me yesterday. Though I wanted to buy a horse in Basingstoke, we decided against it because I'm not a horsewoman by any stretch of the imagination and once we near Winchester Castle, if anyone pegs me as a novice, the king will never believe I'm an Egyptian princess.

I try not to lean against the big blue belt but, after a few hours, I cave and let myself rest into his armor. His chest is not as comfortable as before with the buckles digging into my spine. I'm also not surprised to discover it's a long, boring ride down the London-Winchester Road as they call this muddy tract. I guess all major roads in England lead to royal castles. At least in the thirteenth century.

Finally, four square turrets come into view. Orange and red pennants flap at each corner and I know a building this magnificent has to be Winchester. My heart jolts as I sit forward and point. "There it is!"

As the words leave my mouth, a crackle of energy skitters up my spine. I zone in while electricity continues along my arms out the tips of my fingers. Rolling my eyes to the heavens, I pray this is the sign we've been waiting for.

"What are you feeling?" Noah whispers.

"We're close." I turn and look at him no matter how much I shouldn't. "I know it."

"Thank God," he mumbles, tapping his heels and asking for a trot.

"I'll second that," Amir says, slapping his reins.

As we near, the feelings coursing through me jumble into a ball of nerves roiling in the pit of my stomach. I have no choice but to go with it. Listen to a sixth sense I haven't even come close to developing. Winchester looms in the foreground of an ominous sky, presiding over the landscape like Mount Olympus.

"What if they don't believe us? What if we can't get in? What if they lock us in a cell and leave us there to starve?" I ask.

Amir reins his horse into the lead. "King John has done that and more many times. He is the most ruthless, vile, hated king in all of Britain's history. But that doesn't mean we abandon our mission."

I gulp, never so unsure about anything in my life.

"I'll do the talking," says Amir, tapping his heels.

We follow him along fifteen-feet high city walls. A stench bites my nose as we near a brook. Men with wheelbarrows are dumping refuse into the water. I glance down and see a bone and then another. "Yuck."

"Welcome to the middens," Noah mumbles in my ear.

We ride on and a cathedral comes into view, dwarfing the stone curtain walls. Two enormous, round towers stand either side of a pointed arch bearing a life-sized statue of the king. I'm awestruck until my gaze shifts lower to a severed head and two dismembered hands while the overpowering stench of rotting flesh nearly makes me wretch.

Behind me, Noah releases a long grunt.

"Halt in the name of King John," bellows a guard. Though the gates are open, the entry is blocked by pikemen. I'm beginning to detest pikemen. "State yer business."

"We've traveled from afar bearing a missive for the king." Amir shows the guard the sealed letter he wrote at the church in Basingstoke while I do my best to keep my head down.

The man takes the note and turns it over in his hands while the other guards stare at us as if they're prepared to attack on command.

I'm wondering if the soldier can read as he taps the missive in his hand and moves toward Noah and me. "From the Continent are ye?"

"Aye, sir," says Noah. "Bringing a message of peace."

The toad runs his tongue across his lips as he gives me a perverse once-over "And a pretty one at that. Have a wee peek at those eyes."

I hastily lower my gaze to my hands as the guard gives the missive back to Amir. "Very well. Present yerselves at the castle gates and see what the sheriff has to say about yer *message of peace.*"

Inside the walls, we pass tiny cottages arranged at chaotic angles. We weave our way through them while activity bustles around us. Oxen lumber toward the market, drawing heavy carts laden with grain. A black-robed friar preaches from atop a wooden box, surrounded by a circle of admirers. Beyond, a monk wearing a habit with a crucifix swinging from a belt of rope leads a donkey toward the cathedral.

We continue on until we reach a gatehouse nearly as large as the one we just passed through. The closer we move to the castle, the more my skin tingles. But I'm not feeling evil grip me as it did when Grand Master Li mentioned the Qiang. Still, chakras flow through me like never before. I sense an invisible aura encircling my body, connecting me with the earth and the universe.

Is this a sign that we're on the right track? Given days with no sensations whatsoever, I can't help but to believe it is.

At the castle gate we undergo similar scrutiny as we did at first except after the guard examines the missive, the sheriff is summoned and we're asked to dismount.

A bell from the cathedral announces the hour is four o'clock. The sound makes me miss watches and cell phones. And light switches would be nice; hot water from a tap. Everything here is such a chore.

Through the gateway is a courtyard and, at the far side, a wooden ramp leads to the castle door, which is about ten feet above the ground. The guard hastens down it leading a man dressed in blue robes, and when they reach us he is introduced as the Sheriff of Winchester. There's a dagger hanging from the belt secured beneath his distended stomach. His assessing eyes shift like a lizard's while he asks more questions. I continue to play the demure princess and stare at the ground. They all seem to look at me as if *I'm* the gift from the Holy Land. I guess it doesn't matter as long as we're allowed an audience with the king.

The Qiang are close. I know it because I want to jump out of my skin. Push past these idiot guards and look into every nook and cranny until I find them.

We're told to dismount and the horses are led away by a stable boy.

"Earl Marshal will want to have a word afore yer given an audience with the king," says the sheriff. "He fought beside the Templars in Jerusalem. He'll know what to make of ye."

"I would have thought no less," Amir replies. God, he's good.

I'm excited and terrified at the prospect of meeting William Marshal. He's one I clearly remember from Bashir's history class—I even stayed up late and researched him in my cubby. And though he's the Earl of Pembroke, they refer to him as Earl Marshal or The Marshal because of the reputation he earned as a knight on the tournament circuit, and because he's tasked with keeping order in the kingdom. Which is no easy task with King John messing things up all the time.

I steal a glance at Noah. Nothing escapes him while he stands with his feet wide and his hands on his hips, towering over everyone—the perfect image of a bodyguard for a princess.

At the point of pikes, we're escorted up the castle's ramp. Honestly, after this, I hope I never see a pike again.

It's dark inside and there's a torch burning on the passageway wall. Farther on, we're led into an enormous room lined with tables and benches. Similar to the hall at the Tower of London, the walls are covered with ornate tapestries depicting hunting and rural scenes. To my left, a fire with gargantuan logs crackles in a hearth that must be twenty feet wide and is nearly high enough for me to walk into without stooping. At the far end is a raised dais with a long table. By the size of the chair in the middle, I wonder if that's where King John dines with his closest barons and advisors, at least those who are still loyal to the crown. The chair is hewn from wood, it's boxy with a straight back like FitzWalter's and doesn't look comfortable.

Noah tugs my arm as we're shepherded into another room. All four walls are decorated with tapestries of dragons and fountains in blues, ivories, and shades of gold. Candles in an ornate candelabra dripping with wax burn atop a table with a bench on either side. We're instructed to wait. The sheriff tells two guards to remain at the door.

"This is where we need to be," I whisper to my comrades as I take a seat. The energy pulsing around me is too powerful not to recognize. "I have no doubt."

Amir gives me a nod. "Now all we need to do is figure out who's the target."

Noah climbs onto the bench beside me. "My bet's on the king or Marshal."

An older man comes in. His robes are similar to the sheriff's, but he's taller and wears an impressive sword with a jeweled hilt at his hip. His beard is gray yet his shoulders are square, his eyes hawkish like a predator. This man has seen death beyond anything I can imagine. I sense his aura. If I raise a finger to do harm, he'd not hesitate to take my life, nor would he bear remorse. His commanding presence swells through the room and, when I meet his gaze, a shudder courses through me.

The sheriff shuffles in beside him. "Rise and bow before William Marshal, Earl of Pembroke."

At last we meet one of the great men on our list.

Chapter Seventeen

"Wherever you go, go with all your heart." - *Confucius*

A charge whispers through the air as William Marshal takes his time assessing us. When his gaze shifts to me, I feel as if he can see clear to my soul—see our ruse. I can't even look him in the eye.

"The sheriff tells me ye've come from the Holy Land," he says at last, his expression impassive and showing no hint of emotion.

Amir brushes his fingers down his tunic and bows. "We have, my lord. Bearing a missive from Sultan Al-Adil for King John."

"A Mussulman?" Marshal sounds flabbergasted while his eyebrows draw together and he studies Amir. "'Tis difficult to believe. I'll have ye know I rode beside King Richard on the Third Crusade. We marched into the Holy Land and drove out Al-Adil's brother Saladin from Acre and Jaffa, though we failed to recapture Jerusalem. You'd best have a better explanation than that. No one in Christendom would entertain guests sent by an Ayyubid sultan."

"We thought the same at first, my lord." Amir licks his lips and I know he's freaking out. "But we have Al-Adil's word that he is seeking an alliance."

"Preposterous."

"Not when the Mongols are threatening to take control of the Silk Road. The sultan intends to face Genghis Khan's army to ensure trade from the east, but first he desires a truce with the Christians." Swiping a hand across his mouth, Amir is turning pale. "To be forthright, such a truce may only be short-lived, but might purchase time to plan the Fifth Crusade."

"Wise for men so young. Yet I daresay a mite foolish." Marshal strokes his gray beard, narrowing his gaze. "With this truce, ye propose to leave Jerusalem in the hands of the Mussulmen?"

"I believe with Al-Adil's missive he opens the door for many things." Amir looks at me, then back to the earl with a shrug of his shoulders. "And if his army is fighting the Mongols..."

I exhale. *Smart, Amir.*

Marshal's features brighten at the inference. "An interesting proposition."

Folding his arms, the earl stands silent while tension swells through the air. "I agree such news ought to be delivered to the king. Though I caution ye, John is no fool." He drums his fingers. "Pray tell, from whence do ye hail? Yer speech is strange to me."

"Ah..." Amir shifts his feet. "My brother and I were born in a small village near Naples. Spent our first years in a convent. We were fortunate to be fostered by the son of a wealthy merchant who took us on a pilgrimage—*peregrinentur*," he says in Latin. "Though we had meager beginnings, we found our way through the Order."

My heart pounds. Damn, I should have focused more in Latin class. If anyone in England can see through us, it is this man. A thin-lipped smile plays on the earl's lips giving nothing away.

"Many men of lowly birth rise to greatness." The Marshal's gaze shifts between my two companions. "So, where is this missive ye have brought from the sultan?"

Amir produces the vellum bearing the seal he so carefully inscribed, then he gestures to me. "Presented by his daughter, Princess Genesis."

The Marshal's brow furrows. "Genesis?"

"*Mansha* in Arabic, but her father felt it best to use the English translation."

"Of course," the earl says, regarding me and bowing politely. "My lady."

I glance at Amir before I curtsy. "My lord." Raising my finger, I exhibit the ring. The pink quartz sparkles with the gleam of sunshine coming through the window. "My father entrusted me with this ring to give to the king as a symbol of his sincerity."

"Very nice, indeed." Marshal takes my hand between his warm palms and looks me in the eye. "Tell me, how did a pair of Knights Templar come to accompany an Ayyubid princess to England?"

"Ah..." Think! I should have thought through my alibi a little better. Except I was told to keep my mouth shut. "My father felt it was the only way I would be allowed safe passage through Christendom."

"And he entrusted yer care to these men?"

A hundred explanations buzz in my head, the most plausible being I'm Sultan Al-Adil's eighteenth daughter born to one of the lesser wives in his vast harem. But belittling my importance would do nothing to help our cause. "He did, my lord. And may I add these men have performed their duties respectfully, and loyally, just as my own brothers would have done."

"I'd expect no less from members of the Order. Their vows of chastity and obedience are sacred." Earl Marshal releases my hand and bows again. "I must admit it comes as a great surprise to greet the daughter of the sultan at King John's court. `Tis almost too remarkable to believe."

"We feared the same." Noah steps forward. "But with the raids of the Mongol army along the Silk Road, Al-Adil needs a truce, even if it's temporary."

Who knew? Noah isn't too bad at impersonating a Templar knight, either.

The Marshal taps the missive in his hand. "I've heard of this Genghis Khan and his army." Marshal gestures to a guard. "Ye will be given quarters and presented to King John in the hall before the evening meal. The Whitsun feast is on the morrow. I trust ye will celebrate with us."

"Of course," I say. "It will be my pleasure to partake in English festivities."

"Very well." His eyes turn black and deadly. "But heed my caution. I am the king's protector. If at any time, one of ye lifts a finger to harm the king or threaten a member of his court, I will personally have ye flayed."

"I've just met with the steward," says Amir, pushing into my room—or *chamber* as we were told when the guard led us "above stairs". It's quite a climb, four stories up in the east tower. The chamber is not exactly what I would have expected for an Egyptian princess. The bed's a bit short. I imagined a four-poster with a canopy but this one isn't any larger than a twin. The headboard is elegant, hewn of dark wood with a trellis of roses carved into the frame. The room is small as well but the hearth is made of marble which must have cost a fortune. There are also two wooden chairs and a table sitting off to the side.

One of the nicest features is the window embrasure. The castle walls must be at least five feet thick and on either side of the embrasure are recessed seats with embroidered cushions. Noah and I have been sitting across from each other admiring the spectacular view. Beautifully manicured green gardens speckled with vibrant purple and magenta flowers stretch all the way to the River Itchen.

We both shift our attention to Amir as he strides across the room. "The guards said you'll be taken to the king's throne room and presented to him. From there we'll proceed to dinner."

I brush my hand over my hair and knock off my circlet. "The throne room? That sounds intimidating. Can't I just sit beside him at dinner and give him the ring?"

"Sorry, it doesn't work that way."

My gut twists into a gazillion knots. "Is there some sort of protocol I'm supposed to follow? Have you ever been introduced to a king?"

"I met Pharaoh Ka in the Pre-dynastic era," Amir says as if it were no big deal. "Just curtsy and let the king do most of the talking."

"What if he tells me I'm a fake?"

"Marshal should have ascertained that already."

"I think you ought to rehearse," says Noah. He hops to his feet, pulls a chair away from the table, and sits. "Okay, I'm the king. Wow me."

Amir stands beside him. "I'll be the steward."

I retrieve my circlet and reposition it on my head. "I really don't have a good feeling about this."

The brown belt rests his hand on the pommel of the sword at his hip as if he were born to be a Templar knight. "On the bright side, they probably have no idea how Egyptian princesses behave. To them you're the infidel."

I shake my head. "Wait, I thought they were the infidel."

"It depends which side you're on." Amir clears his throat and squares his shoulders. "Introducing Lady Genesis of Egypt!"

I pretend to step through a doorway. "How close should I go?"

The makeshift steward shrugs. "I have no idea. There's probably some sort of carpet on the floor. I wouldn't step off it—or beyond it."

"Okay." I walk forward, pick up my skirts, and dip into the most graceful, most obsequious curtsy I can manage. "Your Majesty—"

"Wait." Amir holds up his palm. "Henry VIII coined the phrase 'your majesty'. You should use Sire or Your Grace."

"He's not her sire," says Noah.

I clutch my arms across my stomach while a wave of nausea hits me. "Oh my God, I'm going to screw this up. It's way too easy to misspeak."

"You got this." Batting his hand through the air, Amir blows a raspberry as if I'll be meeting some ordinary run-of-the-mill king. "Just remember English is your second language. You can't screw up."

I don't believe him but I still go back and try the whole curtsy thing again. "Your Grace, it is with great gratification to meet you at last."

Noah snorts. "Great gratification?"

I hold my position. "I thought 'my pleasure' was too trite."

With a flick of his fingers, Amir urges me to continue. "It's fine."

"Rise," says Noah. "Tell me, why have you made such a long and perilous journey?"

"Have you not read the missive sent from my father?"

"His cleric will read the missive to him," says Amir. "But that's neither here nor there. You should just answer and try not to antagonize John in any way, otherwise he might not react well."

"I read the damned missive." Noah gives the brown belt a backhanded thwack. "But I want to hear an explanation from the princess' own lips."

I continue with the rehearsal, imagining all sorts of vile ways King John might react if I displease him. Including stretching me on the rack. But I have no option. To complete this mission, I must see him and figure out who we have been sent to protect.

I think.

"That wasn't so bad, was it?" asks Amir. "Once you're finished a courtier ought to be assigned to escort you to the dining hall."

"Won't you two be escorting me?" I ask.

"We're your henchmen. We'll be standing behind you to protect you from attack."

"Is that necessary?"

"In this century it is. Believe me, the king will be surrounded by guards with his most high-ranking man-at-arms standing right behind his chair."

I jam my fists into my hips. "But you need to eat."

Before Amir can reply, a knock sounds at the door. "The king will see you now, Princess."

As a lead weight drops to my toes, I wipe my sweaty palms on my dress.

Oh, God, help! I so cannot mess this up.

Judging by the twelve guards escorting us to the throne room, I highly suspect we didn't impress William Marshal as much as he'd led us to believe, flaying comment and all.

But then, from what I've studied, King John was...*is* paranoid. And he has good reason to be. The tyrant raised taxes more than any king in history, as much as five hundred percent over the course of his reign. He has squeezed his barons of their wealth and led many into bankruptcy. The king imprisoned high-ranking men for nonpayment of taxes and outrageous fines, tortured them, their wives, and their children.

I shudder. Do I really want to meet this guy?

Before I can think of an excuse, we're all standing in a passageway while a voice booms across the stone walls. "Ye hunt in *my* forest and steal *my* deer and ye have the gall to plead for leniency?" This voice is filled with malice and snobbery and can belong to none other than John himself.

"Please, sire," comes a miserable plea. "My father hunted these lands. My family is facing starvation without—"

"Silence!" booms the king. "For yer insolence, ye will be flogged with no fewer than five and twenty lashes. Yer right hand will be severed from yer arm and hanged from the bailey wall."

"No, sire, not my hand. My family relies on me to survive!"

I can't believe what I'm hearing. Clenching my fists, I lunge forward only to have Noah catch my elbow. "But—"

He gives me a dead-eyed stare and a single shake of his head. "Remember, ours is not to intervene," he growls directly into my ear. "Get a grip. *Now*."

"Take him away!" roars the king.

I stand helpless, the backs of my eyes stinging as the poor man is led past us, struggling against his captors. I can't even imagine what it must be like trying to feed a family when the boundaries of the hunting grounds keep changing.

It kills me to be a witness to tyranny and not do or say anything. I clench my teeth. I already detest King John yet he might be the one I've come to protect.

Then my body goes numb while our party shuffles forward. I inhale deeply to calm myself. Noah was right. I need to get a grip. This is too important to blow. No matter how much I want to scream, I cannot afford to lose control.

As I reach the archway festooned with red curtains, the steward stops me with a thrust of his hand. Aside from his black robe, he reminds me of the master of ceremonies at a boxing match. He's standing in the center of the archway and pounds his staff on the floorboards. "Princess Genesis of Egypt," he bellows as if he not only must inform the king, but the servants working four floors below in the cellars need to hear as well.

I step forward, taking my first glimpse of King John's court and terror seizes me like it did at a karate tournament when I was thirteen and forgot my kama kata. The throne room isn't terribly large, but it's packed shoulder-to-shoulder with men dressed in colorful robes, knights in chausses and chainmail, monks, and priests. There's even a man with a blindfolded hawk chained to his arm.

My hands tremble and I close my eyes. *Chakra*.

"Come forward," says the king. Dressed in richly embroidered purple robes beneath an ermine cloak, he's seated in a high-backed wooden chair. Not surprisingly, his features are fleshy and quite pale. His red-bearded chin tips upward as he examines me, his expression guarded, aloof, and skeptical.

Alarm whispers across the back of my neck. Is it a sign? Yes. It has to be. Is the Qiang's target in this room? Or is our assailant here?

I scan the eyes of every face, looking for an imposter. I sense deceit, jealousy, fear, intrigue, and a great deal of distrust, but not the intensity of hate—the type powerful enough to motivate someone to live the life of an assassin. Unless the enemy knows how to mask his or her aura.

I shudder as it occurs to me I'm in way over my head. But that's not why my heart is trying to hammer out of my chest. With my next breath, the king could peg me as an imposter and have me put to death. Or worse, have me tortured and mutilated like the poor hunter they just escorted to the bowels of hell.

My gaze stops at the queen who is clearly pregnant. Her throne is much smaller than John's and she regards me with a serene, close-lipped smile, almost as if she's a life-sized doll placed there to adorn the king's right arm. In her I sense goodness and, of all the people present, I'm drawn to her the most.

I give her a polite nod, then shift my attention to the king while I slowly step forward as I'd rehearsed. It feels like I'm floating across the red carpet before I sink into a deep curtsy. I remain in place and say in my most confident voice, "I come bearing tidings of peace, oh great and powerful King of England."

"Is that so?" John asks rather sardonically. "I find yer sincerity difficult to believe. Tell me, why is yer father plying me with his favor when Pope Innocent is actively enlisting the armies of Christendom to take up their swords and embark on a Fifth Crusade and drive the Mussulmen out of the Holy Land?"

Keeping my head bowed, I stare at John's bejeweled pointy-toed shoes. "My father wishes to prevent the Mongol raids on the Silk Road. His motives are as simple as that."

"A truce? With Al-Adil? Ha!" John plants his feet square on the floor. "Though I haven't met yer father face-to-face, I understand Al-Adil would sooner ride into purgatory than ask me, the pope, or any governing authority in Christendom for a truce."

"Not at all, Your Maj—*um*—Grace." My thighs start to shake from my excruciating curtsy, and I chance looking up. Amusement etches the king's fleshy features. I might be ignorant in his eyes, but if I'm going to assert myself as a princess, I have to do it now. Straightening, I remove the ring we bought from the blacksmith in Basingstoke. "My father offers you this gift as a symbol of his sincerity."

John motions to one of his knights who, in turn, retrieves it from me and takes it to the king.

After examining the pink quartz, John slips it on and taps his fingers on the throne's armrest. "The craftmanship is admirable. Perhaps Al-Adil has a point in his quest to protect the Silk Road, though one might better believe he intends to control trade from the east. However, presenting me with the hand of his favored daughter *and* this ring from Egypt. I must consider his..."

What!

King John keeps talking, but I can't hear him because my ears are ringing. What did he say? My hand? What the hell does he intend to do with my hand? Cut it off like the poor peasant the guards just took to the dungeon?

No. Of course not. Even an ignoramus from the twenty-first century knows the hand of a favored daughter can mean only one thing.

God!

I steal a backward glance at Amir whose sheepish expression reminds me of my cat Rufus slinking away after he knocked over a glass vase. Amir is dead. He knows it. My fingers are twitching in anticipation of wrapping around his throat.

"Yer arrival has come at quite an opportune time," the king's voice breaks through my inner tirade.

I try not to scowl—or pass out—when my attention returns to the throne. "Seriously?" I croak, searching for the nearest exit. Damn, the only two are blocked by guards with pikes.

Have I mentioned how much I hate pikes?

"Indeed." Grinning, the king gestures to his right. "Why, only today, Lord Richard de Burgh made known his need of a wife."

Melting might be an option. Or making a beeline for Stonehenge. I follow the line of King John's upturned palm and meet the gaze of an elderly man with a long gray beard and silver hair brushing his mail-clad shoulders. Though reserved, his smile is pleasant and genuine unlike that of his king's. With a lateral scar running from Lord de Burgh's left eye, disappearing into his whiskers, he'd give Noah a run in a ruggedness contest. Maybe more so because the lines etched from the corners of his nose are like caverns, seconded only by the deep crow's feet at the outer edges of his eyes. He has to be at least sixty— old enough to be my grandfather and, to add insult to injury, the man is a good four inches shorter.

My mind races. Panic seizes my chest. We must complete our mission and run for home before I have to pledge eternal love to someone who's almost old enough to be my dad's dad.

Dammit!

I swear Amir will definitely feel the extent of my ire. Just as soon as I get the weasel behind closed doors thick enough to dampen the douche's squeals of pain. I might have expected this sort of thing from Noah, but to be stabbed in the back by the guy I thought was nice totally burns.

Still focused on de Burgh, I force a smile and a quick bow of my head. "My lord." Then I shift my gaze directly to the queen who honestly doesn't look much older than me. And she's pregnant! God, how can she stand to be married to crusty old John?

I scrape my teeth over my bottom lip. Perhaps a plea to Her Grace for feminine interference might postpone this ludicrousness. "Of course, I require some time to adjust. To-to grow acquainted with English customs...ah...l-learn what is expected of an English wife?" My voice ratchets up with my mounting hysteria.

"I suspect that which is expected of a wife in Egypt is the same as it is in England. What say ye, de

Burgh? In bed and on her back, aye?" The king throws up his chin with a deep bellowing laugh, mimicked by all the men in the room including my intended.

"Who cares about the bed?" says some pompous ass who has no clue how stupid he looks in shoes with pointed toes so long I can't imagine how he manages to walk.

I'm ready to bolt, or to be struck dead, or to have some time-traveling vortex hurl me home to the twenty-first century. Now, please?

I glance over my shoulder at Noah and catch him laughing, too. Damn him. I'll have to put some thought into paybacks. For this, I'll need something good. And if de Burgh dares to lay a finger on me, I'll deck him. I'll, I'll knee him where it counts so hard, he'll be singing like Michael Jackson for a week.

For the first time since the king's inquisition began, the queen's expression grows contemplative as she sits forward. With a purse of her lips, she claps her hands. "We must pay heed to Princess Genesis, Yer Grace. Clearly Her Ladyship is weary from her travels. And it is Whitsun, after all. Perhaps we ought to wait until the feast days have ended before she marries."

Before I *marry*? I'm freaking sixteen! I gag as a lump the size of my fist swells in my throat. Were they actually planning to execute the deed tonight? What the hell was Amir thinking when he wrote that missive? I was supposed to give the king the ring not my effing hand!

His Highness pats the queen's arm. "I suppose if the young Egyptian needs respite, it is fair for me to grant it. I shall allow a fortnight." Sniffing, he looks down his nose at me. "Earl Marshal tells me ye lost yer possessions when yer ship capsized. A fortnight ought to grant a tailor time to outfit ye with a new wardrobe and the like."

Out of the corner of my eye, Lord de Burgh appears relieved as he releases a long exhale. Except I'm still freaking out—especially if we don't find and dispatch the Qiang in two weeks.

God save me.

A plainly-dressed man appears from the stairwell behind the royal party and clears his throat. "The evening meal is served, sire."

"'Tis about time, ye groveling imbecile." King John rubs his stomach and belches. "Let us adjourn to the hall before we all starve."

I'm still standing at the edge of the red carpet when everyone bows as John and Isabelle rise. I bow, then quickly switch to a curtsy, feeling as awkward as a penguin on the equator. But when the royal couple disappears through the stairwell, the tension in the air immediately dissipates and the chamber fills with the murmur of voices.

I turn in place like a kid on the first day of school with absolutely no idea if I should follow or go back to my chamber when de Burgh appears beside me. "Ye appeared rather surprised at the king's decision for us to wed, my lady."

My lady?

It takes a second to realize he's referring to me, but the whole lady thing throws me even though they've been saying it since I arrived. "Weren't you?" I ask, "ah...my lord."

He takes my hand and pulls me down the countless spiral stairs. "Truth be told, until ye were introduced to court I had no idea when John might find me a wife."

"Why would the king do the finding and not you?"

"I've been away from England for ten years overseeing the king's interests on the continent. 'Tis time for me to take a wife and no matter whom I choose, I must have John's blessing."

"And you're worried he will not give it?"

"Let us say 'tis easier to have John find a woman who meets with his approval than it is for me to do so."

I ponder his dilemma, but the whole debacle doesn't make a lot of sense to me. Sure, there were a lot of arranged marriages among the nobles, but why wouldn't the baron want to pick his own bride? Because he's ancient or because the king would be within his rights to impose a heavy fine if Lord de Burgh chose the wrong woman? I think I read about that, too.

De Burgh shifts my hand to his elbow as we follow the procession into the enormous hall. I glance back for Amir and Noah but they haven't come through yet.

We proceed to the high table where the royals are seated first. The Marshal takes a place on the king's right. There appears to be a prearranged pecking order while the barons take their seats. I imagine de Burgh isn't at the top of the king's list of important vassals because we're seated at the far end of the table.

After a servant assists me to scoot my chair in, I reach for a napkin, but there's none. What's more, the place setting is nothing like what I would have expected for a royal dinner. Atop a pewter plate rests a single spoon, no fork, and a handful of knives look as if they've been carelessly tossed into the center of the table. Another servant fills my silver goblet from an earthen ewer.

"What is this?" I ask.

The man pours for the baron. "Mead, my lady."

"Yer English is quite good," says de Burgh.

I take a sip, pleasantly surprised at the sweet honey-like taste. "Thank you."

"Where did you learn?"

"Ah...my father employed all manner of tutors for his children." God I hate lying. Should I make up a story about growing up in a harem? I cringe. The more I say, the more I'm likely to forget. "One of my favorite teachers was a eunuch whose native tongue was English."

Where the heck did I come up with eunuch?

De Burgh winces. "Fortunate for ye given your present circumstances."

I lean toward him and lower my voice. "I don't want you to feel like you have to marry me. If you'd prefer someone else, you should make your wishes known now while there's still time."

He practically chokes on his mead. "And renege on a decree of the king? I'd rather face a headsman with a blunt axe."

Cringing, I can't help but think of the gruesome head hanging on the wall above the city gate. Under the table, I pound my thigh with my fist. I need to work harder at dissuading this man. "It doesn't bother you to marry an Egyptian?"

"I'll have to admit, at first I had my reservations...before I set eyes upon ye, of course. But ye are quite comely." His assessing gaze shifts downward, the dog. "Ye appear to be built for childbearing, and ye are a princess, above all. I doubt I could have found a wife as suitable had I spent the next year searching."

I take another drink of mead, this time draining half the goblet. What else can I use? Jeez, de Burgh is acting as if taking a wife is as simple as selecting a shirt from the rack. "What about courtship? Wouldn't you prefer to fall in love?"

"Ah, my lady. I'm far too old to dally in frivolities engaged by men far younger than I. If I do not produce an heir, there will be no one to inherit and my lands will pass to the crown." My intended smooths his weathered fingers across the back of my hand, making me want to slap him. "Ye have nothing to fear from me, dear lady. I have wealth and lands in Kent, and ye will want for nothing. My needs are simple. Bear me a son and ye will live out yer days in comfort."

I want to scream! I'm definitely not having his son. And why the hell can't he say anything about a girl? A daughter will probably manage his wealth and lands better than a son. Regardless, is there no changing his mind? I shift to a new tack. "What about religion? I-I-I follow the teachings of Allah."

"Do we not all worship the same God?" he asks while servants place huge wooden platters of meat on the table—I mean whole joints of meat, roasted chickens. Holy effing hell, they plop a cooked pig's head right in front of me.

I gag, completely losing my appetite. I swear it's the grossest thing I've ever seen.

"Of course 'tis the law," de Burgh continues as if severed pigs' heads are normal fare. "Ye must attend Sunday mass, though, however ye choose to pray in the sanctity of yer rooms shall never be condemned by me."

"Though worship of Islam is discouraged?"

De Burgh removes a dagger from his belt, cuts a hunk of meat off something that looks like roast beef and drops it onto my plate. "It is heresy, my lady. Surely ye knew that before—"

"My lord, do not assume anything where I am concerned," I say as Amir and Noah take their places behind me. "Prior to my introduction to the king, I had no idea my father had offered my hand in marriage."

De Burgh reaches for a basket of bread, his hand stopping in midair. "No?"

"My instructions upon leaving Egypt were simply to give the ring to King John."

"And after?" he asks, taking the basket and putting a slice beside the unappetizing meat on my plate.

"It seems I am the one who made assumptions." Over my shoulder I glare at Amir. "I presumed my Templar guardians were to accompany me back to Egypt."

Chapter Eighteen

"Better a diamond with a flaw than a pebble without." Confucius

Outside the door to my bedchamber, de Burgh gallantly kisses my hand while Noah and Amir stand at a distance, acting the dutiful personal guards. If only I were thirty years older and born in the thirteenth century, I might fall in love with His Lordship. But at the moment I just want him to go away.

"Until the morrow, my lady."

"The morrow?" I ask, tugging my hand from his grasp. "But the king gave me two weeks."

"'Tis the Whitsun feast. Naturally, I assumed ye would be dining with me as ye did this eve."

"Oh. Right. Until the morrow." I manage a curtsy and slip through the door before he can say anything else. I'm positive my teammates are killing themselves to keep from laughing.

My nostrils flare while I listen to de Burgh's footsteps fade down the passageway. Once they've completely vanished, I count to five. Yanking the door open, I glare at the two partners in crime. "Get your scheming asses in here," I growl, keeping my voice low, because the stone corridor is like an echo chamber.

Amir raises his hands and sidles past me. "It wasn't supposed to happen so fast."

I grab the back of his hand and wrench downward, stretching the tendons in his wrist and dropping him to his knees. I keep twisting until he's on his back. Then I jam my knee into his bicep while I crush his throat with my forearm. "What sort of sick game are you playing?"

Amir's face turns from red to blue as he kicks his feet and gurgles something unintelligible.

"Get off him," says Noah, pulling me up and tossing me onto the bed like I weigh no more than a pillow. "We thought the king would take more time—not grant your hand in marriage as soon as you were introduced."

I launch off the bed, aiming a roundhouse at Noah's head but the bastard ducks and catches my arm. We spar, tumbling over the hardwood floor, grappling until he has me pinned on my face in an arm-bar.

I squirm, only making the pain worse. Every way I try to move puts more torque on my stretching sinew. "Let go. You're going to dislocate my arm, you douche!"

"Are you going to stop fighting and listen?"

"I ought to—" He twists harder. "Yeeass. Dammit! But this better be amazing."

As Noah releases me, Amir sits up coughing and rubbing his throat.

Good. He ought to be sore. Kneading away the ache in my arm, I face him. "How in God's name am I supposed to focus on the mission when you've recklessly offered my hand in marriage?"

The brains of this operation gives me a shrug—a stupid shrug as if marrying an old medieval baron is an insignificant complication. "I didn't think the ring alone would be convincing enough. We needed something more substantial, something John wouldn't question."

I pace. He had to say something logical, didn't he? But I'm still pissed. "All right—maybe you have a plausible angle, but why the hell didn't you tell me about it first?"

Noah hangs his head. "We didn't think you would go along with it."

"So, blue belt, you mean to say you were in on the marriage plot from the beginning?"

"No." Amir moves to the hearth and tosses a stick of wood onto the fire. "I dreamed it up while I was writing the missive. Afterward I told Noah, we both agreed to conveniently forget to mention it."

"Conveniently forget? *Deceptively withhold* is more like it!" I eye each of them with a dead-eyed glare. "This is a disaster. What am I supposed to do if I actually have to marry that man?"

"Don't worry about it." Noah pats my shoulder. "You have two weeks."

I parry his hand away. "Thank God I asked for time or else I could be walking down the aisle in the morning."

The dude doesn't take my hint and grabs me by the shoulders. Dammit, my knees wobble as he stares at me with those electrifying eyes. I hate him for disarming me with a stupid look. "You have my word I will not allow you to marry him."

I grind my molars and glare up at him. "Oh, that'll work to our advantage. Fleeing the very court we're trying to protect."

He drops his hands and slumps into the chair across from Amir.

"She has a point," admits the crafty brown belt. He should have thought of all the angles before being so careless with my freaking life.

I cross my arms and pace in front of the fire. "I know I felt something when I first entered the throne room, but any sensations I had were completely wiped out with the announcement of my betrothal."

"Damn," Noah grumbles under his breath.

Sitting back, Amir crosses his ankles. "So, then we can narrow it down to someone who was in the throne room, right?"

"I guess that's a fair assessment." I keep pacing. "What are we looking for? Have you guys seen anyone who seems even slightly out of place? Are most of the Qiang Asian?"

"Nope," says Amir. "They're recruited from all over just like we are."

"Who would want to join them?" I ask.

"Plenty of crazies," says Noah. "Fascist militants, religious zealots from the Middle East, Russians. You name it, there are hundreds of haters out there, and they're just as skilled as we are."

"Do you think they've identified us?"

Amir shrugs. "Who knows."

"I don't think so," says Noah.

"Why not?" I ask.

"Because I can pick one out if I see one."

"Right." Adjusting his sword belt, Amir snorts and looks to the ceiling. "And my name is Julius Caesar."

I step between them and plant my palms on the table. "Would you two be serious for five seconds? If someone who was in the room is the Qiang's target, then it has to be the king or Marshal."

"Probably." Pushing to his feet, Amir holds up his finger. "However, we shouldn't discount anyone seated at the high table at dinner."

He's giving me a headache. "Wonderful. Grand Master Li should have sent an army."

Noah stands as well. "Except he can't."

That's right, they can only send three. I still can't believe how little I know about this. If only I'd had more time with Li before we jumped. "Do we ever send scouts?"

Noah shrugs. "We follow the Grand Master's orders, but we usually go in as a team. Our odds are better that way."

Every question I ask leads to more. "How do the Qiang decide where they're going? I know they can pick their destination, but how do we know to follow?"

"We don't always." Amir gives Noah some sort of nod with his head. "Remember Hitler?"

I gulp. "Seriously?"

"That's why so many non-descendants of Sun Tzu attend the academy. Once we graduate, we fight them in our time."

"Except we don't know where they are. It reminds me of Bin Ladin when he was in Afghanistan."

"But we got him, didn't we?" Noah brushes a wisp of hair away from my face. "Just focus on our plan. You'll start learning the rest once you're yellow belt, but for now we gotta go."

The guys move toward the door and I follow. "You're leaving me in here alone?"

"We're your henchmen. We guard your door." Amir rests his hand on the latch. "We probably shouldn't be in here now, but we ought to avoid a scandal if people see us standing guard in the passageway."

"Are you serious? Who cares about a scandal? You need to sleep."

Shaking his head, Amir frowns. "We've established our cover now. We have no choice but to stick to it."

"We'll sleep in the hallway," says Noah.

"Wait." I drag some pillows and a blanket off the bed. "Take these."

Noah gives me a wink as I hand them to him. "You're not too mad at us, are you, white belt?"

I give his pillows a shove. "Let's just say you're in no position to make assumptions."

愛

The next day I'm not as crabby, probably because the mattress in my chamber is filled with feathers and is the softest thing I've ever slept on. Earlier this morning, a maid named Madeline brought me a large breakfast and, though I told her I didn't need help, she insisted on dressing me. Thank God I only had to strip down to my shift or else she would have been blown away at the sight of my bra and panties.

Now she's brushing my hair while Noah and Amir have gone to the hall to eat.

"What is it like in Egypt?" she asks. Madeline isn't just a maid, she said she's a *lady's maid* assigned by Her Grace to see to my necessities while I'm at court. I swear she's not five feet tall. Her hair's covered by a linen veil and she has a pale, heart-shaped face that reminds me of a pixie.

I think of Bunkerville on the fringe of the Mohave Desert and figure it's probably pretty similar. "It's hot and dry, and it doesn't rain very often."

"How do the crops grow without rain?"

"Canals from the River Nile—but only close to her shores. Very little grows inland."

"Do ye miss it?"

I instantly wonder if Rufus is missing me and if Dad is staying off the sauce, and suddenly a pang of longing stretches my heart. "I do." Everything is so different than I imagined. First of all, no one in Bunkerville would ever believe me if I told them I traveled back in time from the twenty-first century.

A knock sounds at the door and I look up, expecting Noah and Amir to step through.

"Her Grace, requests Lady Genesis' presence in the courtyard," a deep voice announces.

"Shall I tell him ye'll be down directly?" Madeline asks.

"Yes, please."

Things grow stranger by the day. At home I'm never summoned by a queen, I answer my own door, and brush my own hair among so many other things. Even the guard waits for me while the maid pins my veil in place.

My officious escort leads me through a labyrinth of corridors and winding staircases until we exit out into a beautifully manicured garden. I admire a trellis of lavender wisteria while goosebumps rise on my skin.

Sitting on an iron bench, the queen smiles while my gaze shifts from her, to her guards, to the woman standing behind her cradling a baby. Three young children play tag on the grass, two boys and a smaller girl who squeals with delight.

The guard urges me forward while I search the foliage for movement, anything that looks out of place.

Queen Isabelle holds out her hands. "Princess Genesis, what a delight to see ye this morning."

I force myself to smile and focus on her face. There's kindness in her eyes, but is she the target? My gaze shifts to her belly and I'm chilled. Something isn't right. "Thank you for summoning me, Your Grace. It is a lovely day."

The queen pats the bench beside her. "Please do sit. It tires my neck to look up and I'm in no condition to stand."

"When is the child expected?"

Her Grace rubs her baby bump. "By the way she kicks, I am certain it will be soon."

"She?" I ask. "How do you know?"

"The midwife's prediction has been correct on three of my four children, though she thought Henry was to be a lass."

The boys are too fast for the girl and she's losing ground. "Is the tallest Henry?"

"Yes, next is Richard, then Joan, and—" The baby in the nurse's arms squeals. "And Isabella never allows me to forget her for a moment. She's named for her mother after all."

Henry looks my way, then pushes his brother and laughs. He's an attractive kid, though it is beyond my imagination that he will soon be king. But right now, they just look like normal children, laughing and playing.

The queen beckons them. "Come hither, children, and meet Princess Genesis from Egypt."

The three are introduced by name and stand before me like idyllic cherubs.

Henry studies me with a critical eye. "I beg yer pardon, Yer Ladyship, but Master Lawrence says Egyptians are the enemies of Christendom as are the Ottoman."

I suppose it depends who is in power as to who is the worst enemy, but I'm not prepared for such a debate, not even with an eight-year-old boy. "My father would say the Mongols are his greatest threat."

"How am I to believe ye?" the boy asks. The intensity of his stare makes tingles skitter up my spine.

Thank goodness he didn't have the wherewithal to ask about Al-Adil's inherent hatred for all Christians. But still, his question is not only valid, it demonstrates his kingly responsibility to question.

"Be polite," chides the queen.

"He does have a reasonable point. How best for me to convince you?" I drum my fingers on my lips, watching the prince. There are two guardsmen behind us and I gesture toward them. "What if one of them grabs my arms and the other tries to run me through with his sword? If I can get away, will you believe me then?"

The boy looks from me to the guards. "Aye, my lady."

"Heavens no." The queen looks back to the men. "Absolutely not."

"I think 'tis fair," says Henry. "Especially since the princess offered."

Shaking her head, Isabelle slices both hands across each other like a referee. "There will be no bloodshed in my garden."

"I assure you there will not be," I say, standing.

"See?" says Henry. "Please, Mama, I want to see the princess escape yer guards."

After the queen reluctantly agrees, one of the two baffled sentries grabs me around the elbows in a hold Sensei Soto calls captured wings. It's just about the easiest hold in the world to escape from, which is a relief, because I have no intention of meeting my end.

The second guard stands opposite and draws his weapon. "Are ye certain ye want to do this, my lady?"

"Give it your best shot."

With my next breath, I know he's planning to lunge in, aiming a stab to my midriff, but intends to stop before he actually stabs me. I suppose he'd be in hot water if he actually killed a guest of the king. No worries, I can live with a near miss. As he begins to move, I launch myself against the rear guard and swing my legs up over the blade. On the way down, my heel kicks the sword out of the front guard's hand. Landing on my feet, I bend forward, flipping the guy holding my arms over my back like a sack of potatoes.

"Aye ya!" I kiai, unable to help myself.

Then I brush off my hands, step back, and bow to the assailants before I turn to the prince. "Do I have your trust, my lord?"

"God's bones," Henry says, gaping at the guards, his eyes round as quarters.

The queen shakes her finger. "Watch yer language, young man."

"Sorry, Mother." Henry bows to me. "Aye, I believe ye, Princess."

"Thank you."

"But I'm still not certain about yer father." Henry laughs and shoves Richard. "Come, brother, ye're it!"

Another chill shoots through my veins, as I chuckle, watching the future King Henry III run away with his siblings.

The soldiers resume their positions and the queen again pats the bench beside her. "Where did ye learn how to flip a mail-clad soldier over yer back?" she asks.

"It's all mechanics."

"Mechanics? Are ye certain ye're not a sorceress?"

"Absolutely positive. When a girl has dozens of brothers, she learns a trick or two." Needing to quickly change the subject, I look to the queen's swollen belly. "If your babe is a girl, what will you name her?"

"Eleanor."

"I like the name Eleanor."

"So do I." She scoots a little closer. "But that isn't why I asked for yer presence."

"Oh?"

The queen pats my hand, her expression growing intent. "Ye knew nothing about yer father's gift of yer hand. And do not try to deny it to me. I saw it in yer eyes."

I glance to my folded fingers and nod while my face burns. If only she knew the whole truth: My traveling companions stabbed me in the back. And furthermore, I am not here to do anything but find a murderer in our midst. "Yes. It wasn't until the king said I would marry Lord de Burgh when I learned of my father's wishes."

"And I'll wager ye would have performed yer duty and brought the message to the king even if ye knew ye were to be married to a Christian."

"Of course."

"Men. They think they are ever so clever." Her Grace grasps my wrist and looks me in the eye. "I'm sure it will come as no surprise to hear I believe England would be a far more peaceful country if the decisions were left to the fairer sex."

I try not to laugh but end up sputtering a chuckle all the same. "It seems we are of like minds, Your Grace."

"If only I weren't great with child more often than not, my influence might have more of an impact. But such is the lot of women. Ours is not an easy path."

"No, I've discovered the same." A hundred things race through my mind that I know I shouldn't say—like walking alone and choosing one's boyfriend, dating, baths and running water, feminine hygiene, and birth control for heaven's sake.

Before I blurt something I shouldn't, she rubs my hand between her palms. "Ye may not know this, but mine was an arranged marriage with John. Though my father told me whom I was to marry, I had not met the king prior to our wedding day. I had seen but twelve summers when we took our vows."

"Twelve?" I ask, unable to hide my disgust. I clap a hand over my mouth before I accuse the king of molesting a minor. "You were only a child."

"As ye are aware, the duty of noblewomen is to marry well and increase the wealth of her family." Her smile is sad. "I imagine ye are quite young, are ye not?"

Sixteen seems ancient in comparison, but I nod. "I am."

"And ye are not *schooled* in the ways of men?"

Oh, God, is she about to launch into a discussion of the birds and the bees? Inching toward the edge of the seat, I shake my head. How much more of the queen's kindness can I take?

"I know Lord de Burgh is likely far older than ye envisioned yer husband to be, but I want ye to know he is one of the most respected knights in the kingdom. In fact, aside from Earl Marshal who is already married, I do believe I would trust de Burgh the most."

"You would?"

"Indeed. And being that ye are, no doubt, unfamiliar with England's barons, I thought it might ease yer conscience to know ye will be wedded to a good man."

A rock the size of a grapefruit plunges to the pit of my stomach. Why am I not jumping for joy?

Chapter Nineteen

"To see what is right and not to do it is want of courage or principle." - Confucius

Madeline, stands back and adjusts my veil, her blue eyes intent.

"How does it look?" I ask.

"I've never seen a woman as lovely. The lavender suits you, my lady."

I'm a little embarrassed. I expected something along the lines of "fine" or "passable." But Madeline has bent over backward for me, drawing a bath, making sure I'm well fed and well rested.

While I was visiting the queen, Noah and Amir found me another gown. It's nice for this era, ivory with lavender trim which matches the silk veil. Madeline wove it through my circlet and beneath my chin and called it a wimple.

I've seen no mirrors here and rather than looking beautiful, my head feels wrapped up like a baby's swaddling. And regardless if Noah and Amir are trying to make amends, I'm still mad at them. It's not as if they bought me something new because they'd like to see me all dolled up. Their only motivation was to further the ruse of my being an Egyptian princess.

What a miserable idea that has become, especially since we're no closer to achieving our mission aside from a few measly premonitions.

The bell tower is across the courtyard from my chamber and the clanging seems to be constantly sounding off. Without clocks, Madeline has explained it's how they tell the time, but according to her, they don't say it's noon, they say it's nones, or lauds at first light, or prime at sunrise, or terce at the end of the third hour, and so on.

"'Tis time for the feast, my lady."

"Not compline?" I ask. Compline is the worship service before dinner.

Madeline patters toward the door. "The compline bell already rang. Do ye not recall?"

"It's a little confusing, but have no fear, I'll get used to it."

As the door opens, Amir and Noah spin and face me.

"Whoa," Noah says while Amir's jaw drops.

"Don't even try to butter me up." I march past them. "And give the credit to Madeline. She's a magician."

"Shh." Amir follows. "You could get her burned at the stake for that comment."

"Good Lord, get me out of here," I mumble.

"Hopefully sooner than later," Noah adds. "I need to sleep in a real bed."

A twinge of guilt needles at me, but I keep my mouth shut. Their discomfort is penance for marrying me off. At least until I can think of something better.

The chatter from the hall resounds up the stairwell and my stomach jumps. I have no idea why

I'm nervous, but it gets worse as I step out and am swarmed by people.

If I thought it was crowded last night, it's now insane. The smell of freshly-baked bread and roasting meat makes my mouth water while flute and lyre music resonates over the excitement of voices.

"This way, my lady," says Noah, taking my elbow and urging me toward the dais.

The king's table is decorated with a green cloth and flowers. Lots of flowers in whites, pinks, yellows, and blues are scattered atop the table. Flickers of light from the candelabras pick up the iridescent colors. Atop the dais, the barons are chatting but the royal couple hasn't made their grand entrance yet. I figure that's a good thing because I'd look like an idiot if I was late.

Ahead, Lord de Burgh catches my eye and greets me with a pleasant smile. His face is so kindly I can't help but grin back like I would do to my grandfather or to a teacher I respect. But as soon as my lips turn up, I feel like I'm living a lie and soon that poor old man is going to catch the brunt of it.

"You're right in character," Noah whispers into my ear.

"Shut up," I say, barely moving my lips.

Uh oh. The chatter in the hall ebbs to a low hum while everyone turns to stare at the foreign princess. Maybe this ruse wasn't such a great idea. If the Qiang are here, the three of us are an easy target— especially me.

De Burgh moves to the dais steps and offers his hand. "Good eve, Princess. Ye are absolutely a vision of pure beauty."

As he leads me away from Noah, a cool whisper crosses the back of my neck. For a moment I think a Qiang warrior may actually be watching until I glance back at Noah's scowl. Is he jealous of the baron? How would the blue belt behave if John had offered my hand to some mega-hot knight? In fact, there's a blue-eyed stunner watching me. He looks like a movie star dressed in period costume. I give him a nod.

"Do ye know Sir Roderick?" asks de Burgh.

"Who?"

De Burgh arches a sly eyebrow and inclines his head toward Mr. Sexy. "The young whelp slavering over himself. Ye'll do well to stay clear of that lecherous cur. He has a reputation for raising the skirts of unsuspecting maidens."

I giggle and shift my attention to the flowers on the table as my cheeks burn. "Thank you for the warning." I guess sexy men are the same in this century as they are in mine. They know women can't resist them and it makes them behave like wolves.

I'm about to ask why no one is sitting when trumpeters blast a fanfare from the balcony above. The steward moves to the center of the dais. "All good people of Winchester, behold yer king!"

With a rustle of clothing, everyone in the hall bows or curtsys. As my knees bend, I get a tingling sensation like someone's blowing cold air across the back of my neck—I close my eyes and focus. I see a blade, but it's hidden in a scabbard. The vision disappears just as fast as it came.

No!

My gaze darts across the faces in the hall. *Where are you?* If only I could shout, all bad guys raise your hands!

Ahead, the king and his pregnant queen are being led by William Marshal which convinces me we are definitely close to achieving our goal. As soon as the royal party was announced, my senses went on overdrive. Either the king, the queen, or the earl *has* to be the Qiang's target.

I try to catch Amir's eye, but both he and Noah are bowing and I can't see their faces.

The king stops at the top of the dais and spreads his arms wide. "Happy Whitsun, to all. May the Lord bless us with healthy crops this planting season. Let us feast and celebrate our prosperity!"

"Hear, hear!" shouts the crowd as everyone straightens and starts to move. I find it odd that John doesn't mention the negotiation of the Magna Carta and refers to crops instead.

Lord de Burgh holds a chair for me, the same one I sat in last night. "Princess."

"Thank you." After I take my seat, I crook my finger, motioning for Noah to lean down so I can whisper in his ear. "I'm positive they're after John, Isabelle, or Marshal."

"We'll be watching. You focus on the guys at the table." he whispers back. Not only my neck tingles, but I get goosebumps. God, would my hormones stop for second? Next time I need to whisper something important I'd better speak to Amir—except he's standing on de Burgh's side, and I don't need my pseudo-betrothed to overhear what I'm saying.

The musicians have moved to the balcony and medieval tunes swell around us like a Renaissance faire. A swarm of servants heads for the dais, carrying platters of...oh my God, there's a swan on a platter, feathers and all. Except it's not alive. It's sort of taxidermized. And honestly, it turns my stomach. I hope they don't expect me to eat a dead swan.

Worse, two men are carrying an entire roasted pig and set it in front of the king.

"That's a fine sow if I've ever seen one," says de Burgh.

I don't bother to reply while I watch a servant place the swan in front of the queen, grab the neck and lift off the carcass, showing her whatever the disgusting delicacy is beneath.

In a flurry, everyone wields their eating knives, spearing the nearest joint of meat in a barbarian's free-for-all.

"May I cut ye a slice of chicken breast, my lady?" asks de Burgh.

"Huh?" Duh, he's talking to me. "That will be fine, thank you."

As the nobles load their plates, more servants crowd around us. My breathing speeds and I close my eyes, willing myself to a place of calm. Except I can't. In my mind's eye, I see a dagger and it's not in a scabbard now. Nor is it an eating knife like the one de Burgh uses to spear his meat, but a deadly, razor-sharp knife with a blade at least sixteen inches long.

It's here.

Behind me.

Me? I squeeze my eyes to better see it.

Oh, God.

Move now!

"No!" I shout, pulling de Burgh's sword from its scabbard while I launch myself from my seat. Pivoting around Noah, I thrust up the blade, eyeing my target.

Just as the dagger angles for the killing strike, I shove the big blue belt aside, stopping the downward motion of the knife with the cross guard of de Burgh's sword.

Beneath the cloak of a hood, brown eyes filled with hate glare into mine as the attacker recoils. In my mind's eye I see his strike and it's aimed for my heart.

If I don't stop him, I'll be dead in a half-second.

Using the momentum of my defensive block, I flatten the blade. With both hands, I put my weight and every sinew of strength I possess into a swinging attack, eyeing the Qiang's neck. "Aye yaaaaa!" I bellow a blood-curdling kiai.

It's over before my mind registers what I've done.

Women scream as the headless body falls backward, blood pooling across the floor.

Sucking in gasps of air, I crouch in en garde position, ready for the next bout, keeping Noah pinned behind me.

I check left then right while shrieks grow louder and benches screech across the floorboards.

"Protect the king!" The Marshal shouts while guards swarm the dais.

De Burgh's chair topples as he stands. "What the devil—?"

I grip the sword tighter, tuning him out, desperately trying to concentrate. My mind swims as I struggle to focus. Are we still in danger?

"It's over, Genesis." Amir's voice sounds like he's speaking through a tunnel in my head.

As my entire body is wracked by tremors, I realize he's right.

"I-I-I *killed* him."

My gut heaves as I release the sword into de Burgh's hands. Noah and Amir flank me, their weapons drawn.

"We need to move," Noah growls in my ear, his fingers gripping my arm.

"Okay," I squeak, almost passing out when I glance at the dead Qiang warrior. My feet are moving because my teammates are dragging me, otherwise I'd still be standing there gaping in disbelief. I'm in a state of complete shock as we rush into the masses of people frantically trying to escape through the narrow doorways.

"I can't believe it," I mumble over and over, trying not to hyperventilate.

When Amir pushes open the door to my chamber I don't even remember how we got there. Compared to the hall, it's like a sanctuary. As soon as I step inside, I run to the washstand and retch into the chamber pot.

"What the effing hell!" I scream, making my throat burn all the more. Damn, I hate showing weakness, and I clench my stomach and wipe my mouth with a cloth. "W-w-why was he after Noah?"

Amir hands me a cup of water. "He pegged him for sure. They've never attacked us directly before—not on any mission I've ever been on."

Moving beside me, Noah rubs his palm around my back. "Are you okay?"

I nod my head and drink some water, but it tastes like acid. But I'm not okay. I just killed someone. I took a life.

"The dude must have recognized me from another mission."

"God!" I blurt, not capable of anything more coherent. "I can't believe I did that. I just can't. I-I saw him coming and my instincts took over...and now-now." Oh my God, I'm going to faint!

Amir pats my shoulder. "It's not your fault."

"Hell no." Noah urges me into to a chair. "I'm just glad you saw him. With all the commotion, I didn't even hear the dude approach."

"You didn't spot him, did you, Genesis?" asks Amir. "From where you were sitting, there's no way you could have seen him coming."

"I-I saw him in my m-i-i-ind," I cry, wrapping my arms around my midriff and rocking back and forth. "B-but only seconds before he attacked. If I'd been a fraction of a second later, he would have stabbed Noah."

The blue belt thumbs his leather armor. "He would have tried but I could have taken him."

If I wasn't about to puke again, I might laugh at his cocky bravado. But this isn't funny. I'm in shock. Sure I've competed in some tough fights, but I've never faced real-life action. Icy blood races through my veins and I can't stop shaking. I'm here in this room, but I feel like I'm out of my body watching from above. Maybe this isn't real.

I tug on Noah's tunic. "Poke me."

"Huh?"

"Poke me, dammit!"

He drills his pointer finger into my shoulder.

"Ow."

"You told me to do it."

I rub my shoulder. "Yeah, but not so hard it causes a bruise." My stomach roils again. "I'm not dreaming," I whisper, gulping back bile.

Amir claps his palms onto the table and leans forward. "Is the mission over? Did they only send one?"

"That doesn't make any sense," says Noah. "Why would they lure us to the time of the Magna Carta just to off me? They know we'll just send someone else."

"He was a messenger," I blurt, sitting straighter. "He didn't come for the mission. He came as a scout."

Amir throws up his hands. "They're sending scouts now? Then why did he bother to show himself?"

Absently, I grasp Noah's fingers and rub them between my palms. "I saw the hate in his eyes. You've met him before. I'm certain of it."

Looking away, Noah scratches his beard.

It comes to me. "You killed someone he cared about."

"So?" Noah's eyes turn ice cold. "If you go on a mission, you'll end up with blood on your hands. You should have been told that before you leapt."

"She knows it," Amir snipes impatiently. "We're all warriors. But if what Genesis says is true, they're close. Someone at Winchester Castle has to be their target."

"Agreed," I say as angry voices echo through the passageway.

"This is insanity, my lord! If she hadn't acted so quickly, that madman could have killed any one of us."

I stand, recognizing de Burgh's tenor as the door swings open. William Marshal's eyes blaze with fire as he faces me, sword in hand. "Princess," he says as if the word is a curse. "I must take ye into custody forthwith."

Noah draws his sword and blocks the earl's path. "I cannot allow you to do that, my lord."

Amir draws his weapon as well. "Nor can I."

As guards file into the chamber, de Burgh elbows his way beside the Earl of Pembroke—the dude I considered to be the smartest, most rational man of this era. "Ye must at least give the princess a chance to explain."

"No one is that fast," says Earl Marshal. "She's a sorceress, sent to us by our sworn enemy, Al-Adil!"

Noah moves in front of me. "She is no witch."

"See?" says de Burgh. "A knight who has taken a sacred oath vouches for her."

Marshal sneers at the baron. "Ye are blinded by her beauty."

For the first time, I'm almost happy with my engagement. At least someone from this century has my back.

De Burgh squares his shoulders. "What I want to know is who is the man she slew. Where did he come from?"

"He's a Mamluk," says Amir with great authority. "The slave warriors who have vowed to overthrow the Ayyubid dynasty. He must have been following us all along."

Marshal saunters toward Amir. "If this is true, then she has brought peril into the king's court."

"No!" I shout. "My father sent me in the name of peace."

"She speaks the truth." Amir looks the earl in the eye. "She is not your enemy. Your evidence is the corpse in the hall, my lord. *He* is the assassin, not this young woman."

"But she is a pagan sorceress, performing the work of the devil." Earl Marshal thrusts a finger at me. "She must be taken into custody and punished until she repents."

"I will not allow it." Noah moves in front of me. "The princess is innocent. She saved *my* life. I will take any punishment she may have coming."

My every nerve is wound like a spring. Punishment? I did nothing wrong!

Marshal's gaze shifts to the blue belt. "Ye?"

"Aye," says de Burgh. "These men have been sent to protect the princess and they have vouched for her good standing. Her royal blood, mind you. I, too, vouch for my betrothed. Will it not satisfy the king to have the knight she defended bear her penance in her stead?"

Silence fills the room as Marshal takes a deep breath, anger radiating from his aura. He finally gestures to the guards. "Very well. If the Templar feels so strongly about the innocence of the princess, he will indeed feel the fiery tongue of the whip. Seize him."

"This is insane!" I shout, grabbing Noah's tunic. "Can't you impose a fine or something civil?"

This isn't happening. A whipping? I cannot let Noah suffer because of me.

"Let it go, Genesis," he growls through clenched teeth as the guards secure manacles around his wrists.

"Ye dare call her familiar?" asks the earl before he turns to de Burgh. "I will have a word with the king. Given these events, I'm certain he will absolve ye of yer duty to marry this woman."

"I do not so desire." De Burgh grabs my hand. "If ye cannot see her courage, then ye are a lesser man than I believed."

"Courage she has. That is not in doubt." Scowling, The Marshal saunters up to me. "But if I

discover ye have brought evil into this kingdom, I
will see to it ye are boiled alive."

Chapter Twenty

"To be wronged is nothing unless you continue to remember it." - *Confucius*

Numbness paralyzes me while I stand beside Amir in the courtyard. We're surrounded by courtiers who carelessly laugh, standing elbow-to-elbow, watching as jesters tumble and prod each other with wooden wasters. I cringe at the pantomime of last night's slaying, mimicking me taking de Burgh's sword and beheading the Qiang scout.

I still can't believe what happened, but at least I've realized there was no other way. Noah would have been stabbed in the back had I not acted.

The crowd howls with laughter and I lean into Amir, stretching my arm at my side. The thongs I've used to tie a dagger beneath my sleeve are irritating my skin but after the attack in the hall, I decided to carry a weapon. "This is hypocrisy at its worst."

If the bags under his eyes are any indication, he got about as much sleep as I did. Zilch. "It makes you appreciate our time all the more."

"It makes me appreciate sanity."

"Not to mention the Constitution."

My gut wrenches. Our mission still isn't over. I don't need to be reminded that not only the United States of America, but many nations employed the Magna Carta as the foundation of their governments. The rage of anger spreading through me like wildfire makes me immediately scan the crowd for a hooded devil. The problem is there are too many people wearing hoods. I contemplate running through the maze of laughing hypocrites and yanking off their headcovers. Are the Qiang here? Or are the bastards still in the twenty-first century, waiting for news from their scout? What will they do when he does not return?

Shouts and jeers rise as soldiers lead Noah out from the guardhouse. He's bleeding from a scrape on the side of his head.

I clench a fist over my mouth. "God."

"I told him not to fight the king's guards," growls Amir.

"That's like telling a dog not to chew on a bone."

They lash the chain between his manacles to an O-ring on a wooden post. I'd lose my breakfast except I didn't eat—haven't eaten anything since lunch yesterday.

A man-at-arms unrolls a scroll and reads aloud, "Sir Noah Jones, you have agreed to receive twenty lashes on behalf of the Princess Genesis for behavior unbefitting her station."

"Thank God they didn't report you're suspected of sorcery," Amir whispers behind his hand. "If he'd said the S-word, no number of lashes would have kept you from the ravages of this mob."

That only makes me feel worse. "What was I supposed to do? Let the Qiang kill Noah?"

"No."

I suck in a gasp as a guard tears off Noah's shirt, revealing the intricate dragon tattoo on his back while dissent murmurs through the crowd.

"Heathen!" shouts a priest standing near the post.

The mob grows louder, roused by the accusation, cursing poor Noah to Hell.

Clapping a hand over my mouth, I blink against the sting of tears. "This is really happening?"

Amir squeezes my shoulder. "You don't have to watch."

I brush his hand away. "Are you kidding? I must be here for him. I'm the one who should be chained to that damned post."

"No. You did nothing wrong. You saved his life. Remember? Twenty lashes is little price to pay."

Why does Amir always have to be so ridiculously logical? "Don't tell me you'll be standing here without feeling his pain."

His wince tells me he won't.

When a guard cracks a whip on the ground and cackles with laughter, every muscle in my body clenches. The crowd cheers while the torturer hurls the whip over his head and delivers the first strike.

I jolt with pain as a red welt springs across Noah's back, diagonally slicing the dragon in half. I can't believe the blue belt doesn't make a sound, not even a grunt.

The second lash comes, turning flesh into a red X with blood streaming from the wounds Cringing, I clutch my fists across my chest, shaking. Tears stream from my eyes.

This punishment is senseless. Noah did nothing to deserve such mistreatment. And I did nothing except defend him—and I would have done so for anyone on the dais.

I'm repulsed as the flogging continues. It is all I can do not to drop to my knees and weep while every welt turns into a stream of blood. I clutch my fingers around Amir's arm, forcing myself to watch. Noah stands stoically bearing the punishment until the end when his legs finally give out and he's hanging by his wrists.

"Mercy," a woman shouts from the crowd.

"Aye, mercy," come muffled cries, growing louder until the twentieth lash hisses through the air and rips a streak of blood through Noah's mottled flesh.

Are they kidding? They ask for mercy when it's over?

Smirking, the whipman rolls the braided leather and steps away.

Silence swells through the courtyard with the heaviness of death.

The soldiers release Noah's manacles from the post, sending my friend face-first to the ground. A guard swings back with his boot while I rush forward. "Stop!"

The man-at-arms folds his arms and glares. "This is nay yer concern, lady."

I shove myself between Noah and the fiendish guard and thrust my fists onto my hips. "It is very much my concern." I look for Earl Marshal but he's not man enough to attend a public display of humility. Nor is Lord de Burgh. It doesn't matter. In fact, I can take charge more easily without them here. "Take Sir Noah to my chamber and I will see to his wounds."

The guardsmen exchange glances as if they intend to argue.

It's all I can do not throw a roundhouse kick to the side of his face. Instead, I thrust my hand toward Noah. "This man has gallantly escorted me across all of Christendom for the sole purpose of protecting my virtue. I am quite certain in his present state he is completely and inarguably incapable of taking advantage of me." Stamping my foot, I clench my fists. "Carry him to my chamber immediately!"

Flat on his stomach, Noah glances back from my bed. "Whoa, Genesis, remind me never to piss you off." His voice isn't as husky as usual. I figure he's in a lot of pain and trying not to show it, which is exactly what I'd expect from him.

Using a linen cloth, I carefully work the iodine into the angry and raw marks on his back while he hisses—the only sign of his discomfort. If I thought he was tough before, there's no doubt in my mind now. It makes me sick that his dragon tat looks like a misaligned puzzle.

"Why?" I ask. "Because I'll kill you, or I'll curse you out like a medieval shrew?"

"I think I'm more afraid of the shrew than the warrior. After all, I'm bigger and stronger."

"But you don't have her gift of second sight," says Amir, handing me a tincture of antibiotics.

I take the cup and level it in front of Noah's face. "Let me help you with this."

He rolls to his side and takes it with shaky fingers. "I'm not an invalid."

"No." I shove the stopper back in the iodine bottle. "But you're staying here until you're well enough to put on a shirt."

He raises the cup in toast. "The academy always ensures we get the good stuff. I'll be out of this bed by tomorrow."

I can't help but give him a look. "I'll believe that when I see it."

"The tincture is mega strong," says Amir "They add something to the iodine, too, but don't ask me what it is. All I know is the stuff works better than anything my mom ever used."

I examine the bottle. "Not over the counter, is it?"

Noah takes a sip and makes a sour face. "We can't afford to be laid up. Not when we're on a mission."

"All right," I say. "I'll buy that, but if this stuff works so well, then why isn't it available to everyone?"

"Bureaucratic bullshit," says Noah.

Amir snorts. "What he means is it isn't FDA approved."

"Seriously? Then we're guinea pigs?"

"I don't know about that, but I've used this medicine enough to trust it." Noah drinks down the remaining tincture and coughs. "*Yeee-uck.* It sure would be nice if they did something about the taste."

"Wait." I take the cup and set it on the table. "You can't be too healthy tomorrow or else Earl Marshal will send me to the guillotine."

"Wrong country, wrong era," says Amir.

Groaning, I decide it's his turn for one of my sarcastic eye rolls. "He'll have me put to death and it won't be pretty."

"I'll act sore. Besides, the stuff isn't magic. I *will* be sore." Noah rolls back to his stomach. "I'm starved. Can one of you find something to eat?"

"I'll go." Amir shakes his finger under my nose before he starts for the door. "Remember you're supposed to be a princess. You don't get your own food. You send servants to do it."

I snort. "It makes me feel lazy."

"Well, don't get used to it," says Noah while Amir makes his getaway. "You'll be back to being a lowly white belt in no time."

"I sure hope so." I move to the side of the bed and sweep the hair from his eyes. "If I live."

"You will." He hisses. Yeah, he's in way more pain than he's admitting. "You have a gift."

I tug off my stupid veil. "I've never been so unsure of myself. And traipsing around Winchester Castle pretending I'm a princess makes me feel like a fraud."

"If we had princesses in America you'd be one." He grins—scabbed-over gash and all. Even peering up from his stomach, the dude can still make me melt. How can he affect me so much with a mere look? "Besides, Grand Master Li wouldn't have sent you if he didn't think you could handle it."

Blowing a raspberry, I almost spit out my teeth. Have I finally managed to prove myself? "But you said I'd get everyone killed."

"Forget what I said."

I wedge my butt onto the bed beside him. "That's a little difficult to do now. Why are you so hard on recruits?"

His lips disappear before he lets out a pent-up breath. "Because it destroys me to see anyone get hurt. Man, these missions are brutal. And I feel..."

"What?" I whisper, dying to know what he really feels inside.

"Responsible."

Sighing, I brush my fingers over his forehead and study him. The tough guy pushed my buttons because he didn't want to see me thrown into danger. And though I respect him for his valor, if I've learned nothing else since taking the leap into the dragon's lair, being a time warrior is in my DNA. Not that fending off the Qiang cemented my decision, but I can't imagine myself being anywhere but here at the moment. Yes, I lacked confidence at first, but knowing I can see the Qiang, I can help the cause, makes me feel as if I belong here with Amir and Noah. It's my destiny just as it is in theirs. It is a fact rooted in the core of my soul.

I give his hand a squeeze. "You can only be held responsible for yourself. Your actions. Not mine. Not Amir's. Not anybody's."

"I know." Noah pats his pillow. "Come here."

"Why? I might hurt—"

He grabs my wrist and tugs me forward. "Just do something without a reason for once."

I laugh like a nervous dork as I lean low enough to look directly into his eyes. I don't think I've ever been this aware of him, at least not with my eyes open. I hadn't noticed before, but there are flecks of white in those blues. "Beautiful," I whisper.

He smiles again, while shifting his gaze to my lips. Slowly, he inches toward me until his pillowy-soft mouth connects with mine. But it isn't a bursting, steamy kiss of fleeting passion like the last one. This time, he takes his time, gradually parting my lips with a warm tongue while threading his fingers through my hair.

I sigh as his tongue starts to dance with mine. His kiss is unhurried, deliberate, and downright intoxicating. A rush of want courses through my body while I move closer, my hand slipping to his hip, careful not to touch his open wounds.

The door creaks and I jolt to my feet. "Hi, Amir," I squeak like a twelve-year-old girl. "That was fast."

Chapter Twenty-One

"Life is really simple, but we insist on making it complicated." - Confucius

Two days have passed since Noah's public whipping and my chamber has become a hub of activity. Because there were so many visitors for the feast and all the bedchambers are in use, Madeline made up a pallet for me. Lord de Burgh has posted his guards outside the room as well as one inside around the clock to ensure Noah doesn't take advantage of me.

My betrothed is so romantic.

Yuck.

It seems like a constant procession of servants is revolving in and out as well, bringing food, water, wood for the fire. And, of course, Madeline has been told not to let me out of her sight.

I'm sure de Burgh has everything to do with the added activity. After all, what prospective groom wouldn't be a little disgruntled when his fiancée is taking care of a young, totally hot knight in her bedchamber?

If Amir was annoyed by catching us kissing, he hasn't had a chance to voice his dissent. But the worst thing at the moment is, once again, I've lost all sense of the Qiang, and that is making us edgy.

"Aargh!" Noah arches his back as I apply the iodine solution. Since my bottle ran out, I'm using his. "I've had enough of that stuff, okay?"

I guess even the toughest dudes lose it after a while.

At the foot of the bed, Amir crosses his arms. "Just let her finish," he barks.

I take a close look at the lash wounds. They're angry red and scabbing over, and thankfully I don't see any signs of infection. Nonetheless, the blue belt's capacity for being a good patient has run its course. In short, the air in my chamber is filled with angst, we're frustrated that the mission has stalled, and if Noah weren't flat on his stomach in bed I think the three of us would go a few rounds.

Madeline answers a knock at the door.

"Good afternoon." De Burgh steps inside as I finish applying the iodine solution.

"My lord," I greet him. Though he visited twice yesterday, this is the first time he's been to my chamber today.

"If it's not your dashing fiancé," Noah mumbles.

Frowning, the baron's gaze shifts to the bed. "And how is the knight faring?"

"I'd be a hell of a lot better if I were in the courtyard sparring."

I set the cloth on the table. "I'd say he's bad-tempered at best."

De Burgh offers his elbow. "Well, my dear, I think perhaps ye might do well with a stroll through the gardens."

Chewing my lip, I look to Noah. I really don't want to leave him, even though he's turned into a salty ogre.

The blue belt flicks his hand. "Don't mind me. Go on and get some air."

"You might as well," Amir agrees. "I'll watch the sore-headed martyr for a while."

Reluctantly, I place my hand in the crux of de Burgh's elbow. "Thank you."

I might not want to marry him, but the baron did stand up to Earl Marshal on my behalf. Besides, if I don't keep up with the pretense of being a princess betrothed to this guy, I have no doubt the king will arrest us and have us all hung, drawn, and quartered.

We step into the gardens manicured with beds of flowers and rows of hedges and I take in a reviving breath which helps to lighten my mood. "Goodness, I did need some air."

"I thought as much." His Lordship picks a purple flower and twirls it between his pinchers. "Though I did not agree with yer decision to allow the Knight Templar to convalesce in yer chamber, I do understand yer attachment to the fellow, especially after he took yer punishment."

I finger the dagger lashed to my arm beneath my sleeve. "Sir Noah and Sir Amir have behaved honorably toward me. I trust them both more than I trust my own father." I say this because as far as de Burgh knows, it was Al-Adil who betrayed my trust in the first place.

"I would think no less of Templars. They take their vows of chastity very seriously."

"Yes," I say, swiping a hand over my mouth.

De Burgh stops and waves the flower beneath my nose—it's more like a stem with several tiny buds. "Do ye know what this is?"

"No, but it smells nice."

"My mother thought so, as well. She had the servants place vases of lavender all around the castle when I was a boy—at least when they were in bloom. She dried them, as well, saying a home infused with lavender will always be blessed."

I take the flower and inhale the fragrance once again. "It's really nice."

De Burgh rubs the blooms between his fingers, then holds them to my nose. "They're more aromatic when they're crushed."

"Oh." My eyes pop. "That is fragrant."

He gives me a wink—one that reminds me of a dirty old man and I suddenly remember how much I do not want to marry a father figure. Turning away, I continue down the path.

I consider running as he follows, wishing he'd leave me alone. Sure, in his time, it's normal for a wizened knight to marry a teenager, but it's sleazy and sick where I come from. "I cannot stop thinking about how lovely ye looked in the lavender wimple on the eve of the Whitsun feast. Ye do know you have intoxicating eyes."

I watch the stones pass beneath my feet, staring anywhere but de Burgh's face. He's buttering me up, I know it and if he tries to kiss me I'm going to knee him where it counts. He might be a nice guy, but I'm about as attracted to him as I am to a slug.

"I take it ye're not accustomed to compliments," he says.

"Not exactly." I don't usually get many compliments...except from Rex...maybe Ziana, and a few from Noah of late.

"Well, ye'll grow accustomed to them after we're wed."

I trip and stumble. By the way my toe throbs, they must have put a boulder in the middle of the pathway.

"Do ye miss yer home?"

Stepping outside with my intended is proving a bad choice. "Yes."

"I'd venture that's where ye learned to wield a sword."

"I did."

"It seems rather odd, a royal woman becoming proficient."

"All of my father's children are taught to fight from a young age, both male and female." Yep. I'm living a lie that gets deeper by the day.

De Burgh watches me out of the corner of his eye. "I must remember to keep a tight inventory of my weapons when we argue."

I chuckle, imagining throwing daggers if I actually do end up marrying him, which may happen if we hang around in this time period much longer.

The baron smiles as well. I'm glad he's not an ogre like the king, or even like Earl Marshal. "If only I'd had ye in my army at Normandy I mightn't have spent ten years trying to win back the king's French holdings."

"Ten years?" God, I was six when he started. If I thought there was a void between our generations before, I'm doubly aware of it now.

A breeze picks up. More like a wind. It whips my veil and it cuts through my dress as if I've jumped into an ice bath. Gasping, I reach inside my sleeve and wrap my fingers around the dagger as I turn in place. Even with the wind, an instant chill puts me on red alert.

A shadow moves behind the hedge.

Adrenaline darts through my veins as I sprint toward the end of the row, drawing my knife from its hiding place.

"Princess!" de Burgh calls after me, his weapons clanking as he follows. Ignoring him, I charge head-on for a stone fence, raise my skirts, and hurdle it. To the left, the shadow catches my eye. I chase it beneath an awning, it's dark and as I reach a solid wall, I don't see anyone.

"Aargh!" I groan, turning in place.

"My lady," says de Burgh, gasping for breath. "W-what made ye rush away as if ye were being chased by a demon?"

"Not chased but chasing." I look beyond him but see no one but the princes, Henry and Richard, riding their ponies. Henry waves and I shudder.

De Burgh's mouth tightens in a grim line. "Earl Marshal's fears are founded."

"No they are not." I sheathe the dagger. "I thought I saw..." God, what do I say? Can I tell him?

"What, pray tell?"

No. Telling de Burgh anything about our mission will put my life and the lives of my teammates at risk. "The man at the banquet—the one I killed?"

"Yes."

"I think he might not have been alone."

Alarm flashes across the baron's face. "Is the king in danger? Why did ye not say something earlier?"

"I-I can't be certain. And after Earl Marshal accused me of sorcery, I needed to be sure before I jumped to conclusions." God, I sound like an idiot.

"I must inform the king at once."

I hold up my palms. "Tell him I believe there *may* be another threat."

"My lord!" calls a servant, hastening toward us. "The king has decreed court will move to Windsor on the morrow."

"'Tis a good thing as well, what with danger lurking within the walls of Winchester." De Burgh clasps the man's shoulder. "Assemble my men. There may be an assassin in our midst and the best way to trap an interloper is in the open. I'm off to seek council with Earl Marshal forthwith."

"I hope you're right," I whisper under my breath.

"What was that, my lady?" the baron asks.

"Um...will we be traveling to Windsor come morning?"

"Indeed we will." He takes my hands and pulls me right in front of him. "And there we will wed, my love. I must spirit ye away to my castle in Kent. Far away from the treachery here."

I try to turn my face, but he plants a sloppy kiss on the side of my mouth. "Go. Gather yer things. Ye and yer knights will join the de Burgh retinue."

"Yes, my lord," I say, wiping my mouth and starting away, praying Noah will be well enough to ride.

愛

I should never assume anything when it comes to Noah. The next day, he's dressed and leading the way to the stables. Though he winces when he heaves up on the strap to buckle the saddle's girth.

I feel his pain as I rub my hand down the destrier's mane. "Will you be able to ride?"

"Did I ever say I couldn't take a little pain?"

"No, but your back looks like hamburger meat and you're going to have to rename your tat to the fractured dragon."

"Ha." He cuts me a look. "I like it, white belt."

Behind us, Earl Marshal strides into the stable, his expression grim as usual. "By the king's orders, ye are to remain at the rear of the royal procession."

De Burgh skirts around him, panting as if he's been running. "My men will take up the rear with the princess and her guards, not to worry, my dear. And *ye* will ride with me in my coach."

Noah's eyes narrow as his jaw twitches.

"Are we under arrest, Your Lordship?" asks Amir, leading his horse out of a stall.

"Presently, no." The earl rubs his hand over the pommel of his sword. "However, after learning there may be another assassin in our midst, the king will take no chances."

Smoothing his fingers around the crest embroidered on his tunic, de Burgh adds, "And it seems there are those who believe ye may be the assassin's target, my dear."

"Me?" I was wondering when they'd come to that conclusion. Medieval minds are a quandary.

The baron takes my hand, bows, and kisses it. "All the more reason for ye to be safely under my protection."

Now both sides of Noah's jaw are twitching.

I try to tug my fingers away, but de Burgh holds tight. "Sir Amir, I want ye and Sir Noah to flank the wagon. If the Mamluks have sent another assassin, he ought to be easy to spot in the open."

"God willing," grumbles The Marshal under his breath. "But know this, Princess, if any harm should befall the king, I will hold ye and these Templars responsible. And I will not be lenient as I was before."

I finally tug my fingers away from my enthusiastic betrothed. "We're here in good faith, my lord. We have no hidden schemes."

"So say you." William Marshal, the man whom history loves, turns on his heel and marches out.

"Tyrant," I grumble under my breath.

"Do not fret, my love." De Burgh urges me out the double doors. "The earl is responsible for the protection of the king. Should anything go awry while we are on procession, he will be held accountable."

I look out over the hundreds of men-at-arms readying themselves to march. There is no way the Qiang will attack now. The odds are definitely not in their favor.

Atop the wall-walk, trumpets sound while King John leads Isabella from the tower. I crane my neck to better see the royals. "Where are the children?"

De Burgh bows along with everyone else. "They stay here with the Bishop of Winchester and their tutors."

"You mean they don't travel with their father?"

"Oh, no. Children are frail. 'Tis far too dangerous to take them about the kingdom. And John never stays in one place for more than a fortnight or so. The queen will remain here as well, given her condition." De Burgh arches an eyebrow, looking up at me with a curious glint in his eye. "Ye cannot tell me yer father took ye along when he traveled about Egypt."

"Um...of course not. Besides, Father has many wives and dozens and dozens of children."

"I'd surmised."

"Oh?"

"When a king has dozens upon dozens of children, it is of no consequence for him to send one to make peace with his greatest adversary. Even a young woman as beautiful as ye."

"Ahem." Noah clears his throat behind us. "Where is your coach, my lord?"

"To the rear of the dogs."

"Dogs?" I ask.

De Burgh points to a group of foot soldiers, all leading large dogs by torturous-looking collars. "The king's greyhounds."

"Is it necessary to restrain them so savagely?" I ask.

"Oh, my dear, ye do have a kind heart. Unusual for an Egyptian warrior princess." He offers me his elbow. "Will ye never cease to surprise me?"

Poor man. If he only knew the surprises to come.

In front of the dogs is a wagon cage carrying falcons. The birds have leather hoods over their heads and their legs are tied to a roost. *Savage*.

"Do we bring along sheep, chickens, and goats as well?" I ask.

"Not this day. The royal procession will only camp one night on the road to Windsor."

"Then we'll arrive tomorrow?"

"Aye. Late afternoon should all proceed as planned." He leads me toward a wagon covered with blue canvas and gestures inside. "My lady."

I take a moment to survey the castle walls, breathing deeply and willing myself into meditation. Something here is unsettling and I look to Amir. "I feel like we shouldn't be leaving."

"Why is that?" asks de Burgh.

Because I can't focus.

"But this is the path set before you," says Amir. He's so good at being cryptic. Me, on the other hand, I'm more like Noah. I never beat around the bush. I just want to find the assassin, stop him, and go home.

I scrape my teeth over my bottom lip while I climb inside the wagon. There is a low bench covered with silk pillows that looks a whole lot more comfortable than sharing a horse with Noah. When de Burgh climbs in after me, I decide I'm wrong about comfort. I long for Noah's arms around me as he navigates the reins. I long for the beat of his heart against my back, the warmth of his breath teasing my neck.

Silk curtains shroud the windows and I pull them aside. As the baron asked, Noah is already mounted beside the wagon and his gaze shifts my way. I want to blow him a kiss or mouth, "I love you", but I just smile and waggle my fingers in a tiny wave. "How is your back, sir knight?"

"Feels like a nest of angry hornets have used it for target practice."

"He's doing rather well," says de Burgh, gently tugging me back on the bench. "I'm surprised he's able to sit a horse."

"So am I." I let the curtain drop, praying he makes it.

Chapter Twenty-Two

"Never give a sword to a man who can't dance."
- Confucius

I see a child riding a pony with another close behind. The first sits taller than his companion. They're laughing, racing, and jumping their mounts. I'm laughing, too, until a cold sweat breaks out over my skin. A cloaked man leaps from the brush. He's wielding a Japanese sword and it flickers blue as he slices the razor-sharp blade aimed at the child's neck.

"No! Noooooooo!"

My throat burns with my panicked screams. I jolt up in the blackness of night, sweat streaming from my brow made colder by the English night air.

"Genesis!" Amir's urgent but hushed voice comes through the flap of the tent de Burgh provided for my comfort.

"We have to go back," I croak, shaking. Dark shadows dance around me and I can't make out the definition of Amir's face. "They're not after anyone on our list."

"What in the name of our Lord has happened?" demands de Burgh as the hazy light from his lantern shines through the gap. "Sir, if ye dared lay a hand on her—"

I spring to my feet, my head smacking the canvas of my tent. "My knights would never think of such a thing!"

"My dear." De Burgh leans inside with the lantern. "Whatever happened?"

"I'm sorry. I just had a bad dream." I'm still shaking, but now I know where the Qiang will attack. My gaze shifts between my companions, trying to alert them. "Please, my lord. We must all return to our beds."

"Are ye certain, my love? I could sit beside ye until ye fall asleep."

"No!" I say far too forcefully.

In a blink, suspicion fills de Burgh's eyes.

"I'm flustered is all. I-I would prefer a moment alone to pray if you will allow it, my lord." Turning my head, I cringe. *Will he leave already*?

The corners of Noah's lips turn up and he swipes a hand down his mouth. Blast him. I'm trying my best to play my part and I've already spoken to de Burgh about worshiping Allah. I thought the praying idea was pretty quick thinking on my part.

"As ye wish," says the baron. He kisses my forehead then turns to my companions. "I expect the two of ye to remain awake and vigilant."

"Yes, my lord," they repeat in unison.

"And when we arrive at Windsor, yer guardian duties will be over." De Burgh swings his lantern between the two of them. "I suspect the pair of ye are anxious to return to yer order. And mark me, it is past time to do so."

Noah splays his fingers at his sides while he and Amir follow the baron out.

Things are growing more precarious by the minute. I watch from the opening in the tent flap as de Burgh walks off, his lamp light fading as he goes. Damn, now several other guardsmen are up as well.

"What's the deal?" whispers Amir. The two of them are still outside as they were told.

I'm ready to jump out of my skin. We can't stay here any longer. "We've been wrong all along. The Qiang aren't after John or Marshal or Langton. They're after *Henry*."

"A child?" asks Noah, too loudly if you ask me.

"Keep your voice down," I say, pulling down the flap to the tent and pretending to go back to bed. But I kneel right by the entrance where they can hear me. "Think. It makes all the sense in the world. Sure, King John signs the Magna Carta but, two weeks later, he and the rebel barons are at war again and the document isn't resurrected until Henry takes the throne next year. Don't you see? If Henry is assassinated, the Magna Carta will be dead forever."

"Holy shit, she's right!" Noah whisper-shouts.

"There's no time to waste," Amir growls through the canvas.

"I told you I felt something in the garden yesterday. There was a shadow and then I saw Henry and Richard riding their ponies. Dammit, I should have listened to my inner voice."

"We should have listened to you after you came upstairs."

I did try to tell them, but there were too many people in my chamber. Worse, I wasn't sure about the sign. God, I'm so inept at this. What if my inexperience *does* get us all killed?

"Is the camp settling?" I ask. "Can we slip away?"

"Not yet," says Amir. "De Burgh's men are watching us."

"Genesis." Noah's voice is lower now, barely discernable. "I want you to stay there—"

"Here? No! We can't be separated."

"For now," he growls. "As soon as everyone goes back to sleep, Amir and I will sneak over and quietly saddle the horses. Do you think you can slip out the back of your tent in about a half-hour?"

I scoot back and test the rear canvas. I can lift it about six inches but ought to be able to get it higher if I can wrench the stakes out of the ground. "Yes."

"After you slip out, skirt along the tree line. Carefully. The last thing we need is for you to trip. It's darker than ink out here."

"Okay."

I crawl back and reach under the skirt of the tent, my fingers combing through damp grass as I blindly feel for the rear stake. Brushing it with my fingertips, I push my head against the canvas to gain a few more inches—far enough to work it back and forth.

How could I have been so stupid? Every time I saw Henry, I got a chill. Why the hell can't I pay attention to the signs like I did when the assassin tried to kill Noah? But that sensation was so incredibly intense. In comparison, the chills were much less noticeable with Henry.

If I make it back to the academy, I'm asking Grand Master Li for lessons—at least more information on what to expect when I'm thrust into insanity. How dare he send a complete novice on a mission as important as this?

Worse, what if we're too late? What if I fail? What happens if the Qiang win?

"Damn it, Genesis," I spit through my teeth in a heated whisper. "Failure is not an option!"

I bear down and tug up with everything I have. The spike inches up a little—just enough for me to exit. I scurry to the front of the tent and raise the flap slightly to see if Noah and Amir are still there.

Thank goodness they're gone.

Has a half-hour passed?

Not likely.

I sit on the edge of my blanket and drum my fingers on my knees. Waiting is torture. I meditate and that helps, but I'm way past ready to bolt.

None of us has a watch. What are they going to do? Cuss me out because the moon hasn't shifted enough? Screw that!

I'm going.

Quickly, I slide my feet into my shoes, grab my satchel and wrap my cloak around my shoulders.

I hope the boys are working fast because I'm too jumpy to wait any longer. I slip out through the gap I've made. Crouching at the edge of my tent, I scan the campsite. A soft light glows from the fire pit. I see no one else until the wagon catches my eye. A pair of guards are chatting quietly—probably the two on duty.

I pick up my skirts and tiptoe toward the horses.

Stepping on a twig, it snaps loud enough to wake the dead.

Help!

Ducking, I hide in the shadows. The guards look my way as my heart thunders in my ears.

"Did ye hear that?" one asks.

The other shrugs. "Probably the wind."

As he speaks, a breeze rustles through the leaves above and I let out a breath, not moving until the guards lose interest and resume their conversation. But this time, I move on my tiptoes.

"Hey, guys," I whisper, barely able to make out Amir and Noah through the shadows where the horses are tethered about fifty feet outside of the camp.

"Perfect timing."

And I was worried about the movement of the moon? I step near the destrier and let him sniff my hand to ensure I don't spook him. "How did you get past the guards?"

Noah clasps his fingers together and makes a step, giving me a leg up. "Amir told them he needed to take a leak while I slipped around the back."

"Smart."

"Let's hope so," says our mastermind. "Once we're on the road, it will be next to impossible to double back to Windsor."

My gut squeezes. I hadn't considered that. "I'm not wrong," I say as Noah mounts behind me, his grunt of pain barely discernable.

"We're counting on it." Reaching around my waist, Noah takes up the reins. "We're walking out of here quiet as a mouse."

I smooth my finger over the cross tattooed on his hand and lean against the wall of his chest. I no longer care about the buckles. It's so comfortable riding with him now. I really missed this when I was in the wagon with de Burgh.

"Know what I'm going to do as soon as we get home?" he asks, his voice deep, familiar, and oddly comforting.

"What's that?"

"I'm giving you riding lessons."

Clapping a hand over my mouth and nose, I stifle a laugh. "I hope that's a promise."

愛

The pre-dawn sky hovers, shrouded in cobalt as the spire of Winchester Cathedral etches black on the horizon. We've ridden hard and the horses are spent. I pat the destrier's neck. "Just a little longer, big fella."

"I've been thinking," says Amir as the stench from the town wafts over us with a gust of wind. "We might run into trouble if we try to ride through the main gates."

"Because we just left?" I ask.

"Not only did we leave, we were told to keep to the rear under the watchful eye of Lord de Burgh. They don't trust us."

"Look over there," says Noah, pointing to a farmer's cottage and a man illuminated by a lantern swinging in his hand. "I'll bet he can help us."

"He's hitching an ox to a hay wagon." I crane my neck for a better view. "What if he's like everyone else and doesn't believe us?"

Amir pats his satchel. "We still have coin."

Noah cues the horse toward the farmer. "Or we can give him our horses."

I elbow his ribs. "That's dumb, how will we make it to Stonehenge without horses?"

"We'll need to worry about that later. If we can hitch a ride with our friendly farmer, then he'll have to stable the horses for us anyway. No self-respecting peasant is going to haul hay with a destrier in his prime."

Amir trots after us. "True, but Genesis is right. If we don't ride in, we'll have to find a different way out of the castle."

I don't like it. These horses have carried us everywhere. "How far is Stonehenge from Winchester?" I ask.

"It's west." Amir is rarely ever that sketchy. Cleary he doesn't know. Not exactly, anyway.

"It can't be too far," says Noah. "We've been traveling west since we left London—and Britain is just an island."

"An island with sixty million people or so," I add. "It's not that small if you don't have a car."

"Hello, friend!" Amir hollers, putting an end to our conversation. The brown belt does the talking as usual. It turns out the farmer is no fan of King John even though Amir is very convincing about needing to stop a murder. The man is obviously poorer than dirt and I swear by his reaction he'd give away his firstborn in payment for two sturdy horses. Moreover, he's not only smuggling us through the city gates, he's taking us all the way to the castle stables where he's delivering his load of hay. In fact, the man delivers a load of hay to the stables three times a week.

As we hide under the hay, I pray nothing will go wrong.

"Ha-chew!" Good Lord, I think the sneeze comes from Amir.

"Ye'd best not do that after we reach the road," says the farmer, cracking his whip.

"Allergies," Amir whispers. "I'll cover my nose. Don't worry."

My nose is tickling, too. "We all better cover our noses."

"I'll take the wagon around the rear of the stables. Ye'll have to stay put until I tell ye 'tis clear, else we'll all end up in irons."

"No sneezing," I growl.

The journey into the city takes forever. Everyone in the county must know our friendly farmer because he stops and talks as if he has all day. And if I thought horses were slow, oxen move at a snail's pace in comparison.

"Do not shift a fraction of an inch," the farmer growls as he pulls the wagon to a stop.

The ground beyond crunches. "Good morn, Danny."

"'Tis a fine morn."

"Ha-chew," comes a muffled sneeze from Amir while my heart roars in my ears.

"What was that?" asks the man.

"Nothing overmuch. I've a wee bit of a sniffle. Margaret's brewing again."

"Oh, aye. If ye're ailing, do ye need some help unloading?"

"No, no. Go on about yer business. I'm feeling well, especially now I've had some air."

It's a good thing I have my hand over my mouth because the air in the medieval towns I've been to is anything but sweet. And the stable reeks with manure. Heck, I know why they call hay sweet—the saying has to be from the Middle Ages, because it smells so much better than most other things.

"Very well, then," says Danny. "Just give us a holler if ye need anything."

"Will do."

The crunching of the footsteps fades.

"'Tis clear," whispers the farmer. "But I'd best not hear of any skullduggery."

As I sit up and push away the hay, Amir is already hopping off the wagon. "I give you my word, we are here to stop a crime, not to commit one."

"I just hope it's not too late," whispers Noah, his face is pale. The ride must have been hard on his back. "Now where to?"

I wish I was certain, but all I know is the same evil feeling that woke me up last night is stirring in my blood to a boil. "Follow me." At a crouch, I skirt around the stable buildings, heading for the field beyond the garden. "Henry was riding his pony in my dream."

Reaching inside my sleeve, I draw my dagger. I'd prefer a sword like Amir and Noah, but there's no time. I lead them along the hedge to the place where I saw the two boys. But the field is empty aside from sheep grazing in the grass.

"Damn. I was sure he'd be here."

Amir looks up the towering wall of the castle. "Now what?"

"We have to find a direct route inside," Noah growls through his teeth.

I rest my fingers on his arm. "Maybe you should stay here."

He bats my hand away. "Have you lost your mind?"

"I can tell you're hurting by the tightness at the corners of your mouth."

"Save it for your grandma. I'll worry about my back after the mission."

"Yeah," Amir agrees. "He's over the worst of it."

"Speak for yourself." Noah's whisper is barely audible, but I'm standing close enough to catch it even if Amir doesn't.

"Once we're inside, where to?" asks the brown belt.

"Give me a minute." I sheathe my dagger and step into the corner where I saw the shadow. Placing my hands on the stone wall, I close my eyes and force myself to concentrate.

"Come on, Genesis," says Noah. "Time's ticking."

I whip around and give him a shove. "Do you think I don't know? It's not like I have a virtual reality device strapped across my eyeballs. Now shut up and give me a little room."

The two guys look at each other and shake their heads. Why in God's name do they assume I have all the answers? I squeeze my eyes shut and concentrate, but I don't get anything. Damn! Was I wrong about returning to Winchester?

Have I ruined everything?

Where are you, Henry?

I summon all seven chakras, focusing on my root, sacral, solar plexus, heart, throat, third eye, and crown. I breathe slowly while the vortex of meditation envelops me and allows me to see only one thing. *Henry.* The boy who will be king. The child who, with William Marshal, brings the Magna Carta to life forever.

By the time I open my eyes, I'm flooded by a sense of spiritual unity. I'm calm but more confident than I've been since setting foot in King John's England. I turn to my comrades and take a deep breath. "Let's go."

Chapter Twenty-Three

*"By three methods we may learn wisdom. First,
by reflection which is noblest; second, by imitation,
which is easiest; third, by experience, which is the
bitterest." - Confucius*

Checking my ten and two to ensure we're not being
watched, I lead the way through the servant's
entrance. After being outside, I can barely see a
thing in the dimly lit corridor, but my ears are honed
so sharply, I swear I can hear an ant crawling up the
wall. But it's still too risky to proceed until my vision
adjusts. Caution takes over and I hold up my hand
and signal the guys to stop.

"Princess Genesis?"

Before recognition sets in, my heart nearly leaps
out of my chest. Thank God it's her and not some
rankled guard. I take in a calming breath.
"Madeline!" I chirp, sounding like I've just found a
long-lost family member. "I'm so glad we found
you."

She steps under a wall sconce, illuminating her
concerned expression. "Why have you returned, my
lady?"

I want to grab her shoulders, look her in the eye
and insist she stop calling me that, but I must keep
up with the charade for a little longer. Nonetheless, I
do plant my hands on her upper arms and firmly

squeeze my fingers and level my gaze. "What I am about to ask is a matter of life and death. Do you understand?"

Her eyes flicker to Noah as she nods.

"You must keep it to yourself—at least until we've determined the danger is over."

"Danger?" she squeaks.

I grip a little harder to ensure I have her attention. "We believe there is an assassin in the castle."

"Here? Now? But ye're as aware as I the king has gone to Windsor—"

"The assassin isn't after the king," growls Noah.

"What's the fastest way to the nursery?" I ask. "A route where we won't run into guards who want to stop us."

"The assassin is after the children?"

"Henry," says Amir.

"But Henry isn't in the nursery. He's with Master Lawson in the king's apartments. The solar. I-I just came from there."

"Will you show us?" I ask.

The maid nods. "This way."

As we climb the spiral stairs, the higher we go, the more my skin crawls.

When a shrill scream echoes through the stairwell, my heart slams against my chest.

Are we too late?

Shoving Madeline aside, I tear off my veil and run. "Henry!"

"Help!" cries a muffled voice.

"Move!" Noah races ahead of me and kicks open the door.

Three Qiang stalk toward the tutor. The slight man trembles, barely able to hold on to his sword as blood streams from his temple. Beneath the table, tiny Henry clutches a child-sized sword. But his hands are sure and solid.

The assassins whip around and face us, brandishing medieval swords rather than the Samurai I saw in my nightmare. One smirks at Noah. "You've met your match, Jones. You won't be going home this time."

Though he's speaking a foreign dialect, the earpiece translates and I understand him perfectly.

"In your dreams, asshole." The corner of Noah's mouth ticks up. "Leave now or I'll kill you first."

Before I blink, all three attack. Noah deflects, buying a second for Amir and me to race through the doorway. The smallest of the Qiang leaps in front of me. Attacking like a viper, she goes for my jugular, aiming to end this quickly. I duck, positive she takes a lock of hair as the weapon hisses above me.

The fight is on with weapons clanging, but I can't check my teammates to see how they're doing. With a full-length sword, the girl's reach is much longer than mine with only a dagger. She knows it, too, hacking at me as I back to the far end of the solar, barely able to defend myself with my measly knife. I grab a chair and throw it at her when a battle-axe on the wall above the mantel catches my eye. Transferring my dagger to my left hand, I use the next seat as a launching pad. Sailing through the air, I rip the axe from its blackened iron nails, land on the far side of the hearth, and face my opponent in a crouch.

"Bring it, sister," I seethe, steeling myself for her next attack.

She chuckles with a deep, eerie cackle sauntering toward me. "You dare to fight me? I will murder you."

With a feral scream, she spins, aiming for my legs. My mind's eye sees it coming and I block with the axe, but her blade hacks through the wooden shaft. No wonder the axe was on the wall. The timber is so dry, the handle is as brittle as a matchstick.

Lunging in, I blitz with the dagger, but she's fast enough to deflect.

She bares her teeth and, with a burst of speed, the witch unleashes the fury of hell. I barely escape the thrusts of her sword, moving too close to Amir who's neck deep, fending off a guy a head taller.

With nowhere to go, I leap onto the table. But I can't stay there. Hopping again, I stretch for the iron chandelier suspended by chains. Thank God it holds as I raise my feet, swinging and landing on the far side next to the table. The tutor has taken refuge beneath and passes up the hilt his sword.

Gripping the handle, I barely catch sight of Henry's terrified eyes while I prepare for the next assault.

The enemy girl mirrors me as I vault onto the table. Snarling, she launches herself across the top, wielding her weapon in both hands, pointed downward, ready to plunge through my chest.

I don't even breathe as I take a step off the line, swinging the sword fast enough to catch her hip.

"Aargh!" she screams as she lands askew, stumbling and teetering on the edge of the board.

Leaping, I throw out a split kick aimed to knock her to the floor but she counters with a backward flip, landing smack in the middle of the table. Blood from her hip splatters the wood, but she doesn't give it a glance as I prepare, holding my weapon in *en garde* position.

I go for it first, our blades clashing with blurring speed. Harder. Faster. Deadlier than I've ever imagined. This girl is better than me and if she gets inside my guard I'm dead.

"Aargh!" she screams again as she drops to her knees, blood pooling around her.

I skitter away to the far end of the table as it dawns on me. Henry has just sliced through her Achilles tendon.

Still on her knees, she glares and sneers, raising her weapon. "You will die."

"Not today," I seethe.

But I can't kill her—not unless she attacks first. It would be like killing a wounded soldier on a battlefield. I'm a warrior. Not a murderer.

Ahead, Noah is backed over a chair by his opponent. Before the bastard can lunge in with a killing strike, I throw my dagger, hitting him in the throat.

The girl on the table shrieks as she draws back her blade, aiming to kill the big blue belt.

I lunge with a sideways attack, but Noah rolls, turns, and drives his blade into her heart.

In the mayhem, I look for Amir. He's standing over his lifeless opponent. The brown belt pans his sword across the solar. "God strike me dead. It's over."

"Damn," Noah curses. He's panting and the back of his tunic is soaked with blood. "Maybe I'm not healed yet."

Sheathing his sword, Amir nods. "Then we'd better not waste any more time."

Peering under the table, I return the weapon to Master Lawson. "Thanks for thinking fast. I wouldn't have survived without this." My gaze shifts to Henry, the future King of England. I offer my hand. "Hey there, young prince. You were very brave. I am duly impressed by your attack."

As he stands, he grips my hand with the force of a vise and wraps his arms around me. "Y-ye are?"

"Absolutely. You injured the enemy and that gave me the upper hand."

He's shaking now, his eyes shifting. "But I was afraid," he whispers.

"We all were afraid," says Noah, patting the boy's shoulder.

"You have the heart of a lion." I run my free hand along Henry's back as I usher him out of the room. "You saved me."

He's still clinging to me with the little sword in his fist. "Who were those people?"

Amir catches my eye as I consider my answer. "They were sent here by the Mamluk." It's a fib, but close enough to the truth. "And they'll never bother you again."

I drop to one knee and rest my hand on his shoulder. "One day, you will be a great and powerful king. You will do good deeds in the eyes of your kingdom. From this day on, I want you to remember that a man with goodness in his heart will always conquer a man with evil."

"Will ye be here to advise me?"

"No, but Earl Marshal will. He is an honest and loyal servant to the crown and his experience both in battle and at court will be of great value."

"But he's so old."

"Do not confuse advanced age with feebleness of mind. With age comes wisdom, and His Lordship has it in spades."

Henry's bottom lip pushes out just any other little boy would do. Except this one has just fought for his life in his own home. Even more, this one will be one of the greatest monarchs ever to live.

"Promise me you will listen to the Earl of Pembroke," I say like a mom.

Henry turns his toe inward. "I promise...but I'd rather it if ye were with me, too. Ye're smart, and pretty, and better at sword fighting than most of the men in Father's army."

"You've won an admirer," Master Lawson says as he steps beside us.

A clatter comes from the stairwell as guards pour into the passageway. "Release the prince or meet yer end!" bellows the man-at-arms.

The tutor steps in front of the guards' lances. "Stop, ye fools! The princess and her knights have saved Prince Henry from the Mamluks."

Henry faces them as well, shielding me with his little body. "He speaks true. If the princess and her men had not arrived when they did, I would have met my end and Richard would be the heir—no thanks to ye. In my opinion, ye are all a mob of laggards."

I force a frown, trying my best not to laugh out loud.

The man-at-arms lowers his weapon and walks to the solar doorway. "God on the cross, how did those assassins spirit inside the castle walls?"

"I certainly didn't see them," says another.

Amir claps the man on the shoulder. "Send for Earl Marshal straightaway and tell him what has happened. And do not forget to let him know Henry is safe under your command."

The boy tugs Amir's tunic. "But ye and Princess Genesis saved me. Not the king's men."

"That's right." I muss his hair. "However, the Winchester guardsmen will see to your safety now."

My attention is drawn away by Noah. His hands are planted on the table and his face is blanched. I rush in and slide under his arm. "Are you cut?" I want to refer to the Qiang leader as a bastard, but not in front of the kid.

"Yeah."

Amir moves under Noah's other side. "We're taking him to Her Grace's guest chamber."

"Aye, sir," says the man-at-arms. "I'll send up a healer."

"I'll take care of him," I say. There's no way on earth I'll entrust Noah's health to anyone who hasn't attended modern medical school.

愛

Amir manages to peel off Noah's clothes before he drops face-first onto the bed. He has a six-inch long gash on his hip and half the welts on his back have opened and are bleeding.

"We never should have traveled with the king's caravan," I say, taking the last of the bandages from my satchel.

"We had no choice." Amir grabs a bottle of antibiotic powder. "Aside from the queen, every man on our list was heading for Windsor—and Langton would have joined them there as well. It was the best decision we could have made with the information we had."

"I don't buy it." I douse the cloth with iodine solution and set to work. "I need more practice. Next time we're not going to cut it so close. And next time, no one is going to get hurt."

"So says the novice on her virgin mission." Amir's sleeve hikes up while he mixes the tonic. His wrist is purple and swollen.

"You'd better ice that."

"Right, I'll just head to the mountains and search for an ice cave." He tosses the spoon on the table. "Don't worry about me. We just need to get the big fella fixed up so we can head out of here."

"Remember you traded our horses to get inside this place."

"Dammit." He helps Noah drink. "We have some coin left. I'll go down and find a couple of nags."

"How about one for me?"

"Can you ride?"

"Probably. I've spent enough time watching Noah."

Amir heads for the door. "I'll see what our money can buy."

I look at my patient's back and exhaustion weighs on my muscles like wet blankets. "He needs rest. Heck, we all need rest after riding all night. Can't we wait until the morning?"

Gripping the latch, Amir shakes his head. "Believe me, now the mission is over it's imperative for us to head for home before someone realizes you're not a princess and we're not knights."

Before I can think of something else to convince him to stay just for tonight, he slips out the door.

"Don't worry 'bout me," Noah mumbles into the pillow. "Though I could use an injection of caffeine about now."

"Coffee," I purr. "A double latte might do the trick."

"Latte?" He snorts. "I'd peg you as one of those sweet, caramel mocha girls."

It's hard to believe he's half-dead and joking. I work in the iodine, barely able to keep my eyes open. "No way. I'd rather have a shot of espresso than the sweet stuff."

"What about beer?" he asks. "Or wine. I imagine you've tasted all kinds of stuff since your dad owns a bar."

"Not me." The welts aren't bleeding as badly toward the small of his back. "Besides being underage, Dad drinks enough for the both of us and then some."

"Sorry."

"Don't be." I move to his hip and press around the wound, examining it.

"Sssssss."

"This needs stitches."

"I thought it might." He raises his head a fraction. "Look in my satchel. I brought a tube of superglue."

"Seriously? Will that get you in trouble?"

"Maybe, but after the last mission I bought a bottle, peeled off the label and brought it anyway."

I find the glue and twist off the cap. "You ready?"

"Just don't get it on your fingers otherwise we'll be stuck together until we get home."

"Good point." I turn in a circle, looking for something to tug his skin with. "I'll use a candle."

"Smart." He snorts. "The first time I saw you I knew you weren't just a pretty face."

"You sure about that?" I ask, applying enough pressure with the candlestick to slightly open the wound. Then I run a thick line of glue across the wound's lower lip and quickly replace the cap. "I thought you hated me."

He chuckles and I wonder what he really thought, or the actual reason he tried to discourage me. If he was Rex I'd ask, but for some reason I'm afraid with Noah. What if he rejects me? What if he says something I can't handle?

I place my fingers a good three inches either side of the laceration and pinch the skin closed, blowing to help dry the glue.

"Would you do that to my back, too?"

"Glue the bits of skin together? Dude, your dragon will still look like mismatched puzzle pieces."

"No, there isn't enough glue to paste my back together. But would you blow on it? Your breath is soothing."

"Oh." My heart flutters a bit as I glance at his face.

"Please?"

"Okay, but I don't want to hear any rumors going around the academy about Genesis giving great blow jobs."

He cracks up, then winces with pain. "Don't make me laugh."

"It wasn't a joke."

"What? Did you get teased at your last school?"

Pursing my lips, I blow on the red-raw lash marks just like he asked. "Sort of. I wasn't popular, that's for sure."

"Neither was I."

"Huh?" I stop blowing for a moment. "I'd think you'd be the coolest guy in school."

"I don't know about that. I kept to myself. Maybe I was a little too arrogant."

Now that I can believe. "So, the kids thought you were stuck up?"

"Yeah." He licks his chapped lips. "And we moved all the time. My dad is a career military man, Marine Colonel Maximillian Jones."

"Wow, I never pegged you as a military brat."

"Military, yes. Brat? My dad would murder any kid who acted like a brat."

He's quiet while I continue pursing my lips and blowing, but I'm going down fast. About to collapse, I snuggle beside him. "You mind if I close my eyes for a minute?"

"You'd better be quick. If I know Amir, he'll be back up here cracking the whip in five minutes."

I cringe. "You need to use a different metaphor."

Noah laces his fingers through mine and kisses the back of my hand. "Know what, Genesis?"

"What?"

"I want you with me on every mission. You did awesome and it's only your first time."

I don't think he could have said anything nicer. "Thanks. That means a lot."

Closing my eyes, I fall asleep almost instantly but I swear only mere seconds pass when someone bolts through the door.

"What is the meaning of this!" booms a deep, angry voice.

Chapter Twenty-Four

"The object of the superior man is truth" -
Confucius

His eyes blazing, de Burgh marches through the doorway thrusting out his arms. "First I learn ye have been instrumental in saving the prince from three Mamluk assassins and now I find ye—a *princess*—on a bed with a knight who has made a solemn vow of chastity?" The baron bellows so loudly, the chandelier overhead tremors. "This is a preposterous state of affairs! How in God's name could ye demean yer station as if ye were a common whore?"

I push to my feet, taking his tirade until he blurted the word whore. "Are you effing serious?" At the moment I can't bring myself to act medieval. "Excuse me, but we rode all night to save the prince. Not to mention, Sir Noah was severely injured in the fight and, after I dressed his wounds, I collapsed beside him."

I saunter forward. "How dare you insult me?"

As de Burgh's gaze shifts to the bed, guilt weighs on my chest until I can hardly take a breath. "There are rules of—"

"But you're right," I say, my shoulders dropping. "I have a few things I need to be honest about."

"Ye're in love with this knight?"

Noah doesn't even budge. Great. Now's the time I need him to stick up for me and I'm on my own. I take a second glance at him and wonder if he slept through the whole thing.

Amir chooses now to appear in the corridor and he's staring at me with one of those "I told you so" expressions.

My attention is brought back to de Burgh as he clears his throat. "Well? What is it ye have to tell me?"

How much can I say? Will I be stuck here forever if I tell the truth? Probably. "Whether or not I'm in love with Sir Noah is not in question. The crux of the matter is I cannot marry you."

The little baron puffs out his chest. "Cannot or will not?"

"Cannot," I say. Amir starts to interject but I hold up my hand and stop him. "Al-Adil of the Ayyubid Dynasty sent us here to stop the Mamluks, but he is not my father."

Rage flashes through de Burgh's eyes as he wraps his fingers around the hilt of his sword. "Lies! How dare ye come into England...into the king's court and claim to be something ye are not?"

"The ruse is my fault, my lord." Amir comes to the rescue regardless of if I want him to or not. "We suspected the Qia—er—the *Mamluks* were planning to attempt to assassinate the king and the only way we thought we could get close to him was to have Genesis impersonate an Ayyubid princess."

De Burgh scowls. "And toy with my heart?"

"Again my fault," Amir says, taking responsibility like a soldier. "I'm the one who decided to offer her hand in marriage. Genesis didn't even know. But I thought it would take the king a few months to find her a suitable husband and—"

"By that time we planned to be long gone." Stepping forward, I grasp His Lordship's hand. "I am truly sorry to have hurt you. It was not my intent."

He smirks. "Ye are terribly young, though yer beauty gave me hope that ye might one day care for a withered soldier such as me."

I give his fingers a squeeze. Yes, I thought of him as a grandfather, but of all the people we've met, he has proven to be the most genuine, most loyal—at least to me. "If I were ready to marry anyone, you would be at the top of my list."

"Except ye are not of noble blood I presume?"

"Not even close."

Amir moves to the bedside and shakes Noah's shoulder. "You awake, dude?"

He doesn't budge.

"No!" I cry, dashing across the floor and pressing my fingers against his carotid.

Amir wipes a cloth across Noah's forehead. "He's lost too much blood."

"We need to get him..." I incline my head toward the door. "You know."

De Burgh's spurs scuff the wooden floorboards as he steps behind me. "Allow me to send for my physician."

I nearly choke. "I don't think—"

"We must take him to a Templar healer." Amir wrings the cloth between his fists. "My lord, how far is it to Stonehenge?"

"The ancient standing stones?"

"Yes."

"I know of no Templar order near there."

"It is not an order, but an old monk who heals lives nearby." It's another lie, but I trust Amir to know what's best. "We must make haste."

"But 'tis a day's ride, near enough. Perhaps a half-day at a fast trot."

Amir takes Noah by the arm and heaves him over his shoulder. "Then we ride immediately."

"Very well," says de Burgh. "My men and I will see ye there safely. We can take the Roman roads until we reach Amesbury."

"No, my lord." I kiss the baron's cheek. "You must leave us and return to the king. In the coming days he will need every ally he has. Earl Marshal was right. I am a seer, and this I can say with absolute certainty."

愛

The horse beneath me snorts, taking gargantuan breaths with his every galloping step. We have to be riding as fast as the knights in the joust. Miles back, my feet fell out of the stirrups and I'm bouncing in the saddle like a cowboy on a bronc.

"There it is!" shouts Amir, holding his reins with one hand and, with the other, gripping the lead line, towing Noah strapped over the back of yet another horse.

An arrow hisses past my ear. "They're shooting at us!" I shriek, not daring to glance back, but lowering myself against my mount's neck. "Keep your head down."

"Stay at my flank," Amir hollers. "I'm not about to lose now."

Everything was fine until we rode through Amesbury and a mob of masked outlaws tried to rob us. Amir bolted through their barricade, giving me no choice but to dig in my heels and follow. *Nothing like riding lessons by fire.*

Another arrow hisses above my head. "Yikes!"

The brown belt looks over his shoulder. "Drop your satchel!"

I'm holding on for dear life and he wants me to drop my satchel?

"Do it!" he shouts.

I move the reins to one hand and grip the horse's mane for added stability, then whip the bag over my head and throw it back.

I breathe an enormous sigh of relief when the thieves stop to grab it, giving us a chance to race into the mammoth circle of Stonehenge. It's overgrown with grass and vines, looking little like the picture-perfect monument of modern day. But there's still no mistaking the giant, expertly excavated rock.

Amir jumps down from his mount and pulls Noah from his horse.

"I'll walk on my own," mumbles the big blue belt.

Thank God.

I swing my leg over my horse's withers and slide to the ground. Running to Noah, I grab his hand and pull his arm across my shoulders. "We're going through together whether you like it or not."

"Hurry, those assholes won't be detained for long." Amir runs into the outer circle. "We need to stand in the center of the blue stone horseshoe."

I follow as fast as I can but the ground is rocky and difficult to traverse and Noah is leaning on me heavily.

Ahead of us, Amir disappears and I drag Noah to the spot. We stand there for a second and nothing happens while the voices of the thieves echo from the east. "There they are!"

The dark cloak of one of the crooks flaps in the distance.

"Can't we travel when someone is watching?" I ask, pulling Noah down to the ground. As soon as we are hidden by the fallen stone, I get my answer. Suddenly we're awash in blackness, hurtling through the abyss.

It's not as terrifying this time. It's almost euphoric as one thing consumes my mind—sleeping in my cubby bed at the academy.

I pray that's where we're headed.

Chapter Twenty-Five

*"He who knows all the answers has not been
asked all the questions." - Confucius*

Noah's arm is still around my shoulder as our feet
lightly touch ground. Red rock surrounds us and,
looking up, I realize we're standing in the middle of
the Dragon's Arch right beside Amir.

He grins. "Wild ride."

"Epic," Noah grunts.

I gaze out over the academy. "It's good to be
home."

In truth, I'm buzzing with relief, but also a little
remorse. I want to see Henry and watch as he
becomes king. I want to tell Isabelle she's a saint for
staying by her husband's side even though she
knows he's a tyrant. I never got to thank Madeline
for trusting me and leading us to the solar. I want to
come to know William Marshal better. He has been
so honored through history I would have enjoyed an
evening beside his hearth listening to his life's
story—*if* I would have earned his trust. But then one
of the bloodiest years in English history would
transpire before King John's death.

Staying there was not an option.

As we make our way down the hill, I realize I'll
never see any of those people again. And though I
didn't want to marry Lord de Burgh, he was kinder

to us than anyone. He was a good man. An honest man. He's what Dad's like when he's sober.

Noah grunts as he steps on the leg with the injured hip.

"Can you make it?" I whisper.

"Damn right I'll make it. No evac for me, that's for sure."

Grand Master Li is waiting for us outside his office, leaning on his staff, his face serene, yet contemplative and assessing. "I see the warriors have come home with battle wounds that need attention."

"Sew me up and send me back to class," Noah grumbles like a typical tough guy, though his face is ashen. His recovery will not be as easy as he thinks.

Once we step onto the cement patio, we stop. "He's lost a lot of blood," I say.

Noah wrenches his arm from my grasp and straightens. "After a day in my rack, I'll be ready to take on the bastards again, sir."

Amir holds up his hand and examines it. I forgot about his wrist and now it's the size of a man's fist. "I'll take Spartacus to the infirmary. Need to have this checked out anyway."

I chuckle at the Spartacus comment. If anyone I know is a great and powerful warrior, it has to be Noah.

Li gestures toward the door. "I'll stop by for your debriefing later."

The Grand Master and I stand in silence while the guys head off, then Li places his palm in the small of my back and walks with me into his office. "You weren't injured?"

"I was lucky."

"Sit," he says, pointing to a cushion on the floor set before a low table with a tea service as if he expected only me for this meeting. He lowers himself onto the pillow opposite. "Tea?"

"Please."

I feel like I'm still in 1215. It's so weird to be here where everything is totally *modern*.

Li pushes a plate of egg rolls toward me. "Eat."

I pick up a pair of chopsticks, take one, and bite into it. "Delicious." In fact it's more than delicious. Saliva is practically pouring out the corners of my lips. I've been eating bland medieval food for weeks and suddenly my taste buds are on hyperdrive tantalized by flavor.

"Have another."

"Thank you," I say, proceeding to devour everything on the plate. Only when the food is gone do I notice Li has filled both our cups and is patiently waiting for my feeding-frenzy to stop.

"Feeling better?" he asks.

"Aside from being exhausted, yes."

He takes his cup and sips, those ultra-intelligent eyes watching me. "Tell me, Genesis, where did the dragon take you?"

He listens thoughtfully while I tell him everything—arriving in London which had been taken over by FitzWalter and the barons. About figuring out the reason for our visit and our list of possible targets. About Noah's joust and taking the purse which enabled us to buy clothes and food. I relayed the journey to Runnymede, then to Winchester and meeting the king, and Amir's trick making me an Egyptian princess sent by Al-Adil to marry an English lord. Poor de Burgh.

Grand Master Li's eyes light up when I mention a Qiang scout attacked Noah at the Whitsun feast. Though he doesn't seem surprised that we headed to Windsor or that I awoke in a cold sweat suddenly realizing the Qiang's target was Henry.

"You battled three?" he asks.

"Yes."

"But they first sent a scout ahead?"

"They did." I take a long sip of tea and lick my lips. "Is that unusual?"

"Quite. Perhaps Noah is too much of a threat."

"He's a threat all right—to them. They even know his name. Things would have been a lot more difficult if he hadn't been with us."

Li strokes his fingers down the long wisps of his white beard. "Hmm."

"Sir?" Chewing the corner of my lip, I adjust the cushion beneath me. "There are a lot of missing pieces in all this. I have a ton of questions."

"Ah yes, there was urgency when you departed which gave me no time to explain."

"But we have time now," I say, making it sound like more of a question.

Li sets down his cup, closes his eyes and draws a long inhale. "There are only a handful of people on this earth with the ability to travel through time— through our gateway. The chosen few are difficult to find. Many...ah...*most* students at the academy cannot, even many of those who are descendants of Sun Tzu. Furthermore, though the gifted are able to travel at a young age, far too young in my opinion, as I explained before, all pass through a phase of settling and the window closes."

"But if the window closes in young adulthood, why doesn't the Alliance recruit younger students?"

"There are many reasons. Maturity is the greatest factor. Strength of the body as well as the mind is another." He raises the pot. "More tea?"

I'm too thirsty for knowledge to sip tea. "No, thank you."

"Many of our students have parents who attended the academy. They prepare their children by encouraging them to pursue martial arts, knowledge of history, and information technology."

I think about my mom and wish she were still alive. It would be so cool to know about her experience at the academy. Did Dad know she was a seer? "But the Qiang live in our time, right? Why don't we send in a bunch of Marines and blow them off the planet?"

"If it were that easy it would have been done centuries ago. They are elusive and constantly on the move. But as adults, many of our graduates dedicate their lives to finding them and putting an end to their treachery."

Li dabs his mouth with a cloth napkin, then neatly places it on the table. "I have kept you too long. You need rest. Fortunately, midterm break is in a few days and you can enjoy some time with your father."

"Midterm break? Isn't it over? We've been gone for weeks."

"Historic space time does not usually correspond with present time. You may be away for months, yet only a few days pass here."

"That's totally wicked, and even better that I didn't miss the break." I get to see Dad and Rex. Jeez, I've missed Rex.

I follow Li as he stands and leads me to the door. "I must remind you that everything that happened on your mission is confidential."

"Confidential," I repeat. Of course I know this but I'm still dazed.

"Yes, Genesis. The only people at the academy you may speak with about your experience are your traveling companions, me, and your senseis."

"What do I say to my classmates? Can I tell them I was on a mission?"

"Everyone has already assumed so."

"But I can't say what happened?"

"Tell them I have sworn you to secrecy."

"Wonderful," I mumble to myself. I can imagine Ziana's inquisition.

Lord help me.

I walk with Li through the corridor of the admin building, but I stop before we reach the reception desk. "I'd like to pay a visit to the infirmary first."

"Give the boys time to rest. Visit them tomorrow."

I start away but then my exhausted mind clicks on the most important question. "Sir?"

"Yes?"

"I need more training on second sight. Will you help me?"

"Ah," he sighs. "That is a request I have heard many times."

Odd answer. "I don't understand."

"It's not a question of being willing. The question is one of aptitude." He waves me away with a flick of his hand. "Time will show us how deeply you will be able to develop your gift. But to your question, yes, we shall resume our sessions."

"I can handle so much more. I know it. I-I'm scratching the surface, only beginning to understand my gift. Just give me a chance."

"Thank you, Genesis. That is all."

My impulse is to convince him I'm ready to start tomorrow. But then my next thought turns my stomach. What if he doesn't want to get close to students because they might not come back?

No. A powerful squeeze deep inside my heart tells me he's more committed than that. I need to be patient. The Grand Master wasn't there to observe us. He didn't see my frustrations as we muddled our way through thirteenth century England. My destiny will unfold in time and no one, not even Li, knows what it is.

By the time I walk into my dorm room, I'm so tired I'm practically seeing double.

Ziana looks up from her computer. "Oh my God! You're back so soon?"

I guess I can't tell her I've been away a few weeks. "Yeah."

Instantly on her feet, she swarms toward me like a hive of pesky bees. "Well, tell me all about it. I'm dying here."

"I wish I could." I shuffle toward the bed while I run a finger across my lips. "But Grand Master Li has sworn me to secrecy."

"He can't do that! I've been on the edge of my seat. And why did you get to go on a mission when you haven't even earned your yellow belt yet?"

I start up the ladder. The sight of my pillow makes my knees wobble. "Lucky I guess."

"You're the freaking luckiest person I know. First you beat me in the tournament and now you go on a mission." Ziana's enthusiasm is giving me a headache. "But don't get too smug, girlfriend. I won the waza contest when we scaled the wall. I proved I'm every bit as good as you are. I should have been picked, you know."

I flop onto the bed and grab the cupboard handle. "Sure." Really, why should I argue with her unabashed arrogance? "I'll bet you'll be next, but for now I need some sleep."

"Oh no, you can't flake out on me. I'm your roommate. I deserve to know *something* about what happened."

Shifting my gaze to her face, it's all I can do to keep my eyes open long enough to reply, "I haven't slept in two days and I can't hold my head up another second."

I slide the Japanese bed doors closed and listen to her huff around the room, swearing like a sailor...for about three seconds.

Chapter Twenty-Six

"We have two lives and the second begins when we realize we only have one." - Confucius

Not surprisingly, they keep Noah in the infirmary for a few days. In fact, he's still there when we're all kicked out for midterm break. I visited him every chance I got, even offered to skip my break and stay to give him some company, but he was brash enough to tell me to "go home, white belt".

The douche!

But I'm kinda glad he did. Besides, this time he only meant for midterm break.

The Greyhound drops me off at the Casablanca Casino in Mesquite but I don't bother to call Dad. Besides, my phone's dead. They gave us our cells as we were leaving and I haven't had a chance to charge mine. My father knows I'm coming because I e-mailed him before I left.

God, I feel like I've been in a time warp—which I have, come to think of it. But even being at the academy seems surreal now that I'm back in my stomping grounds. I need some time to acclimate myself so I walk the four miles.

The dusty street in Bunkerville seems like a ghost town aside from the two motorcycles parked outside the Muddy Hollow—right next to my truck. I run my finger along the side of the Ford, making a bright red line through the dust. Once I hit the curb, I stand on the sidewalk for a while, wondering what things my dad's building has seen in the hundred years it has occupied the corner of First and Main.

Gunfights? Maybe. At one time this was the wild west, after all.

I can't believe I went back in time more than eight hundred years. Was it even real?

Fishing out my key, I let myself in. At the top of the stairs, the first thing I see is Mom's dragon statue and my breath catches. It looks so much like the Dragon's Arch it's uncanny.

The bronze was a family heirloom, but now I wonder if it came from China—from the time of Sun Tzu. I guess I'll never know unless Grand Master Li opens up and tells me everything.

I rub the dragon's head as I move into the kitchen. My duffel falls from my shoulder as I turn in place. Am I really home? Though nothing has changed, I feel like I'm standing in the past, in the time of the 1970s with the olive-green refrigerator humming away.

Rufus hops off the couch and rubs against me.

"There you are, you wily tiger." I stoop to pick him up and scratch him behind the ears which makes him immediately start to purr. "I see you haven't missed any meals while I've been away."

The door to the bar clicks below and I hear Dad's footsteps on the stairs. That sound hasn't changed.

"Genesis!" He opens his arms with a huge smile. "God, I've missed you."

I let Rufus jump to the floor while I wrap my arms around my father. "I've missed you, too."

Dad's embrace is more comforting than I remember. Sincere, as well. "I saw you from the window. Why didn't you call and have me come pick you up?"

I close my eyes and cling to him. He smells like old leather and there's no hint of alcohol on his breath. Nice. "I wanted to walk."

"It's been rough, has it?" he asks, patting my back.

"Rough, but I love being there."

"What do you love about it?"

"Well..." It's so hard to explain. "I guess I feel like I've found my calling. I think I've always been destined to go there."

Taking my shoulders, he holds me out at arm's length, his eyes narrowing. "You've been on a mission, haven't you?"

Goosebumps erupt across my skin. "How did you know?" I whisper.

"You've changed. I can see it in your eyes." Dad pulls out a chair and sits at the table, gesturing for me to do the same. "But you're only a white belt."

Though I've told him about the belt system, I'm positive I've never told him about missions or the fact that white belts don't go on them. "I know...um...but how do you know this?"

Shrugging, Dad turns the cat-shaped saltshaker between his fingers. I gave him the set for Christmas a couple of years ago.

I sit back and cross my ankles. "I can't talk about the mission. Not ever."

"Good girl."

Huh? Why did he say that? Does he know about Mom's past? "Grand Master Li said Mom went to the academy, too. Were you aware?"

"Yeah." Dad looks up, his Adam's apple bobbing. "I attended the Military Academy of Martial Arts, with her."

"What?" A bomb goes off in my heart. Holy hell, WTF? Goosebumps totally erupt across my skin. Both my parents are MAMA alums? "You never told me that."

His gaze slides away. "I was never given leave to tell you."

"Secrets?"

"Always when it comes to the Qiang."

Again, the sound of the Tibetan dynasty makes the room feel like it has been blasted by dry ice. "Oh. My. God."

"Your mother and I went on missions. Her second sight was uncanny. I...*ah*...lost my ability to travel at twenty-one, but she didn't settle until twenty-two. Right before graduation."

I can't believe what I'm hearing. "I thought you met Mom in Half Moon Bay when you were on vacation."

"The past you've been told is all part of our M.O. from the operative protection program."

My jaw drops to my chest. "My entire life is a lie?"

"Not exactly. You've been a witness to everything that has happened since your birth."

"But who are you? Who is Mom?"

Dad gets that hard look in his eye—the one he uses when he's irritated with me. "I'm still your father, and your mother loved you more than anything on this earth. Now that you've been on your first mission, I can tell you this: After graduation, we both joined the CIA as operatives. When your mother got pregnant with you, we decided to settle down. They gave us new identities and set us up with this bar. I liked Harleys and decided to turn it into a watering hole for bikers."

"Holy crapola. So, you didn't win it in a poker tournament?"

"Nah." Dad chuckles. "I don't even like to play poker."

"God, I had no idea."

He thumps his chest. "You're looking at one of the best. That's why I sent you to Sensei Soto. I knew he'd give you a good foundation."

"But you never told me."

"I swore an oath that I wouldn't discuss any of this with you until you went on your first mission. Every graduate must. It's the path we choose."

"So, we keep this between us?"

"Absolutely. No one else knows. As far as anyone outside of the academy is aware, my past hasn't changed."

"Um, what about..." I fold my hands in my lap and squeeze them until it hurts. "What about your drinking?"

Dad's eyes go vacant as a long exhale blows through his lips. "That is a problem. Your mother's passing slayed me."

"But she wouldn't want you to...be soused all the time."

"No." He shoves back his chair. "I know she wouldn't. But we're not discussing that now."

"Of course not," I whisper under my breath.

He knits his brows as if he's preparing to spar. "What did you say?"

I don't want to argue. Not when I have so much to wrap my mind around. "Nothing. It just feels weird to be home."

Dad half-smiles. "It always takes time after you return from a mission, no matter where in the world you go. Rest. The patio will be open for dinner. You can mingle with the guys down there if you want."

The biker dudes. Dad's rugged friends who have always treated me like a princess. Just not an *Egyptian* princess.

"Thanks. I'd like that."

After he leaves, I pick up my duffel and head for my room. I can't effing believe it. My parents fought the Qiang when they were my age.

Shut. Up!

I sleep in the next day but by afternoon, I'm ready to head back to the academy. What am I going to do with myself for a whole week?

Rex.

Even though I can't tell him about the mission, I have to see him.

Outside the D.Q., I cut my truck engine and grin. His lime-green Honda Fit is already here. I'm giddy as I open the door to a blast of super-chilled air.

"It's about time, girlfriend." Before I can open my mouth, Rex smothers me in an embrace. "Hey, you."

"Hey back, dude."

"How's my personal Batgirl?"

"Kickin' butt, you?"

"Glad you're here."

I fluff the neon-colored bangs out of his eyes. "Nice. You match your car."

He blows me an air-kiss, grabs my hand, and drags me to a table. "I already ordered for you."

"My favorite?"

He points to the ice cream just starting to melt. "Still the same?"

"Double hot fudge. At least some things never change." I slide into the seat, noting he has ordered his trademark banana split. "Thank you."

"So how is your kickass academy? Still loving it?"

"Yeah. It's freaking awesome."

"I'm glad."

I dig my spoon into the thick fudge and swirl it around the ice cream making it super chocolaty. "You have a great tan. How was Oceanside?"

"Fun, I guess. You know, vacation with the parents is lame."

"At least you get to go on vacation." Since Mom died, Dad hasn't taken me anywhere. Now I wonder if that's because he's in hiding. Weird. "You look like you've grown, too."

"A little." He waves his sparkly-green fingernails in front of me. "I've been working at Shirleen's Hair and Nails since I got back."

"Cool. You like it?"

"Sure, though she doesn't let me cut hair."

My eyes roll back while I savor an enormous bite of vanilla and thick, warm chocolate. "Mm. This is so good."

Rex takes a few bites as well.

"Are you still planning to go to New York after graduation?" I ask.

"That won't change."

"Awesome." I think back to an e-mail he sent right after I got to the academy. "Hey, what happened after your historical fashion show? Do they want more?"

"Oh my God. They asked me to do it again next year." He pulls out his phone. "I know you were there, but I have a video of the whole thing."

"Cool! What the heck are you waiting for?"

He grins and slides around to my side of the table.

"The picture's a little grainy, but I can't help but watch it five times a day."

I hold the phone and watch the whole thing, pointing out the cheerleaders and their costumes while Rex explains why he chose each one for their particular era.

"It's amazing," I say. "You put so much thought into it."

He slips his phone into his back pocket. "It was all right, I guess."

"All right? Hello? You are effing talented. I mean. What upscale New York salon isn't going to give away their firstborn to have you work for them?"

"Ya think?"

"I know." I shovel melting ice cream into my mouth. "I'd even bet you'd be even more awesome doing hair, costumes, and makeup for the movies."

He snorts. "If I survive high school."

"Just stay clear of the football beasts."

"Yeah. Thanks." He drapes an arm across my shoulders. "If only I still had my own Cassandra Cain watching my back."

Guilt creeps up my spine. We're never going to walk the halls of Virgin Valley High as a team again. "Don't worry. I'm still your Batgirl. You got a problem with someone, call me. I'll be down here so fast they won't know what hit."

I take another bite and as the sweet melty chocolate runs over my tongue, my mind wanders back to 1215 and the costumes we wore. God, knowing what kind of clothes to wear is so important.

A brilliant idea pops into my head. Rex would be an awesome asset at the academy. Wouldn't he? "Can you send me your fashion show clip? I want to show it to my roommate."

"Sure thing." Rex punches his phone, then scoops a bit of vanilla and watches it dribble from his spoon. "When we were on vacation, my dad told me I needed to toughen up."

My eyes snap to my best friend's face as I bite the corner of my mouth. "Seriously? What did you say?"

He shrugs. "It made me think that I won't have you to watch my back in the lunchroom for the next two years."

I lower my spoon. Yeah, we were an awesome duo. "Sorry."

"No, you're following your dream. I would never stand in the way of that." He slices off a big piece of banana. "But I'll bet you'll be happy to hear I went back to Sensei Soto and asked if I could restart classes again."

"Get. Out!" My jaw drops. Rex started karate with me in kindergarten but left after the sixth grade. He wasn't bad, either. He just couldn't bring himself to hit anyone in the sparring ring. "I think that's awesome."

"I like it better now, though I wish you were there."

"Hey, I'll go. You got class tonight?"

"Sure do." He wipes a bit of ice cream from the corner of his mouth. "Sensei says I ought to earn my black belt by the time I graduate."

"That's so cool. I hope you stick with it."

"Yeah, it'll help toughen me up for New York, for sure. At least that's what my dad thinks."

"You're tough in your own way." I grab his hand. "I love you no matter what. You'll always be my best friend, okay?"

He squeezes my fingers. "Best friends till the end, Batgirl."

This is how it's always been between us. We should have been born twins.

Chapter Twenty-Seven

*"Choose a job you love and you will never work
a day in your life." - Confucius*

I've been working out at the dojo with Rex most days. We also went to the mall in Saint George and found a dress. For me, that is. I think it's too short but Rex insisted it looked the best. Anyway, I, Genesis Mans, am now the proud owner of one little black dress and plan to wear it to the next academy dance.

I can't believe my midterm break is nearly over. It's three in the afternoon and I'm lying on my bed trying to read, but Rufus keeps purring and stretching out across my face.

I push him away for the umpteenth time. "You're the most spoiled cat on the planet."

"Meow."

I lower my book and stare at his green eyes. "Why don't you curl up and go to sleep? You're cute, but cats aren't supposed to be annoying."

The doorbell rings and I sit up while Rufus rolls into my lap. "Who do you think that is?"

I'm not expecting anyone and it can't be Rex. He went to Las Vegas with his mom. I decide to ignore the bell until it sounds again. Then a tickle at the back of my neck tells me to answer.

Sighing, I hop to my feet, straighten my t-shirt, and fluff my fingers through my hair.

The stupid bell rings impatiently with two dings.

"I'm coming," I yell, heading down the stairs.

"It's me white belt."

Not even looking out the peephole, I throw open the door, a smile practically splitting my face in two. "Dude, what the hell are you doing here?"

Noah grins and throws his thumb over his shoulder, pointing to his Harley parked at the curb. "I thought you might need a ride back to school."

"But...didn't you go home to Chicago?"

"Nah. Besides, Dad's been transferred to San Diego."

"Oh, so you've come from there?"

"Nope. I took a ride down from the academy."

"You've been at school the whole time?"

"Why not? I needed the rest. It's quiet there."

"But you missed me?"

"Yeah." Those uniquely intense eyes mesmerize me as he brushes my cheek with his knuckle. After glancing behind, he pulls me into his arms. It feels like being home.

"Really?" I ask, praying he isn't making it up.

He kisses my forehead. "Hey, I don't think I would have taken a four-hundred-mile ride for the hell of it."

He nudges me inside and kicks the door closed behind.

"This is how much I missed you," he says, sliding his hands to my cheeks and kissing me. I mean he kisses me like there's no tomorrow. Noah takes his time brushing his full lips back and forth over mine. Then, as if he's reacquainting himself with familiar territory, his mouth grows more demanding and greedier, totally blowing my mind.

Oh. My. God.

I can't believe Noah Jones drove all this way. He's actually here in my arms and I'm floating like a soap bubble, returning his kiss with every bit of passion I can muster. He feels so good in my arms it's like he was meant to be there forever.

"So," I say, a little breathless while I smooth my finger over his full bottom lip. "Does this mean we're *together*?"

"Yeah." A low chuckle rumbles from his chest. Holy hell, I missed him—everything about him. "I'd let you wear my belt, but there's a rule against it."

"I can live with that." I tug him up the stairs, hardly able to believe he's here. If my lips weren't buzzing I'd have to pinch myself. "You want a Coke or something?"

"You got any mead?"

"Ha." I pull two Cokes from the old fridge and lead him to the table. "How are you feeling?"

"I'm ready to take on the Qiang, baby."

"Seriously? Your wounds are healed?"

"Pretty much." He wriggles his shoulders. "I just need to get back to it. No use whining over a few aches and pains."

"You're amazing."

"Tell that to my dad."

"He's tough, huh?"

"He's a Marine."

I twist off the cap on my bottle, relieved that I can be open with him. "I found out my mom was a seer like me. What's more, she and my dad both attended the academy."

"Both? Wow." He takes a long drink, his eyes watching me. "My dad did as well. A lot of the kids at the school have at least one parent who is an alum."

"Li told me."

"Huh. Even Amir's dad is a time warrior."

"You say that as if Amir is inferior."

"Oh no, he's a mastermind. Remember both his parents are physicists?"

"Yes, I remember all too well. Come to think of it, I still need to come up with something good as a payback for marrying me off to de Burgh."

"Hey, that was all Amir's idea."

"But you went along with it."

Noah swigs his Coke, then snorts. "Because it was brilliant."

"What if I'd been forced to marry him? Eew!"

He wipes his mouth with the back of his hand— the one tattooed with a cross. "I never would have let you walk down the aisle."

My heart skips a beat or two. "You mean that?"

"Damn straight. I would have thought of something."

"All right, then. I'll only make you give me riding lessons three times a week for the next year."

He drums his fingers on his Coke bottle as if he's thinking. "Can I ride with you?"

"Hmm, maybe. But I need to become a proficient."

"You will." He swills another drink. "I think I miss riding double the most."

My stomach flips. God, I miss it, too—having his arms surround me while the big destrier ambles across the English countryside. "But I'm glad we're here. I mean you're here with me. In this time."

He belches. It's kinda cute. "And tomorrow we'll swap our medieval horse for a Harley and ride double like we did in 1215. How's that?"

"I like it." The rumble of laughter comes from the bar below. "Except I'll have to convince my dad that you're a safe driver."

"Leave that to me."

"Oh, so now you're the slayer of ties fathers have with their daughters?"

"Never. But you said your dad rides a Harley, doesn't he?"

"Uh huh."

"Then I'll do my best to show him I'm good enough for you."

I can't doubt him. After all, he's Noah Jones. "So, back to Amir. How about making him do my laundry for the next six months?"

"Not unless you want to run around in dirty clothes." Noah stretches out his legs and crosses his ankles. "Make him write an essay for you."

"Do you think he'll do it?"

"I'll ensure he does. Besides, he can whip up an essay off the top of his head. One that would take me a week to research."

"Okay, you're on."

The door to the bar clicks.

I jolt in my seat. "It's my dad," I whisper.

Just as the words escape my lips, my father appears. "Everything okay, Genesis?"

"Hey, Dad," I say as we both stand. "This is Noah Jones. He went on the mission with me."

My father assesses my *boyfriend* with the deadliest, most sober stare I've ever seen. "That so?"

"Yes, sir," Noah says like he's talking to his colonel father.

"You keep her safe?"

The blue belt squares his shoulders. "Protected her with my life, sir."

I scoot beside him and thread my fingers through his. "This fearless warrior took twenty lashes for me. He has a mottled dragon tattoo on his back to prove it."

Dad narrows his eyes. "You did that for my girl?"

Whoa, my father is acting like one of his tough-guy biker patrons.

Noah nods. "Want to see it?"

"Yes."

I cringe as I help Noah raise the back of his shirt. The lash marks are puckered and still red. A sharp gasp fills my lungs. "You're not as healed as you said."

The blue belt pulls down his shirt and eyes my father. Height-wise, they're evenly matched, though I'd never want them to come to blows. "It doesn't hurt much."

My dad actually smiles. "Well, then, son. I'll be counting on you to have her back from now on, understood?"

"Yes, sir."

"Good. Because your adventures have only just begun."

Dad grabs a glass of water and sits with us. "Let me tell you about the time Genesis' mother and I traveled to France during the French Revolution..."

I watch Noah's face as we listen to Dad's story. It reminds me of the challenges we faced in 1215. But more than that, it makes me think of the perils to come. What else will we encounter during our time at the academy? Where will we go? Who will we meet?

Noah gives me a wink and I can't wait to find out.

Author's Note

A word of note for all the karate buffs out there: My style is Bobby Lawrence Karate popular in Utah and based on Kenpo. I earned my black belt in November of 2018 at the Bobby Lawrence Karate tournament held at Utah Valley University in Orem and was awarded a second degree a year later. Master Lawrence trained extensively with Grand Master Ed Parker Sr., Master Richard Callahan, and Sifu Chen. My instructor in Saint George is Mr. Marc Wilson, a fifth-degree black belt. Bobby Lawrence Karate is an ancient, traditional, modern, and eclectic system of karate developed by Master Lawrence. All of our instruction is in English. Therefore, the karate moves and strikes depicted in this work of fiction are written in English, which I feel also provides a more pleasant reading experience for everyone.

Oh, and just an FYI, the Chinese symbol for love has been used for scene breaks:

愛 ài

~ Amy

About the Author

Known for her action-packed, passionate stories, Amy Jarecki has received reader and critical praise throughout her writing career. The author of more than 35 novels, she won the prestigious 2018 RT Reviewers' Choice award for *The Highland Duke* and the 2016 RONE award from InD'tale Magazine for Best Time Travel for her novel *Rise of a Legend*. In addition, she hit Amazon's Top 100 Bestseller List, the Apple, Barnes & Noble, and Bookscan Bestseller lists, and has earned the designation as an Amazon All Star Author. Readers also chose her Scottish historical romance, *A Highland Knight's Desire,* as the winning title through Amazon's Kindle Scout Program. Amy holds an MBA from Heriot-Watt University in Edinburgh, Scotland and now resides in Southwest Utah with her husband where she writes immersive fiction. In her free time Amy studies karate, Mandarin Chinese, and hikes the Santa Clara hills.

Find out more about Amy's books and sign up for her newsletter on https://amyjarecki.com.

Other Books by Amy Jarecki

Highland Force series:
Captured by the Pirate Laird
The Highland Henchman
Beauty and the Barbarian
Return of the Highland Laird - a novella

Pict/Roman Romances:
Rescued by the Celtic Warrior
Deceived by the Celtic Spy

Stand Alone Titles:
The Chihuahua Affair
Virtue: A Cruise Dancer Romance
Boy Man Chief (YA action/adventure)

Lords of the Highlands series:
The Highland Duke
The Highland Commander
The Highland Guardian
The Highland Chieftain
The Highland Renegade
The Highland Earl
The Highland Rogue
The Highland Laird

CPSIA information can be obtained
at www.ICGtesting.com
Printed in the USA
LVHW040542060721
691875LV00016B/2115